ANUBIS

GUARDIAN SECURITY
SHADOW WORLD

BOOK ONE

In the Shadow World, he was the God of Death, and he was called many names. The monsters who he hunted called him Anubis. Those who saw his face died. To Guardian Security, he was a number, a surgical weapon they wielded against monstrous evil. One woman called him Kaeden Lang. Anubis never meant her to be anything except an interlude, a moment of light in the darkness of his life, a one-time escape from the ever-present haze of death. He committed an unforgivable sin—he saw her again—and again—and again. She held back the shadows that threatened to consume him.

Sky Meyers made a grave mistake six years ago. She fell in love— only to have the man she knew as Kaeden Lang disappear. Now, his daughter needed him to save her life. As the office manager for the State District Attorney, Sky accessed national databases in a desperate search for her baby's daddy only to discover the man she knew as Kaeden Lang didn't exist. She'd already lost the man she loved; she couldn't lose her daughter.

Other eyes noticed Sky's search. Abruptly recalled and informed of the existence of his daughter and her illness, Anubis slipped through the shadows to help Sky—but found death threatened more than his daughter. In her attempt to find Kaeden Lang, Sky unknowingly jeopardized his Shadow World existence by alerting an enemy Kaeden Lang can't eliminate—only Anubis can.

ANUBIS

GUARDIAN SECURITY—
SHADOW WORLD SERIES
BY
KRIS MICHAELS

PRINT EDITION 2018

ALSO BY KRIS MICHAELS

THE KINGS OF GUARDIAN:

GUARDIAN SECURITY— SHADOW WORLD SERIES:

CHAPTER ONE

ANUBIS STUDIED THE WAVES THAT ROCKED THE YACHT for tell-tale air bubbles. A deadly silence had hung in the air since he killed the motor. The quiet settled around him like a well-known lover. A dull orange haze lined the eastern horizon of the vast Pacific Ocean and spread a pale golden light against the billowing cumulus clouds signaling the start of another normal day... for some.

He straightened from the bow of the ship, tracking the air bubbles as they moved from aft of the two-hundred-foot floating palace. Correction, the floating morgue. His target had been making his way to the United States, but his journey ended fifteen miles off the coast of California. Technically the event was still in international waters. Yi Bao lay dead inside his stateroom. The crew was unconscious and adrift in the yacht's lifeboat. They'd wake up in an hour with one hell of a headache, but they would have a radio, and they'd be alive. As for Bao's minions, their deaths had been... peaceful. The poison he'd used to lace their dinner worked quietly and efficiently. They went to sleep, never to wake. Anubis felt no remorse at the loss of their lives. If you choose to align yourself with the devil, you will reap what you sow. Bao, the demon's head, had died the way any true demon should die. Awake and fully cognizant of what Anubis was doing to him. Bao had crossed the line of acceptability—even for demons—and the international security community had authorized his extermination.

Hiking the backpack stuffed with the contents of Bao's safe over his shoulder, he followed the air tank trail from the port to the starboard side. The boat rolled under his feet, untethered and drifting with the waves in the open sea. He glanced at the speedboat tied to the starboard side of the vessel. It was his escape. The man currently rigging the yacht with explosives appeared from the darkness when Anubis had flashed the all clear. His orders for this assassination had been clear. Bao's demise must look like an accident at sea. The demolition specialist was sent to ensure only toothpick-sized pieces of the yacht would be found. Normally, he would rig an explosion, but the powers-that-be wanted the specialist to ensure the destruction of the craft. Anubis understood the reasoning behind the order. Bao had led the powerful international Triad. Any indication of an assassination would cause problems, and the Triad had already caused death and maiming within the Guardian family. It wasn't often he took pleasure in his job, but in Bao's case, he made an exception. Anubis ensured the man would never hurt his organization again.

The diver surfaced and pulled his oxygen tank's mouthpiece from his mouth, treading water as he looked up at Anubis through his facemask. The power of the waves would have made it impossible for Anubis to tread water so easily.

"We have five minutes and seventeen seconds. Finish your business. If you aren't in the boat by the time I get there, I will leave you." The man put the mouthpiece back in his mouth and slipped under the water.

Cocky son of a bitch. A smile spread across his face. He liked that. He walked down the length of the yacht to where the speedboat pulled against the rope that bound it to the luxury ship. The diver had levered himself into the stern and was shedding his flippers and tanks. Clutching the backpack in one hand, Anubis looked at the waves and judged the pitch and roll of both boats. His muscles tensed and he vaulted over the rail, dropping to the deck of the smaller craft as it started its upward pitch. He stood and grabbed the knot in the rope pulling it free. The speedboat's motor roared to life. Anubis braced his weight on his back foot, fighting gravity and the power of the propulsion of the speedboat. He lunged forward and grabbed the seat adjacent to the diver.

The boat barely skimmed the top of the water, lifted into the air at a forty-five-degree angle by the power of the racing engines. Fuck, he'd survived ten years as an assassin only to die now of a broken neck because the demolition specialist was fucking insane. Speaking of violent deaths… He glanced at the person piloting the boat—and did a double take. Son of a bitch, no wonder the man had brass balls. Anubis recognized that profile but shelved the thought. The man's code name was Smoke; he was an underwater demolitions expert, and that was all Anubis knew for a fact. He damn sure wasn't going to strike up a conversation with the bastard that might distract him from flying the boat over the waves. Anubis didn't feel much like dying, at least not today.

At a vivid flash of light, Anubis whipped his head around. The entire sky lit with the violence of the explosion. The man beside him let out a whoop of pure, unadulterated excitement and laughed almost manically as he pushed the throttle even farther forward, urging the bullet they were riding in to go faster. Fucking hell, it figured. The man was insane.

The trip to the small marina that rested in the snug cove surrounded by the city of Santa Barbara took far less time than it should have. About a mile offshore, Smoke throttled back and brought the boat out of its hypersonic flight. Anubis unclenched his fingers from the seat. He'd bet the metal frame under the leather padding had dents from his grip. After they tied up the boat, Smoke grabbed his gear and climbed up to the pier. He reached back and offered Anubis a hand up. Anubis narrowed his eyes at the man. He dropped down and launched from a crouched position straight up, landing on his toes at the edge of the wooden pier.

"We should do that again. Oh, you're supposed to call Alpha, priority, Omega." The man gave him a wink and a wicked smile before he threw his tanks over his shoulder and walked, barefooted, toward the end of the pier. Son of a bitch, he'd seen all types, but that man... yeah, there was a screw loose somewhere in that one's brain.

Anubis looked across the bay. The sunrise painted the boats with a rich golden hue. The hills surrounding the area took on a mystic look as a low fog hung along the coastline. He gave Smoke time to clear the area before he followed him to the parking lot. Anubis made a casual walk around his vehicle. He dropped down on the pretense of tying his shoe to check the undercarriage of his SUV. Assured there was nothing attached to the undercarriage, he popped the doors, threw his backpack in the passenger-side seat and climbed in. Before he'd gone a mile, he palmed his phone and called the number he knew by heart.

"Operator Two Five Two." The distant, professional voice was the same today as it had been ten years ago.

"ID Six Four Nine for extension Seven Zero One," Anubis replied.

"One moment, Six Four Nine."

"Alpha."

He recognized Jacob King's voice. The man had taken over the Shadow World along with guiding the helm of Guardian's overseas operations. Anubis respected the man and his past. He once was the skipper of Alpha Team. That meant he wasn't a paper pusher and knew the perils of being in the field.

"Anubis."

"I pass you—Cobalt."

Anubis immediately replied with his code word that would let Alpha know he wasn't compromised. "I pass you—Azure."

"Report."

"The mission is complete. Ancillary documents obtained, without incident." *Well, except for one crazy-ass underwater demolition specialist.*

"Understood. Implement Option Daniel One."

Anubis's head jerked toward the phone as if he'd been slapped. "Repeat your last, Alpha."

"Implement Option Daniel One."

Anubis blinked at the command. *Fuck!* "Affirmative." He powered down the phone as he waited for the traffic light to turn green. Calculating the quickest route, he turned left from West Cabrillo Street onto State Street. As he passed over Mission Creek, he chucked the cheap burner phone he'd purchased yesterday out of his passenger side window hard enough to send it over the pedestrian walkway and into the water below.

On Highway 1, headed south, is mind raced with questions for which he had no answers. Option Daniel One was basic code and referred to the biblical story of Daniel in the lion's den. Gabriel, the original handler of the Shadow World, had invented the option when one of the first SW operatives had been compromised. The directions were clear. Go to Guardian's closest safe house in the area you were currently assigned and standby. He was being pulled from the field because somehow someone had shined a light on him. Anubis gripped the wheel of the SUV and drove carefully, observing every traffic law. He had miles to go before he'd have answers. Fuck, he shook as he put distance between himself and the harbor in Santa Barbara. The drive through Ventura took longer than it should. Traffic, even at seven thirty in the morning, was bumper to bumper. He tapped the steering wheel with his thumb, agitated by the drivers around him. Point Magoo State Park passed by in a blur as his destination, and answers to his questions, drew nearer. He entered Malibu's city limits and continued along Highway 1, traveling just past La Piedra State Beach. He slowed looking for the address he'd memorized when he'd accepted the case. He traveled on until he saw the gated drive. He turned in, punched in his code and waited as the gates opened. Eucalyptus trees lined the drive and hid the mansion from the roadway. Anubis pulled into the circular drive and parked. He damn near ran up the steps and entered his code again on a keypad outside the door. The locks disengaged. Anubis entered the massive foyer and listened as the locks re-engaged after him. He knew it could take hours for someone to reach the safe house and debrief him, but that fact didn't help the constant questions that kept circling through his mind. He rubbed his hand over his face. A line of dried blood circled his wrist. The gloves he'd worn protected his hands as he worked, but Bao's death had still managed to stain his skin.

He did a quick visual of the premises and headed upstairs. He needed a shower, and it was something to do other than sit and wonder what, or who, had compromised him. He opened the first door on the right and closed it. A library. The next room was an adjacent office, and the third was a bedroom. He stalked over the plush carpet and went through the open bathroom door. He turned on the taps and stripped out of his boots and clothes. He spun on his heel and headed for the walk-in closet. There were slacks, jeans, and shirts of various styles and sizes hanging from the bars. He found a pair of jeans his size and grabbed a shirt. The built-in dressers provided an assortment of undergarments. He grabbed a pair of socks and fresh briefs before he returned to the bathroom. The steam coming out of the shower beckoned him with the promise of a brief slice of heaven. Anubis stepped under the rain head and closed his eyes.

Nothing. *Nothing* should shine a light on him. He approached every mission with a meticulousness considered obsessive... except for the mission in that hellhole of a third world country almost six years ago. In truth, he should be dead after that one. He'd endured the torture the minions of the man he'd killed had dealt out, waiting for a chance to escape, or at least find a way to take some of the bastards with him. Bengal was the reason he was alive today. He'd never forget a debt that could not be repaid. He had few friends and Bengal was one.

Anubis went back over each mission he'd completed for Guardian. He had no fingerprints that could be traced; scar tissue obliterated any possibility of identifying him in that manner. Lifting his hand up, he examined the pads as if they could provide an answer. Meticulous pre-planning for every event he was assigned ensured there was no security system to capture his likeness. Several of the operatives in the Shadow World knew him by sight, but only by his code name. His aliases were disposed of like yesterday's trash as soon as he'd completed his assigned event. Dropping his head and rolling his shoulders, he drew a deep breath, and then another. There was nothing to do but wait.

He washed quickly and dressed in the clothes he'd selected before he headed downstairs to find the kitchen. The grandeur of the kitchen didn't impress him. He wasn't one to covet wealth, although, by any standard, he'd become very wealthy. Anubis found a can of soup and opened it, heating it in a bowl that he'd triple washed and rinsed for over five minutes. Overly cautious? Perhaps, but when you work with poison for a living, you tend to make sure things you eat and drink haven't been compromised.

He'd just sat down to eat when he heard the door locks disengage. Anubis was up and pinned to the contours of the wall within the span of two heartbeats.

"Ani, you piece of shit, where the fuck are you?" Bengal, or rather, Zane Reynolds bellowed from the foyer area. His muscles relaxed, and Anubis returned to the table as he yelled back, "In the kitchen."

He sat back down, picked up his spoon, and listened for Zane's tread on the floor, but as usual, the big man moved like the cat he'd been named after—silent, powerful and deadly. He also lived in the light, no longer an apex predator in the Shadow World.

He entered the kitchen and headed straight for the table where Anubis sat. "Who do you know in Merced, California?"

Anubis stopped mid-swallow. He played the name of the city through his mind and came up with a blank. The spoon found a resting place on the napkin he'd fished from the middle of the stack. He finished what soup was in his mouth. He gave himself a second to spin the name of the city through his mind again. He shook his head. "Nobody? Why?"

Zane elevated an eyebrow at him and reached into his suit pocket, pulling out a sheaf of papers. "Because someone ran a partial of your DNA through the Combined DNA Index System."

"CODIS? My DNA? Impossible. Besides, we aren't listed in CODIS." Anubis leaned forward. "What do you mean, partial?"

Zane pulled a second sheet of paper out of the stack. "As in it matches fifty percent of your markers. Enough that all the bells and whistles at Guardian went off. We track every input into all the national systems. When your markers lined up, *we* got the hit, not the lab tech that works for the Merced County Sheriff's office."

A graph filled the sheet Zane pointed to, with arrows indicating matching markers. Another page slid from the stack. A photograph of a man in his mid to late twenties. He didn't recognize the face. The next page was a Guardian-run dossier on the guy, one Mitch Canaga, lead lab tech for the criminal investigation unit of the Merced County Sheriff's Office. Anubis shook his head and let his gaze drift up to Zane's. "I've never seen this guy. Again, I ask, what do you mean, partial? My family's dead." They'd been brutally murdered in a home invasion while he was stationed overseas. His mother, father, and little sister died after the bastard that broke in, bound them, poured drain cleaner down their throats, and then cleaned out their house as the acid slowly ate his family's lives away. Samuel Avery, the perp who committed that heinous act, was out on bail when Anubis found him. He was the first person Anubis had ever killed that wasn't shooting at him. The bastard's death paid Anubis's price of admission into the Shadow World. If he had to do it over again, he wouldn't hesitate. Except now that he knew *how* to kill, it would have taken much, much longer for that bastard to die.

"We know about your mom, dad, and sister." Zane pulled out the last sheet from the stack he brought with him. A little girl with dark brown hair, golden eyes and a capricious smile stared back at him. Anubis ran his hand over his face and glanced away from the picture. It could have been his little sister, Thea. The family resemblance was that strong.

"Who is she?"

"Kadey Meyers. Her mother is—"

"Sky Meyers." Anubis finished for him. He sat back and tried to deal with the onslaught of emotion that name pulled forward. Sky was... fuck, she was the woman he didn't deserve and the woman he couldn't release.

"Yeah. I take it you didn't know?"

"Fuck, no." He turned his glare up and focused on Bengal. His gut, heart, and head fought for dominance. His gut told him not to get involved. He wasn't what they needed in their lives. His heart... fuck, his heart wanted to run out of the safe house and drive however long it took to find Sky and his daughter. And his head? His head told him to weigh all the options, develop a plan and assess the possible outcomes before he made a move.

"You've got a daughter." Zane used one finger to push the photo closer.

Anubis drew a deep breath and shrugged. "Doesn't matter. I can't do anything for them except bring death to their door." That was his gut talking. Loud and clear.

"Death is already making its way to their door, my friend. Kadey has a heart condition called Ebstein's Anomaly. It is when one of the valves in her heart is malformed. In most kids, it's mild; not with her. She needs surgery. Jewell thinks maybe her mom is using her connections to look for you."

Anubis's stomach twisted violently. The soup he'd consumed rose with the bile, lodging in his throat. He stared at the picture. His daughter was sick. He elevated his eyes to his friend. "I can't. I'm a Shadow."

"You can. Guardian has your back on this one. I'm assuming her mom is someone special?"

Anubis stared at the picture. "After you bailed me out of that mission, I came back here, to Fresno, to recuperate—a town where I knew nobody. Hell, I hadn't been in the state before. I laid low for the first three months before I went stir crazy. I met Sky at a bar. We hit it off, and one thing led to… well, it led to two months. I left in the middle of the night. An assignment."

"You kept in contact with her?"

Zane's question got a head nod. He had checked in on Sky through black door acquaintances. At first, never directly and never requesting any information about her, just making sure she would be all right. He made sure she'd been offered a good job in Sacramento, ensured things happened to provide her an affordable place to live. The last time he'd checked through those contacts, about six months after he left, she was working for the District Attorney as an office manager.

Then he'd done the wrong thing, and he'd done it more than once. About four years ago, he called her when he was in California, and they hooked up. Just a hook up at a cheap hotel in Davis, a town southeast of Sacramento.

He'd expected questions and to end up talking half the night, but Sky shocked the hell out of him. She didn't want to know anything about him or why he left, even though he had a perfectly good cover story to use. Hell, he should have suspected something when she wouldn't answer any of the questions he'd asked about how she'd been. Anubis rolled that thought around. Nah, he figured it was her way of keeping him at arm's length for leaving her so abruptly. Sky made it clear she was there for the sex—the fantastic, red-hot-orgasmic-rock-your-fucking-world kind of sex.

It was so damn good that one intense night led to more. Every time his work brought him to California, he called. The sex between them was so hot the devil's balls roasting in hell were frostbitten in comparison. The last time he was in the state before this mission was… damn near two years ago. Anubis was actually looking forward to calling her after he'd debriefed Bao's mission... but now? Fuck, now he had a daughter. *A daughter.* How the fuck was he supposed to wrap his mind around that?

Anubis shook himself out of his own head. Continuous questions spun while his mind was stuck on "reboot" and none of this shit would give him any answers. He moved a piece of paper off Canaga's picture. "Who is this guy to Sky?"

"He is her second cousin."

For some reason that bit of information made him feel better. In another life, he could have loved Sky. Maybe he *had* loved her, but he didn't have another life. He didn't exist. If he were to vanish off the face of the earth tomorrow, no one would know to grieve his loss. He stared at the chubby cheeks of the little girl who smiled so innocently into the camera. *He was a father.* "Okay, she needs surgery. Why is Sky trying to find me? Is the procedure that risky?"

"All surgery is risky, especially open-heart surgery, but there is another reason Sky is looking for you. There is always substantial blood loss during this type of operation, and your daughter will require multiple transfusions." Anubis froze as the realization hit him. He stared at the man across the table from him. "My daughter is Rh-null."

"She is. You know how rare your blood is. How rare hers is. There are only ten active Rh-null blood donors in the world. The hospital refuses to operate until a blood supply is located. You are her only chance."

Anubis donated his blood routinely until he joined Guardian. The International Blood Group Reference Laboratory in Filton, England, maintained the world's database of rare-blood donors, the International Rare Donor Panel. Before he became the man he was today, he'd been listed on that panel. As far as that group knew, he was dead. "What about the Rh-null people on the list?"

"There are none in the United States. The two that were listed on it died. One, of course, was you, the other died of old age about two years ago."

Anubis stared at the picture. The sparkle in the little girl's eyes shone like a beacon into his cold, hardened soul. That smile penetrated the vault where he'd sealed his emotions just like a heat-seeking missile found the ass end of a jet engine. "There is no other way?"

Zane shook his head. "Not according to the docs we talked to."

"I'll need the engineer to redesign my old cover."

"Name?"

"Kaeden Lang."

"It may take a few days to set it up, but I know Jacob will push this through as fast as he can."

"I'll make an anonymous blood donation." It would solve everything. Sky and Kadey would be safe from the danger that flew in a constant satellite around his life.

"We thought of that, but that is a risk Guardian isn't willing to take. If you are up there, you can control the situation. Once your rare blood type hits the medical system, doctors and researchers will have a field day, just like they did with Kadey."

Anubis knew Bengal's assumptions were true. When he'd been on the registry, the medical community hounded him relentlessly for donations for research. He'd given as much as he could, but the demand was never-ending.

"Go up there and get the lay of the land. We didn't have time to get an in-depth report on Sky's past or the acquaintances in her life. Jewell is working that as we speak." Zane leaned back in his chair and rubbed his hand over the five o'clock shadow he sported.

"Guardian has a doctor up there we trust to do your workup. You have an appointment in three days to do the screening to ensure your blood is viable. We can control what he puts in the system, but what happens after that? My lady is good, but from what she tells me, the medical systems are unbelievably easy to compromise. Thousands of access points and no definitive way to regulate who goes in and reviews patient information. The honest people stay honest, and HIPAA rules put some teeth into prosecuting those who are caught, but…"

Anubis sat back in his chair and played with the corner of his little girl's picture. "You're telling me I need to make contact."

"I am." Bengal leaned back and met Anubis's stare.

"Sky obviously did not want me to know about her daughter." Anubis remembered every word and every touch they shared when they were together. *Why hadn't she told him that he was a father? Probably because he showed up, fucked her and left.* Hell, he didn't blame her for not telling him. Still, it was a sucker punch.

"Newsflash. The kid is also *your* daughter and that little girl needs you." Bengal tapped the photograph with his finger.

Anubis rolled his shoulders and looked up at the ceiling. He'd put his life on the line countless times without a second thought, but this? Fuck, he didn't have the skills to do… family. Not anymore. He'd given up that part of his humanity long ago.

"Where's your head, brother?" Bengal's voice brought his wandering mind back to the kitchen and the conversation at hand.

"I don't know how to do or to be… this." He was honest. He reserved deception for the people they used, not the people with whom he worked.

"One step at a time." Bengal cleared his throat and leaned forward on the table, bracing on his forearms. "When I came out into the light, man…" Bengal shook his head. "It's like being born again. You need to relearn every-fucking-thing."

"I'm not stepping out like you." He had no intention of leaving the Shadows. He was damn good at what he did and taking out the scum of the world was his calling.

"Yeah, I get that. Only you can make the decision to stay or walk away."

"If I walk, it won't be toward the light."

"I know, man. That is always an option, but you don't need to make that decision. Yet."

Anubis nodded as he considered the facts. He could ignore his daughter's situation and hope that she'd find a donor, or he could man up and head north. His eyes fell on the picture again. The mop of curls and the brilliant smile left him no choice. "I'll also need access to my off-shore money. I'll give you an account number so funds can be transferred."

"I won't need an account number. Guardian will foot any cost and the hospital bills. I'll have accounts set up in Sacramento, checking and savings, plus you'll have several credit cards in Lang's name."

"I'll still need access to that money, so put it into those accounts. She's my daughter. I need to make sure she's taken care of."

Bengal looked across the table at him, and a sly smile spread across the man's face. "I'm sure the mother and the little girl will benefit from your generosity."

"Shut up, man. Has Sky been dealing with this alone?" He re-routed Bengal's propensity for bringing up his assumed humanity… or lack thereof.

"From what we can tell, yes. Again, we didn't have time to work through this the way we'd like, but according to the information Jewell was able to put together, Sky's expenditures are minimal with the exception of things for her daughter and now, the medical bills. We do know she's struggling to pay her debt."

"Do you have that brief here?"

Zane pulled another paper from the interior pocket of his suit. "Here is everything we could compile. Jewell is working a complete background on her. We have your back on this one. You have a daughter, Ani... *a daughter*, and she needs you. Whatever it takes."

"As long as it takes." Ani automatically finished the words he'd lived his life by for the last ten years.

CHAPTER TWO

SKY MEYERS PULLED UP IN FRONT OF HER modest home. The single-story detached had been a steal and a godsend when she first moved to Sacramento almost six years ago after she'd accepted a job with the State District Attorney's office. The old owner contacted her realtor when she was searching for a place to live. Sky had offered full asking price and signed the papers within hours of seeing the house. She'd been five months pregnant at the time with a great job and a salary she'd never dreamed of making.

A twist of her wrist turned off the car, and she let the sudden silence surround her. With the exception of the small breaths coming from the child safety seat strapped securely on the back seat of the late model Honda, it was blissfully quiet. If only she could mute the thoughts screaming through her mind as easily.

Sky closed her eyes and drew a deep breath. Her nerves had frayed to the point of breaking. Her body and soul hurt, and with each new blow, her heart crumbled a little bit more. Kadey's case of Ebstein's Anomaly was survivable if treated surgically, and normally, the small atrial septal defect didn't overly concern the doctors as it could be fixed during the same surgery. Sky shook her head. The doctor's words two weeks ago fell like a death knell. *"I'm sorry Sky, but Rh-null blood is the rarest blood on record. Donors with Rh-null blood can donate to anyone with any Rh-negative blood type, but they can only receive blood from those who are also Rh-null."* The doctor put down the pen he'd been holding and leaned forward. *"Do you know if her father is Rh-null?"*

Sky wiped at the tears that threatened to fall. Kadey's father. The man she fell hopelessly in love with—and the man who she'd allowed to repeatedly shatter her heart—as far as she could tell, didn't exist. No, loving Kaeden was an addiction she couldn't beat. She leaned her head back against the headrest and stared sightlessly at the dull gray cloth fabric covering the visor of her car. It was almost as if she'd dreamed up Kaeden Lang. She could see him in her mind's eye. Three inches over six feet tall, dark brown, almost black hair and his eyes... they were golden with long dark lashes that made them... irresistible. His year-round tan accentuated his body. Kaeden was strong and muscled without being bulky. Was he classically handsome? No, but he was arresting. So much so that a casual conversation, while she was waiting for her girlfriends to arrive for a night out, changed her world. Kaeden Lang was a seduction that held her captive, even to this day. He was her Kryptonite and drug of choice.

Sky rolled her head and looked down the street as her mind wandered. The man was quiet, brooding at times, but always kind and the sex was literally life-changing. Sky had jumped into the relationship with a naive ease. Kaden Lang had captured her heart and then crushed it beyond repair when he left without explanation, and then he opened the wound that she'd stitched together, bit by bit. She'd lied to herself and believed she'd started to heal until her phone rang, and he was on the line. His call came when Sky was at her lowest. She'd nearly died delivering Kadey, struggled with postpartum depression, and had lost her mom to cancer. When Kaeden called, she wanted to feel something good. She hated that she still wanted him, but she did, so she left Kadey with a friend and drove to Davis, California and met him at a hotel... like a whore. She'd compounded her weakness by doing the same thing every time he called after that. Kaeden Lang was a bastard she couldn't resist, even though she knew, deep in her soul, she was probably one of many. That was why she'd never told him about Kadey.

Sky sniffed and brushed away a tear. After the last time, she woke up in that damn hotel, alone, she'd promised herself she wouldn't go if he called again. So, she made herself go on dates, meet people and even found someone who cared enough to stick around, but...

Sky clenched her fist so hard she felt her stubby nails biting into her palm. The bastard. Why? She wanted to ask him why he had walked away from her. She'd give anything to know. They were so happy, or at least she thought they were. She would have followed him to the ends of the earth, but, out of the blue, he left. One week later she found out she was pregnant.

Sky glanced at her daughter in the rear-view mirror. Kadey was everything to her. Her entire world. She'd risk anything to find the one man who might be able to save her. In order to find Kaeden, she'd used her professional connections within the police department to run his name, and they'd come up with nothing, although she'd seen his California driver's license with her own eyes. Her cousin ran Kadey's blood through the national database looking for matches. There were none. Sky had even contacted the IRS through the DA's office, but Kaeden Lang had not filed a tax return. According to every agency she used to track him, Kaeden Lang did not exist, and yet his child slept in the car seat behind her.

Sky didn't regret a single thing she'd done while searching for Kaeden, but the DA had discovered she'd used her professional contacts for personal reasons, and he'd suspended her pending an internal investigation. She knew they were slow rolling the inquiries so she wouldn't lose her insurance, but it was inevitable that she would be fired—for doing whatever it took to save her little girl's life.

Sky ran both hands through her brown hair and pulled on it in desperation. She was chasing ghosts, had no income, and her savings had dwindled to nothing. Worse, she teetered on the verge of losing her health insurance. Despair rolled in wet tracks over her cheeks. She had no idea where to turn or what else to do.

Her phone chirped with a text alert. She looked down and closed her eyes. Trey. No, she couldn't deal with him now. The two-year relationship with a man she'd hoped would be 'the one' had soured over the last year. Trey had changed… or maybe she'd changed. He was manipulative, selfish and demanding, but she'd still clung to the relationship. Trey's lack of empathy and understanding over her concerns about Kadey had driven a wedge between them, yet she still clung to the breadcrumbs of caring and kindness he sometimes bestowed on her. She hated herself for not breaking off with him, but she was so… alone.

Sky dropped her head and let the tears fall. She stifled silent sobs, unwilling to release the pain aloud as if her audible distress would solidify the reality of her situation—there was no other avenue to pursue, and no one left to reach out and hang onto. Utter desolation enfolded her and ate through the essence of her soul.

"Momma, are you sad?"

Sky jumped, brushed away her tears, and turned a brilliant smile toward her daughter. "Nope, remember what Momma said about the dust making her eyes water? I got a big sniff of dust, sweetie."

"Okay. Can I watch Dora?"

"Sure, baby." Sky pulled her keys out of the ignition and went around the car before carefully extracting her daughter from the car seat. The wind swirled the little girl's curls into her face. Kadey blew raspberries trying to get the hair out of her mouth. Sky turned them out of the wind and drew her finger down her daughter's cheek pulling the hair back. "Silly hair."

"Silly hair." Kadey echoed Sky's words and then yawned and dropped her head onto Sky's shoulder. "I'm tired, Momma."

Sky pressed her lips to Kadey's forehead. "I know baby. We can take a nap."

"After Dora." Kadey yawned and nestled closer to Sky.

"Sure honey, after Dora." Kadey would most likely be asleep before the program even started. Sky sniffed away the lingering effects of her sobs.

"Is it dusty?"

"It sure is." It had been "dusty" since her cousin called and told her that he'd struck out on the CODIS match. That had been her last hope. Ever since it had been so… damn… dusty.

Sky juggled Kadey and her purse to insert the key into her deadbolt. It was a familiar dance. She hip-checked the door sending the stubborn, solid oak slab inward.

"Dora?" Kadey whispered as Sky laid her down on the couch.

"Sure." She grabbed the remote and turned on the television. There was no need to change the channel; it was always on the one that played Kadey's favorites. Sky grabbed a chenille throw off the back of the couch and draped it over Kadey. "I'm going to go get us a snack."

"I'm not hungry." Kadey's eyes tracked the little cartoon girl on the television.

"Five bites?"

"Two." Kadey smiled up at her mom.

The negotiation tactic was new, but she'd go with it. "Four and I'll let you take a bath in the big bathtub."

"With bubbles?"

"Yup."

"Okay, four."

Sky would tempt Kadey to eat more than four bites with some cinnamon granola and yogurt, her favorite. She bent over and kissed Kadey again before she headed into the kitchen. She looked back over her shoulder checking one last time before she turned the corner to the kitchen. The house was old and didn't have an open floor plan. She'd love to be able to keep a constant eye on Kadey, but she'd learned to adapt.

Sky turned the light on in the kitchen. "Oh God!" She grabbed her chest and fell back against the corner of the door. Kaeden Lang leaned against the counter in her kitchen. He'd changed. He was broader and heavier, but still very much the man she thought she'd loved.

"I understand you need me?"

Sky quickly glanced over her shoulder making sure the shocked gasp she'd let out hadn't startled Kadey. Turning her eyes back to the man in her kitchen, she narrowed them and held his steady gaze as she tried to breathe. She stared at the man, mute, as her mind raced to formulate some type of response, instead of launching into a thousand questions.

"Sky?"

She shook her head slowly. With pinpoint, laser focus, she aimed all the helpless anger and desperation she'd accumulated over five years at Kaeden. *If that was his name.* "Do I need you? Me…" She jabbed her forefinger at the middle of her chest. "… need you? No, *I needed* you five years ago. *I needed* you when I spent twenty-seven hours in labor delivering your daughter and going through an emergency C-section. *I needed* you when I was a single mother with postpartum depression. I needed you when my mom died of cancer. I needed you every time I woke up alone in that fucking hotel in Davis." Sky stopped and drew a deep breath before she continued, "*I no longer need you, Kaeden, but *your baby girl*? *She* needs you." Sky whisper-hissed the words.

"Why didn't you tell me about her?"

His question floored her. "Why didn't I… What? Would knowing you'd fathered a child have made you suddenly appear in our lives? I'm many things when it comes to you, Kaeden, but stupid isn't one of them. You would never have stayed." She glared at him, daring him to deny the truth.

"I'm here now." Kaeden crossed his arms over his chest. His eyes held hers without flinching from the rage that gripped her.

Sky grabbed at the first full thought that flashed through her brain. "How did you know I was looking for you?"

"My people reached out to me." He shrugged as if it was nothing.

"Your *people*?" Sky's head popped back. *What the!* "You have *people*?

"Yes."

Kaeden's facial features didn't change, not one iota, and the statue impersonation pissed her off even more. Sky almost hated him at that moment, and still, her traitorous body found everything about the stoic man sexy as hell. *No! That was not happening again!* Ever. Sky shook, trying to discipline her wayward thoughts and with a feral determination pointed the conversation back to him. "You're going to have to be a little more forthcoming than that. Are you in a flipping gang or the mother-trucking mafia? And for goodness sake, could you please tell me your real name?"

A small chuff of laughter floated across the room toward her. "Flipping? Mother Trucking?" A crack in his steel façade, finally. The sexy bastard.

"I have a daughter who is a parrot. Don't you change the freaking subject! Who the heck are you?" She wasn't letting him off so easily.

The man before her shrugged. "You know who I am. I don't belong to a gang, and I'm not in the Mafia. I'm... I work overseas for... a security agency."

She heard Kadey cough, and as much as she wanted answers, Sky's attention whipped to her daughter in the front room. She glanced over her shoulder before she glared at him and pointed her finger at his chest. "I never knew you, don't pretend like I did. Stay right there. Don't you dare disappear. Again." She tiptoed out of the kitchen and down the short hall to the living room to check on Kadey.

"How sick is she?"

Kaeden's whisper came from right behind her. She jumped and spun around almost clipping him with her shoulder. Sky stepped away from him and pulled her hands through her hair. Kadey was sound asleep on the couch. She looked down at her baby and the surge of love she always felt cascaded through her once again. "She needs an operation to fix a valve in her heart. The doctors are guarded when they talk about time. She could stay like this for months, but then again, her valve's ability function could be compromised at any time." Sky put her hand on her neck and rubbed the tension that built there. "According to them, the operation is relatively simple. She also has a small ASD... a defect in her heart that the surgeons will repair when they operate. If they can operate. Her blood is rare."

Kaeden walked over to the couch and crouched down beside it. His eyes traveled over Kadey. "She's Rh-null."

Sky shook like a leaf in a windstorm. She reached out and put her hand on his strong shoulder as she whispered, "Yes, that's right. For the love of God, please tell me you are, too." Standing unassisted right now wasn't an option.

He reached up and covered her hand with his. The warmth of his rough hand spread through her immediately. "I am."

"Will you donate blood before you leave so she can have her operation?" Sky closed her eyes and prayed that the man she once thought of spending her life with would agree.

"No." Sky clutched her gut as if he'd hit her.

Kaeden stood up and turned around to face her. "I'll donate blood, and I'll stay until we know for sure she'll be alright. Our blood is extremely rare, and I won't risk leaving in case she needs more."

Sky gazed up at him. A new scar ran from his ear down to his chin. Other than that, Kaeden looked almost same as he had the last time she'd seen him—a little over two years ago. Except he wasn't. This wasn't the version of the man she'd meet years ago in Fresno, and it wasn't the version of the man she spent stolen nights with, he was... different, colder... more distant. The last two years had been hard on him. She shook her head, still in disbelief at his words, "You'll stay?"

Kaeden turned his head toward her and elevated a single eyebrow. "I'll stay until she's received what she needs." Sky trembled, the impact of his words, that he was here in her home ready to save her daughter's life meant everything. Kaeden had come back, and he'd agreed to help. "Thank you." She couldn't help the tears that fell. Kadey would have the surgery. She'd have a chance at a normal life. For the last four months, she hadn't allowed herself to hope. A sense of relief flooded through her and Sky leaned into him only because she couldn't stand on her own. Her eyes closed as his arms slowly wrapped around her. She said a prayer of thanksgiving to God for sending this man back into their lives, if only to donate his life-saving blood.

A knock sounded at the front door, and Kaeden no longer held her. In the time it took her to open her eyes, he was plastered against the wall and peeking out the blinds toward the front door. Sky ran her hands up and down her suddenly chilled arms. This man—this distant version of Kaeden—scared her. A second knock followed the first, and Sky made two steps toward the door before Kaeden stopped her with a hand on her arm. Nothing violent or harsh, but enough to still her immediately.

"Do you know a man who drives a silver Prius?" Kaeden's muscles were tight and bunched.

Sky nodded. "Trey Cross, he's… we've dated." She didn't want to admit that to Kaeden.

A third knock, this one much louder and more insistent, followed the first two. Sky peeked at Kadey who tossed in her sleep. "I need to answer the door before he wakes up Kadey."

Kaeden relaxed his hold before he whispered, "I'll leave through the back. I'll be back tonight. Don't mention my being here to anyone." He glanced at Kadey. Was he suggesting if she told someone he was here, he wouldn't help Kadey?

"Don't you dare threaten to leave us again, Kaeden, not when she needs you." Sky grasped his forearm and felt the taut, roped cords of his muscles under her hand.

He lowered his arm breaking the contact. "I'll be back tonight. Don't mention to your lover that I was here."

Another knock, followed by Trey's voice calling her name snapped her head toward the door. She looked back at where Kaeden had been and scanned only an empty room.

"Momma? Someone is at the door." Kadey sat up and rubbed her eyes.

"Yes, baby. I'll get it." Sky covered the distance and opened the door.

"What took you so long to answer the door and why the hell didn't you answer my text?" Trey's grey-blue eyes darted immediately past her into the front room.

"Please mind your language. I haven't looked at my phone, and I was in the kitchen. I was going to get Kadey a snack." Sky moved out of the way and let him in.

"Hey, kid." Trey acknowledged Kadey.

Kadey pushed her curls out of her face. "My name's Ka-dey." She gave Trey a disapproving look before she turned her stare toward the television and her beloved Dora.

"Right. Whatever." Trey followed Sky into the kitchen and mussed Kadey's curls, flopping them back into her face as he passed.

"Where have you been?" Trey pulled her into his arms, and Sky couldn't help noticing the difference in the how she felt in Trey's embrace versus the way she'd felt when Kaeden had held her. Trey put her on edge, made her tense, while in Kaeden's, she felt protected and safe. Sky moved out of Trey's grasp and looked around the kitchen. "I need to finish getting Kadey a snack." She used the excuse to create distance from him. She headed toward the cupboard that held the granola and pushed up on her toes to fish it out.

"Have you heard anything else on bio dad's whereabouts?" Trey hopped up onto the counter next to her and grabbed an apple out of the bowl. His messy dishwater blond hair fell into his eyes.

Sky shook her head. "No, I haven't heard a thing." Not necessarily a lie, she knew where he was, or at least she knew he was near. She pulled open the fridge and took out the yogurt.

"You've checked with all the police agencies the D.A. works with?" Trey took a huge bite of the apple as Sky portioned some vanilla yogurt into a small plastic bowl.

"Yes. That's why I was suspended, remember?" She closed the lid on the container and put it back in the refrigerator.

"Your fault for getting caught. And the blood thing didn't work?"

"You know it didn't." Sky dropped the serving spoon into the sink and braced herself on the countertop. How had Kaeden known she was looking for him? What had she done that had caught his 'peoples' attention? The IRS check? The California Law Enforcement Terminal entries that the Sacramento Police Department had performed? What security agency did he work with? She needed to ask him when he came back. Because he *was* coming back. He had to.

Trey put his hand on her waist, and she jumped. "Hey, settle down. You're strung tight aren't you?"

"Yeah, well, dang it, I've earned that right." Sky snapped at him.

"Woah, now. Don't take your shit out on me." Trey pulled his hand from her and took a step back. "I can leave, it's not like I don't have options."

Sky drew in a deep breath, she shouldn't have snapped at him. "I'm sorry, I'm just exhausted."

"Right. I can tell by the ton of luggage under your eyes. I'll spend the night, and you can get some sleep without worrying about getting up to check on the kid."

Sky blinked at the suggestion. Trey had *never* spent the night. That wasn't what they'd agreed upon. It was the only rule

Sky had ever made or enforced. "Stay?" She parroted the word back and gawked at him.

"Yeah, I mean I can keep an ear open for the kid. You can get some sleep, so you don't look like you're fifty years old. Don't worry, I'm not going to jump you in front of your little princess." Trey sat the half-eaten apple on the counter. "Not like we've been able to *do that* lately anyway."

He pulled her into his arms, but she held herself away from him. The dig about not having had sex was true. They hadn't slept together in about six months—but it was a cold, cutting comment. Sky's entire world was imploding, and he was taking shots at her for not putting out? He'd finally crossed a line she wouldn't ignore. He didn't care about Kadey's condition, Trey wanted her rested so she'd put out. Sky stepped back breaking his hold. "I think it would be best if you left. Now."

"What?" A shocked look crossed his face, but it was replaced by anger within seconds.

"I'm not going to be in the mood to '*do that*' with you for one heck of a long time." Sky used her fingers to quote his words. "My primary concern is my daughter. I won't allow you to spend the night. That would lead to Kadey asking questions I don't need right now."

"Why not? How much longer are you going to pretend that you don't have a life outside of that kid? She's young. Tell her we're friends and that sometimes grownups spend the night."

"Ahhh… no, when and if I have that conversation with my daughter it will be about a serious relationship." Sky grabbed the granola to sprinkle it on top of the yogurt.

Trey snatched her arm and turned her. His grip bit into her arm and the granola in her hand flew onto the floor. "Serious relationship? As if the last two years of putting up with your drama hasn't proven I'm serious?"

Sky broke free of his hold and went to the corner to grab her broom and dustpan. His reference to her drama wasn't new. He hated dealing with any of the emotional wreckage Kadey's diagnosis and Sky's subsequent actions had caused. She talked to the floor as she swept, instead of meeting his eyes, "The fact that you don't understand why I don't want to deal with this now is another problem, Trey. Look, right now, I'm not capable of giving anything to anyone other than Kadey, and you should see that. My child is the only thing I can focus on. If that makes you mad, well, then… I'm sorry, but I just don't have the capacity to do anything except take care of my baby. I can't take care of you, too." She swept the crumbs into the dustpan. As she straightened, she glanced at Trey. His eyes narrowed and his fists clenched. Sky shrunk in on herself. It wasn't the first time she'd angered Trey, but it was the first time she wondered if he'd strike her. She paused with the dustpan in her hand, hovering over the trash can.

"Ungrateful bitch." Trey spun on his heel and stomped down the small hallway.

Was she? Had she led Trey on? No. Her shoulders bunched up when the front door slammed. Sky drew a shaky breath in and released it. "Way to mess that up."

"What did ya' mess up?" Kadey asked as she came into the kitchen.

"Ahhh… I messed up your granola. I spilled some." Sky dumped the granola from the dustpan into the trash can and put the broom and dustpan away.

"Why is Trey mad again?"

"You know, baby, I'm not sure." *Other than wanting sex and not getting any, oh, and her standing up for herself.*

"Oh well, we can't cry over spilled milk, right, Momma?" Kadey moved her step stool to the counter where her snack waited.

Sky smiled at her little girl. She had no idea why Kadey picked that saying, but she'd go with it. "That's right, honey. Let me wash my hands, and I'll get you some more granola for your yogurt."

"Then a bubble bath in the big tub!" A huge smile radiated from Kadey's face.

"You bet. Yogurt, a tubble of bubble and then we can read books until bedtime."

"Tubble of bubble! Get clean, no trouble!" Kadey repeated the nonsensical saying they'd made up.

"No trouble," Sky repeated as she handed Kadey a spoon. *If only.*

CHAPTER THREE

"JEWELL KING." THE VOICE ON THE OTHER END of the phone was familiar, yet it wasn't the person with whom Ani wanted to speak.

"Zane Reynolds, please." Ani glanced up as Trey Cross stormed out of Sky's house. The way the door reverberated on its hinges pissed him off. There was no way his daughter was still asleep now—not that Anubis needed another reason to hate the man.

"Zane is in a meeting, what can I do for you?" The chirpy professional tone told him that Jewell hadn't recognized his voice yet.

"I'm not sure. I'm used to doing things… in the dark." Ani smiled as the typing sounds in the background stilled.

"Well, hello my old friend." Jewell's voice softened as if she actually believed that Anubis was her friend.

"It has been awhile." He watched the Prius reverse and hightail it out of the neighborhood about as fast as a preschooler on a scooter, because… Prius.

"I told myself if I ever spoke to you again, I'd thank you for everything you did for Zane and me. So… thank you. If you ever need anything, just name it."

"Ah, well then maybe I won't need to speak with Zane. I need a dossier on one Trey Cross." Ani saw the lights go out in the kitchen. The linen drapes kept Sky and Kadey from his view, but he knew they were in the house.

"What level, garden variety or…"

"I want to know the brand of tweezers he uses to pluck his nose hair." Anubis wasn't playing games. If the man was the one Sky wanted in her life, he damn well better be a good guy. If not, Anubis would ensure he disappeared from his daughter's world—without a trace.

"Well alrighty, then. One nose-hair-level dossier coming up."

He heard her keyboard sing.

"Um… dude? This guy, he's up in Sacramento with you… right?"

A tingle of anticipation ran up Anubis' spine. "Yes."

"Are you sure you got his name right? There are three Trey Crosses in California, one is eighty-seven, one is in maximum security lock up at the Super Max facility in Lompoc, and one is seven years old."

"I have a license plate number." Anubis watched lights turn on at the other end of Sky's small house.

"Well, duh. That would help." Jewell's sarcastic reply made him chuckle. Bengal had his hands full with this one that was for sure. He popped off the license plate number and listened as she worked the keyboard.

"Okay, well first off his name is Arnold T. Cross. Let's just see what his middle name is… Oh, this is a gem. Arnold Treynor Cross. Goodness, no wonder he shortened his name."

Anubis shifted as he listened to Bengal's woman. He pushed against the small out building at the side of the yard adjacent to Sky's neighbor across the street. The view gave him unimpeded visual access to her front door. He'd locked the back door and activated a cheap, but effective, magnetic balance sensor on the outside frame. He'd also placed pressure sensors under all the windows of her home. Until he could obtain more advanced tech, old school at the back door would do. If someone was outside trying to get in, he'd know.

"Okay, I have a complete dossier in the works. How can I get this to you? I'm assuming you don't have a secure email out there?" She left the question hanging.

"No, but I'll need to have access to the information. In our section of the organization, we have dead drop email accounts."

"Of course. I can work that for you. Give me a couple hours and then call back. Wait... no, strike that, Zane's going to drag me out of here in about an hour. He's stupid crazy about only letting me work ten hours a day, but I'll have this for you first thing in the morning. Is that okay?"

"Perfect."

"Cool. Hey, while we're working together, what am I supposed to call you?"

He shook his head at Jewell's question. Yes, Bengal must have his hands full. "You don't. I-call-you. Good night." He disconnected the burner phone and pulled out the cheap sim card, snapping it in two. One piece flew toward the street, the other the top of the small structure he was using as cover.

Anubis leaned against the shed and continued to watch the world flow around him. Cars came and went. Dogs barked up and down the neighborhood. The few children who lingered out in the chilly September evening grumbled and complained when adult voices called them inside for the night. Ani glanced at his watch. According to the pattern set the previous nights he'd watched the small house, the light in Kadey's room should go out soon. He'd wait until the little one was asleep before he returned to talk with Sky.

Anubis ticked off the things on tomorrow's schedule. He would drive out to a private practitioner that Guardian had cleared and sanctioned to have his blood drawn and tested. He hadn't had a physical in the true meaning of the word in years, and there were some questionable needles used to patch himself up on occasion. Making sure he hadn't acquired something he could give to his daughter was essential. He'd need Sky to advise the doctors performing Kadey's operation that she'd found an Rh-null blood donor.

No, he couldn't think of them as his family. Anubis had no certainty he could live a life outside the shadows that Guardian cast. Even if he could turn his back on Guardian and walk away from the profession that had claimed him, Sky obviously didn't want him in her daughter's life. Six years ago, he'd allowed himself to forget "Anubis" for a short time, and while he healed physically, he'd allowed himself to fall in love. The result? He wounded a woman he'd never intended to hurt and fathered a baby girl that he now needed to protect. He would protect her, with his life if need be… but, in reality, the easiest way to protect her was to stay out of her life.

The moment he looked at the picture Bengal pushed across the table, he knew he'd do anything to protect his daughter. That pile of dark brown curls and the perfect Cupid's bow lips… yes, he could see the family resemblance. She looked just like her aunt and grandmother, two people, she'd never be able to meet. Anubis shook his head. The little angel looked like his sister Thea when she was that age. He'd been twelve when his little imp of a sister was born. Back then, she was an amazing little person that worshiped the ground he walked on, and he could deny her nothing.

Anubis watched the neighborhood settle into the evening and wondered what his daughter was like. He yearned to see her awake, listen to her talk, watch her expressions, see her laugh and smile. He needed to strangle those thoughts. Emotion couldn't seep into the equation. It would be best if he treated the entire situation as a mission. He knew the parameters of this event. His objective was to follow through, ensure Sky and the child were safe, healthy, and financially secure, and then walk away. This time it would be forever.

Anubis hoisted away from the building and after a long searching sweep of the area, moved out of the shadows. He crossed the street and went to the back door. The lock took only seconds to manipulate. He let himself in quietly. Walking silently through the laundry room and into the kitchen, he paused. Expecting silence, or perhaps the television, the sound of Sky's soft sniffs drew him toward the interior of the house. He carefully worked his way into the living room without making a sound.

She sat on the couch, hugging an old ragged teddy bear. Strain showed on her face and tears fell down her cheeks. Whatever sent her lover away earlier must be weighing heavily upon her. For the first time in one hell of a long time, Anubis wasn't sure what he should do or say. So, he said nothing. He allowed his boot to scrape the floor.

"It's real? You're here to help?" Sky looked up at him, her big brown eyes begging him to answer.

"I am here to help you. I'll take care of everything, including any hospital bills." Anubis glanced around the room. His eyes stopped at the framed pictures he'd noticed on the wall earlier in the day. They showed mother and daughter in front of a Christmas tree, Kadey with Santa, and portrait photos of them together, each one about a year apart if he'd have to guess.

Sky followed his eyes toward the hallway at the back of the house. "She's asleep."

"I know. I was looking at the pictures." Not one of the displayed photos had his bud Arnie Cross in them. Anubis filed that information away, pleased the man hadn't infiltrated the displayed memories.

"She's my world." Sky reached for a tissue and blew her nose.

"I didn't know you were pregnant." Anubis sat down across from her. A gentle pulse of warm air pushed across the room when the furnace kicked on.

"Would it have mattered if you had? I obviously wasn't enough to keep you from going."

"It wasn't you."

Sky let out a bark of laughter. "Oh, please, don't give me the old, 'it wasn't you, it was me', speech. I think I deserve some answers."

"Answers I probably cannot give you." Figuratively, his hands were bound, and he had a gag order in place. If he told Sky anything about his life, he'd not only endanger her and Kadey but the people who walked with him in the shadows.

"Did you always know you were going to leave?" Sky worried the seam on the side of the teddy bear with her fingers rather than look at him. He understood the need to know and yet not wanting to know.

"Yes. I was only in Fresno to recuperate, although I didn't expect to be called away so suddenly. I couldn't explain why I was leaving. I felt it was easier for you if I just disappeared."

"Right, because every pregnant woman wants to wonder what she'd done to make the man she loved run away in the middle of the night." Sky gave a half-hearted laugh and threw the bear aside.

Anubis watched the bear, but his mind focused on her words. "You loved me?"

"I thought I did, once upon a time, but you messed that up." Sky pulled her legs up into the chair and wrapped her arms around them. She leaned forward placing her chin on her knees. The woman was beautiful, even when exhausted. Thick brown hair fell past her shoulders. She had large, beautiful brown eyes and a smile that could light up a room. Anubis hadn't seen that smile since he'd returned. "You'll come to the hospital with me tomorrow?"

"No. I have an appointment with a physician tomorrow to have my blood drawn and tested. I will have the results sent to Kadey's doctor."

"I'll get his name for you…"

"I have all the information I need to ensure the tests are sent. You should notify Dr. Erickson that you have found a donor and the test results will be forwarded to him tomorrow."

"How do you have that information? Wait, let me guess, your people?"

"Yes."

"They'll want to schedule the surgery soon." Sky bit her bottom lip before she spoke again. "Thank you for coming back. I don't think I said that before. You're giving her a chance to live."

"She's my daughter."

"No, she's Kaeden Lang's daughter, but from what I've discovered, Kaeden Lang doesn't exist."

"He does now, at least for a short while." They sat in silence, looking at each other as if the quiet could strip away the results of years of separation and secrecy. Whatever damage he'd done to their relationship, nothing could erase the memories of their days and nights together. Anubis kept them tucked away from everything and everyone. They were his and his alone, precious memories that sustained him in the darkest of nights.

"Will you answer some questions?" The quiet lilt of her voice floated across the room and returned him to the present.

"If I can." He would tell her what he could, which wouldn't be much.

"What government organization do you work for? Are you a spy?"

Anubis chuckled and shook his head. "Like James Bond? No, I'm not a spy. I work for a large security concern, and I perform my duties overseas, exclusively."

"Doing what?"

Sky's gaze leveled on him and he held the connection. "My job. I won't elaborate."

Sky dropped her gaze and whispered, "Is it dangerous?"

Anubis drew a deep breath and relaxed back into the recliner. "It's dangerous only if I make mistakes."

"Do you make many mistakes?"

"I've made one. Hence, the trip to Fresno to recuperate."

"Why did you act like there was a terrorist wielding a gun at my door when Trey knocked earlier?" Sky released the hold on her legs and leaned against the side of the chair. Her eyes were heavy with fatigue.

"I'm still getting used to being back. When I'm overseas, my job requires meticulous vigilance. Perhaps, I overreacted."

"You did." Her eyes dipped closed and then popped open, and she sagged further into the arm of the chair. Finally, Sky yawned and put her head down on the arm. "You've missed out on so many wonderful things. She's amazing, and she's my entire world."

Anubis nodded. He swallowed hard. Her words picked at the scar that covered the place where he stored his emotions. "What about your lover, where does he fit into your world?"

Sky chuckled sadly. "He doesn't. He wanted to spend the night tonight. God, I guess he was trying to be nice, but I don't have the emotional energy to explain to Kadey why he would be here in the morning. He got pissed, again, and stormed out." She closed her eyes again. Her lids fluttered but remained closed.

"How will you explain me to Kadey?"

"Hmmm… you're her daddy. Simple…" Sky's voice trailed off and her breathing tapered into a steady rhythm.

Anubis stared at the woman in front of him. She'd lost weight since he'd known her, probably from the stress she was living under. He stood silently and maneuvered around the coffee table stooping to pick up Sky.

Her eyes blinked open.

"Shhh… I'm just taking you to your bed. I'll watch over both of you."

"I can walk." The effect of her complaint lessened dramatically when her head fell against his shoulder.

Anubis tightened his hold slightly before carrying her to her room. A small lamp on the bedside illuminated the room. He laid her down and pulled an old quilt up from the foot of the queen-sized bed. Turning to switch off the light, he paused. A framed picture sat on the table. It was a stupid selfie taken when they were together. A mistake he never should have allowed. Her thick hair obscured his face almost completely as they wrestled for the phone. They were both laughing and happy. He had deleted the digital version of that photo and destroyed the chip that held it, but not the memory of the night. He'd allowed that one printed photo… and she'd kept it.

Anubis switched off the light and made his way into Kadey's room. He smiled at the furnishings. It looked like all the cartoon princesses of the world had combined in one location and exploded inside the room. It was vibrant and kind of hideous at the same time with countless shades of pink and all things sparkly. The canopy over the twin bed was festooned with ribbons and billowing pink fabric. He kneeled down beside the bed and watched his daughter sleep. Her long lashes fell against her cheeks, and her eyes twitched under her lids. Anubis dared to reach out and push a stray curl away from her cheek.

He moved away before he disturbed her slumber and made a circuit of the home, noting the areas of security he would enhance before he left. Anubis repositioned the chair he'd sat in earlier, moving his back to a corner, and ensuring his vision of both bedrooms remained unimpeded. Of all the surveillance operations he'd ever conducted, this one was the most important.

CHAPTER FOUR

OH NO! SKY WOKE WITH A START. HER heart slammed in her chest as she pushed the covers off her and bolted into Kadey's room. The bed covers were thrown back, the bed empty. Sky swiveled on a dime and yelled, "Kadey!"

"In the kitchen, momma!" *Oh, thank God!* Sky bolted through the small house and skidded to a stop at the kitchen doorway, taking in the sight before her. "We're making pancakes!" Kadey stood on her step stool holding a dripping spoon in the air. A huge white t-shirt draped over her pink pajamas, and a knot at the side kept her from stepping on the hem. Sky glanced from her daughter to Kaeden. The man winked at her and expertly guided Kadey's attention back to the big mixing bowl he was holding for her.

How did this happen and why isn't Kadey freaked out about Kaeden being here? "Ahh… when did you wake up, honey?" Sky moved into the kitchen, ping-ponging her eyes between her daughter and Kaeden.

Kadey shrugged and looked up at Kaeden.

"About twenty minutes ago?" Kaeden asked Kadey. The little girl smiled and nodded.

"And you're making pancakes…" She glanced at Kaeden. The man had the audacity to smile. *Smile!* She had a thousand questions, and he was standing there smiling at her!

"Yup." Kadey held the spoon with both hands and pulled it around in the batter. "See, Momma?"

"I do." I don't understand, but I do see you." She glanced up at Kaeden and mouthed over Kadey's downturned head. *What did you do?*

"Hey squirt, let me finish up with this. We have to put it on the griddle now anyway."

"Okay. Momma, can I watch Dora?"

"Yes, honey." Kadey got off the stool and skipped into the kitchen, the T-shirt waving behind her.

Sky spun on her heel. "What did you tell her?"

"That I was a friend of yours. That I was making you breakfast so you could sleep."

"And she didn't ask any questions?"

"Other than could she help make you breakfast? Nope. Children are remarkably trusting." Kaeden's look lingered on her face. He nodded almost as if he was confirming some unspoken opinion. "You look better rested and just as beautiful as the day I met you."

Oh. Well… oh. Dang it! No… do not let him get to you again! Sky pushed her hair out of her face. No rat's nest that she could feel, but she probably looked horrible. *Who cares?* "Yeah, I doubt that I look anything like that girl. I haven't slept that long or that deeply in months. Thank you for that, too, by the way." Sky rubbed her temples and tried to pull herself together. Why in the hell was she worried about how she looked? This thing with Kaeden was over. Besides, she needed answers to questions and exhaustion was no longer an excuse to put off the discussion that needed to happen. "I didn't ask this last night, but do you want her to know… about you?"

"What does she already know?" Kaeden whisked the batter as he spoke.

"Only enough to satisfy her curiosity. I told her that her daddy loved her very much, but he couldn't come live with us because other people needed him and that he was a good man." *And that I could have loved him with all my heart.* Sky shrugged away the thought. It would never happen. He didn't do relationships. She was just a hook-up for him. It was something she'd learned to accept.

Kaeden looked at her with an intensity that, had she not known the man intimately, would have terrified her. Finally, he spoke, "If you think me being here and then leaving again will be too hard for her, then feel free not to tell her."

"Because you *will* be leaving again."

"Yes." He portioned the batter out, and the pancakes hit the griddle with a low hiss.

Sky poured a cup of coffee and sat down at the small table. "Part of me wants to spare her that pain of the inevitable separation, but she deserves to know her daddy cared for her enough to come back and save her." She saw Kaeden's shoulders stiffen. "You do care, don't you?" Sky had seen him last night; she'd recognized the way Kaeden looked at his daughter. *She* looked at Kadey that way, but maybe she was letting her emotions cloud her judgment. She knew Kaeden didn't have feelings for her, but Kadey was his child. There was no disputing that fact. Still, her own father didn't care if she existed… so…

Kaeden flipped the pancakes. He glanced over at her and nodded, confirming he cared.

Damn, I bet that hurt like a bitch. Sky set her coffee cup down and buried her face in her hands. She mentally slapped herself. She hated when stress made her spiteful and mean and vowed not to let this situation make her any more bitter. She glanced over at Kaeden. He was here; he had admitted he cared for his daughter; it was more than she'd had twenty-four hours ago.

Sky raised her thumb to her mouth and nibbled on the nail. She had no idea what the correct choice was in this matter and said as much to Kaeden, "I'll admit I don't know what to do. Yesterday, you demanded I not tell anyone you were here. If I tell Kadey, she's going to spout that information off to everyone she sees. I need some input."

Kaeden flipped the pancakes onto a plate and turned off the stove. He turned around and sat down with her at the table. "Yesterday was an excess of caution on my part. My profession doesn't allow me to trust people." Kaeden glanced out toward the front room. "If you would allow me to give her some happy memories of me, I would be grateful."

"You make that sound like you'll never come back. One day she may need you again." Sky rimmed the top of her coffee cup with her finger. She brought her gaze to him. His expression confirmed her words even though he didn't verbalize the thoughts. "Again, I'm not sure I know what to do here, Kaeden. Is it fair to introduce you as her daddy and then have you leave us again?"

"Probably not." Kaeden's face remained emotionless.

Sky sipped her coffee and spun the scenario a thousand different ways, but every time she examined the outcome, her heart spoke louder than her mind. She took a pancake from the plate and tore a small piece off. "Look, I want to do what's right by her, and I don't want her hurt, but my heart tells me you deserve to know the adoration that little girl holds for the man she thinks her daddy is. Even knowing that you'll be leaving again, I think Kadey needs to have that part of her life colored in rather than wondering about you for the rest of her life... and *you* should have some of those memories, too... I'll tell her who you are." She dropped the pancake.

Kaeden's eyes tracked the fall of the fried dough before he closed his eyes for a moment as if by doing so he could hide the gratitude that flashed through them.

"Momma! Trey's here!" Kadey's voice broke the moment. "He's getting out of his car, and he's got doughnuts!"

"Okay, baby. I'll be right there." She stood and pushed her hair out of her face. Sky shrugged her shoulders and braced for what was to come. "I need to go deal with this. Are you staying?"

"I am." Kaeden got up and turned the burner on, heating up the griddle again.

"Do I introduce you to him?" She wasn't sure how that would go.

"I'll handle any introductions, should they become necessary."

Sky couldn't help the smile that spread across her face, even if the shadow of happiness she felt lasted only a few seconds. She made it to the front door just as Trey knocked.

He visibly flinched when she opened the door. "Shit, did you just roll out of bed?"

"A couple minutes ago, yeah, and please stop swearing." Sky ran a self-conscious hand through her hair.

"Whatever, and it sure looks like you had a hell of a night. Are you still wearing the same clothes?"

Sky ran a self-conscious hand down her rumpled shirt and jeans. "Yeah, I ah... fell asleep on the chair."

"I can tell. Anyway, I brought breakfast. I hope you've at least managed to put coffee on. Hey, kid."

"My name's Kay-dee!" Kadey's foot stomped when she spoke.

Trey slid his eyes to Sky as if expecting her to reprimand her daughter.

She put her hand on her daughter's shoulder.

"Are you going to let me in?"

Sky opened the door further, moving both her and Kadey out of the doorway. "I brought doughnuts. Do you want the one with sprinkles?" Trey opened the box but held them just out of Kadey's reach and view.

Sky picked her up so she could see into the box.

"No, I want pancakes." Kadey squirmed in her arms, so Sky let her down.

"Then you're out of luck." Trey picked up the only donut with sprinkles and ate half of it in one bite.

Kadey watched him for a few seconds before she spun and walked away. "That's okay, Prince Charmin and I made pancakes." Kadey, still decked out in Kaeden's t-shirt, sashayed into the kitchen.

"Charming, baby. Charmin is toilet paper." Sky called after her.

"Is that a new imaginary friend? She's a little old for that shit, isn't she? Maybe you should have her head checked."

Sky opened her mouth, but Kaeden's voice cut her off.

"Sky, where's the syrup?"

Trey's head whipped around as quickly as Sky's. Sky blinked at the picture of Kaeden standing in the doorway with a day's worth of stubble on his chin, wearing no shoes or socks and his shirt half untucked. The clothes he wore hugged his body just enough to define his impressive build but not enough to call undue attention to him. He held Kadey on his hip as if it was an everyday occurrence.

Trey swiveled his head back toward Sky.

"Kaeden." Sky didn't know what else to say.

"I see." Trey turned his attention back to the man across from him. The disdain Trey had for Kaeden oozed out of every pore in the man's body.

The tension in the room built further… if that was possible.

Trey pulled himself up to his full five-foot-ten-inches and glared at Kaeden, "Where have you been?"

Kaeden flicked a dismissive look at Trey and hugged Kadey closer to his chest. The little girl wrapped both arms around his neck and focused her attention on the cartoons playing on the television. The lack of any answer from Kaeden coupled with a glacial attitude forestalled any other questions from Trey.

Sky stepped between the men, "Trey—"

"*I'm* Sky's boyfriend."

A smile passed over Kaeden's face, and he arched an eyebrow. The expression clearly implied he found Trey's words amusing.

Sky wanted to thump him. Kaeden could close off his facial expressions and be a stone-cold statue when he wanted, so she never doubted for a moment that the smirk was calculated to offend.

"Sure you are." Kaeden turned his attention to Sky. "Syrup?"

"Top right-hand cupboard, second shelf in the back."

"Got it. Come on kitten, we have pancakes to eat!" Kaeden spun quickly sending Kadey into a fit of giggles.

"Not too rambunctious, she needs to stay calm," Sky called after them.

"Got it, no fighting dragons until after breakfast." Kaeden's voice carried over Kadey's giggles.

Trey turned toward her. "What the actual fuck?"

Sky felt her eyes bulge at Trey's words. "Language!"

"Right, like that matters. She's not here, she's with bio-dad and what the fuck is he doing here? I thought you couldn't find him? You said you hadn't heard anything."

"He arrived last night after you stormed out." Not a total lie.

"Did he sleep here? A stranger? *How* did you explain that to your precious daughter?" Trey spat the words at her.

Sky narrowed her eyes at her friend and sometimes lover. "That man is not a stranger, he is Kadey's dad, and yes he stayed here last night."

"Great." Trey dropped the doughnuts on the sofa table. "So that's why you didn't want me to spend the night. Is that why you haven't been putting out? You're cheating on me with bio-dad. How long have you been getting some on the side?"

Sky blinked at the accusation. "I said he got here *after* you left. He had nothing to do with the fact that I didn't want you to spend the night."

"But you'll let him waltz back into your life and move right on in." Trey crossed his arms over his chest. "Look, I came over here this morning to figure out a way to get past last night. Maybe I haven't been the best at explaining my expectations, but I've got a lot invested in this relationship. You know that guy is a douche, he left you high and dry when you were pregnant, and he'll drop out of sight again. Men like him don't stick around to play house."

Sky flinched. Trey had flung a load of truth at her, and she couldn't deny a word of it. "I know that, alright? But, he's going to save Kadey's life. What do you want me to do, tell him to get lost?"

Trey blew a huff of air and shook his head. "If there was any other way for me to get through this situation, *I* would throw him out."

Sky could have laughed at the image Trey's words conjured up. There was no way he could possibly move Kaeden an inch, let alone muscle him out the door. But something Trey said stopped her. She cocked her head and crossed her arms in front of her. She stared at Trey for a long moment.

"What?" Trey spit the harshly hissed question out.

"If there was any other way for you to get through this situation?"

Trey narrowed his eyes and looked at her, almost daring her to continue. Sky put her hands on her hips. She couldn't deal with his selfishness anymore. "This situation isn't about *you*, Trey. For your information, this is my daughter's *life* we're talking about."

"As if that hasn't been explained in finite detail *every* time I'm here! Eventually, this situation will all be done, one way or the other. Sure, I want the kid to get better, but I also want you to know that I'm not going anywhere. Once all this is past us, when he's gone, I'll still be here."

"One way or the other?" Sky couldn't go there. One way or the other and Trey would be here? Her mind was a whirlpool of swirling thoughts.

"Fuck, like you don't know about the risks." Trey's verbal slap hurt more than any physical punch to the gut.

"Why?" Sky elevated her eyes to the man, seeing him clearly for probably the first time, and what she saw disgusted her.

"What do you mean, why?"

"I mean why will you still be here? Why are you here today? We don't love each other. We've never had a passionate romance. Why are you so adamant that you want to be here when he's gone?

Trey reached out and cupped her cheek. His grip tightened on the back of her neck. "Because I've got a lot of time and effort invested in you. I'm not willing to just walk away." Trey pulled her in for a kiss.

Sky twisted away. "I'm not in love with you, Trey. I've been honest with you from the beginning. I used to enjoy your friendship, but you've changed. I'm sorry if you thought there was anything more. I never meant to mislead you."

Trey dropped his hand and glared toward the kitchen. "I haven't changed, you needy bitch. This entire situation has become a soul-sucking event because you've let it dominate your life. Now you're kicking me to the curb, and he's staying here with you?"

Sky gaped at him. "Soul-sucking event? You know what, no, we haven't discussed the logistics of it, but if he wants to stay here... yes."

"Right." He turned toward the door and stopped with his hand on the knob glancing back at her. "When he leaves you, and he *will* leave you, I won't be here to pick up the pieces of your seriously fucked up life."

Sky glared at him. "Is that what you think you've been doing?"

"Obviously. I've never met a woman so unfit to be a mother. You have no job because you fucked up and got caught doing shit that was illegal. You're going to lose this house, and at the end of the investigation the DA is doing on you, you won't have insurance for your precious little baby. How are you going to afford the surgery then? Unless you marry me and get on my insurance, you can't. Not like I'd fucking take you now and good luck getting bio-dad to step up to the plate." A nasty sneer painted itself across his face.

"Get out and never come back." Sky raised her arm and pointed at the door.

"Gladly. You will regret this."

"I'll never regret it. My only regret is I didn't do it sooner." Sky growled the response as the door slammed behind Trey. There was no stabbing pain of regret or sharp emotional sting from the breakup. Trey's departure didn't leave a void. In fact, she felt a wave of relief. She'd fallen into the relationship because she needed to talk out her concerns. She needed someone to unload her fears onto and that someone had been Trey...in the beginning. However, his expectations, needs, and demands had slowly added up to a pressure she didn't want or need in her life, but she had not had the emotional strength to face the drama that would ensue if she kicked him out.

The sound of laughter snapped her back to the present and led her down the short hallway.

"Momma, he put a whole pancake in his mouth! All at once!"

Kaeden's eyes widened, and he pointed to himself innocently. The conspicuous movement of his jaw as he chewed the pancake sent Kadey into another giggle fit.

"He's so silly!"

"He sure is, baby. Sit down on your chair for a minute. I need to talk to you."

Kadey's face immediately fell. "'bout the surgery."

"Yes, about the surgery. You remember how the doctors said you had super special blood and only someone with super special blood could help us?"

Kadey nodded her head and turned her eyes to Kaeden. "Do you have super special blood, too?"

Kaeden smiled at her. "I do."

"Are you going to help make me better?" Kadey spun her fingers in her curls

"I am if it is alright with you."

Kadey stared at him for several long seconds. She jumped down from her chair and ran out of the room.

Sky blinked at her daughter's sudden bolt out of the kitchen. "Kadey! Where are you going? No running!"

"'Kay! Just a minute, Momma!"

Sky started after her only to stop as Kadey came barreling back into the kitchen with the small picture that sat on Sky's night side table. The little girl was pale from the brief physical activity. Her chest heaved with labored breathing. Sky immediately dropped to her knees by her daughter and reached for her. Kadey ignored her and fought to get out of Sky's hold.

"This is you. Right?" Kadey pushed the picture at Kaeden.

Kaeden glanced from the picture to Sky.

She nodded at him; her eyes stung with unshed tears. Her baby knew her daddy without anyone having to tell her.

"Yes, that's me."

"You're my daddy?" Kadey made a valiant effort to climb up on Kaeden's lap.

Kaeden lifted her up and smiled. "Yes, I am."

"Are you done helping all the peoples?" Kadey looked at the picture and then back at Kaeden as if comparing the likenesses.

"Not yet, but I'm taking a break from that so I could come help you, because you are more important to me than all the other people in the world."

Sky's heart broke at his words. She knew she'd never be enough to hold Kaeden. She'd tried to make peace with that years ago, but she wished Kadey could have a relationship with a father figure who would love her the way Sky loved her. She swiped at the tears that tumbled down her cheeks.

"Momma cries when it gets dusty," Kadey talk-whispered to Kaeden before she turned to Sky and smiled at her. "Is it dusty again, Momma?"

"Yeah, baby, it's dusty again."

CHAPTER FIVE

ANUBIS TUGGED THE MEDICAL TAPE AND GAUZE PAD off the inside of his elbow. He'd arrived for his appointment, had his blood drawn, and left the building in seven minutes. Guardian's influence once again paved a smooth path.

He palmed a new burner phone that he'd purchased with cash on the way to his doctor's appointment and called into CCS, the secure intelligence computer center that functioned as the brain of Guardian. Making contact directly with people at Guardian was about twenty miles outside his comfort zone. He preferred facilitated contact through multiple anonymous filters—filters that deliberately removed him from any form of association with his co-workers.

Thankfully, Bengal's woman didn't answer this time, and Anubis chuckled when Bengal's distracted voice boomed across the connection, "Reynolds."

"That name never ceases to confuse me." He purposely forwent any salutation.

"No shit. Took me about three months to get comfortable with it. The report you've requested is waiting in your Shadow World account. There were several flags and concerns. The dude has no criminal record, but he's got issues at work. He's been written up several times and has very little in the way of savings.

Spends money like a drunken sailor on shore leave. Not the type of person I'd want hanging around my family."

Anubis inhaled sharply. He gazed up at the sky and searched the puffy white clouds. "They aren't… I can't do family."

"Bullshit, but I don't have time to debate that with you today, so I'll take a rain check."

"Roger. Copy. Remember to mask my blood work, so alarms don't go off."

"The alarms will go off because Kadey is Rh-null. We will try to mask her name and all her information in the hospital's system, but it will only delay the inevitable. If word gets out that she is having surgery, that logically means another Rh-null donor has been found. The Internal Blood Group Reference Laboratory will contact the hospital, and as we discussed, it isn't like you could just make the donation and leave."

Yeah, like he didn't know that. Besides, after hearing the verbal abuse Arnie laid on Sky this morning, he wasn't going to leave her without knowing the man was warned off. He'd make sure the bastard knew the consequences of continuing any type of contact. He couldn't wait to explain in detail why Arnold Treynor Cross wanted to leave his daughter and her mom alone.

"I can't leave them until Kadey is through the operation and they're both safe."

"And *that* is why we will never debate the fact that Sky and Kadey are your family."

Anubis totally disregarded Bengal's comment and continued the conversation without acknowledging his words. "If the laboratory gets a sample of my blood they'll compare it to other known samples. My past will be resurrected." Like Lazarus, back from the dead.

"We're working that. Unfortunately, the system the lab overseas uses to store information on Rh-null donors isn't online. Jacob sent Lycos to take care of it. He's been tasked with eliminating any physical or digital files pertaining to who you once were, although he has no idea why he's deleting a dead man's data."

Anubis chuckled. "He has an idea. The man's a genius."

"True, but he can't connect you with your history. Nobody can."

Bengal's words were meant to reassure him, but Lycos was one of the few who Anubis trusted, so his reassurance wasn't needed.

"We're here if you need us. Keep us posted."

"Understood." Anubis ended the call and with practiced ease disassembled the burner phone, throwing pieces away as he walked. He had another in his pocket and two in his vehicle. He'd already dropped Sky and Kadey off at the hospital. They had a scheduled appointment, and Sky would explain to the doctor that they had an anonymous Rh-null donor who had reached out to her. Anubis glanced at his watch. After circling his vehicle and conducting a thorough visual assessment, he got in and booted up his tablet. He logged into the small email provider and signed in to his Shadow World account. He accessed a draft email that Bengal had dropped into the account. It held Cross's dossier. He scanned the information and noted the paltry sum in the man's bank accounts. The dossier listed the man's lineage. His extended family wasn't exactly on a solid citizen platform, but Arnie was benign at first glance. He had two speeding tickets within the last five years. A trespassing arrest during college for attending an environmental protest and chaining himself to a bulldozer. *That explained the Prius.* He was an accountant with a large firm downtown. Anubis kept reading and didn't like what was coming to light. Arnie had been written up four times in the last year. Anubis accessed the attachments. He'd give her credit; Bengal's woman was thorough. The letters of admonishment from the man's supervisor had escalated to letters reprimanding the jerk for his declining work performance and caustic attitude. The latest of which was a week ago. Cross had written a scathing reply, and it was attached to the supervisor's reprimand. It was difficult to decipher the man's sprawling handwriting, but he managed… and growled deep and low inside his chest at the fucker's words. Anubis re-read them. *'My issues revolve around the daughter of my fiancée and her life-threatening illness. The situation is complicated by the impending surgery of the little girl I consider a daughter. I can't explain how hard this time is for us.'*

Anubis finished reading the fantasy accounting of Arnold Cross's life. The letter from the head of HR directed the supervisor to remove the document from Cross's personnel file due to extenuating circumstances. Anubis seamlessly slipped firmly into the Shadow World he lived in as he finished dissecting the dossier. His mind notched the facts into his memory like any other case. Arnold Treynor Cross was a Class 'A' bastard. He'd used his relationship with Sky and Kadey to weasel out of his poor work performance and bad attitude. His gut told him that Cross wasn't going to take Sky kicking him to the curb lying down. No, Anubis had profiled enough men to know Cross would show up again and again. A sneer made its way to his lips—not if he had anything to say about it.

He deleted the dossier after another read-through and signed out of the email account. There would be no digital trail since the email wasn't sent to anyone. It was old-school tech, but it worked well.

Anubis tapped the steering wheel of his rented SUV and stared into space. He examined everything that had happened in the past few days carefully. In order to clarify his goal, he needed to remove his emotions and examine the situation. Besides the blood issue, he needed to provide for them financially in a manner that would not drag them into the death and destruction that populated his world, and that meant he could not stay. Granted, Cross was a dick, but he was a manageable dick. His background check revealed small problems, nothing too dramatic, just another asswipe looking to get a leg up by using another's misfortune. Anubis ground his teeth. His purpose here wasn't to teach Cross a lesson, but he'd add that line item to the mission. Just. Because. He. Could.

A sneer pulled at his lip. His disdain for Cross pulsed through him just as surely as his blood pumped through his veins. He needed to tamp down the territorial fierceness. He needed to do what he was here to do and leave. Sky was an adult, and from what he could see, she was a fantastic mom, even though her choices in men left a lot to be desired. First him, and then Cross. Anubis released a sound, not unlike a growl. He was not like Cross. Cross was… a bully. The man was nothing special, and that gave Anubis pause.

The average, vanilla people of the world were the ones that worried him the most. Anubis could gage a target's move based on his intense studies of the vile people he hunted. Sadists, psychopaths, rapists, pedophiles, murders, drug lords, arms dealers, mafia bosses, he'd assimilated into the life of so many sick, perverted people that the world's normal was his abnormal. He'd executed seventeen primaries. Sixteen for his country, and one for his family. The people he had to kill to get to the targets bumped that number up to twenty-four. Collateral damage was something that his specialty allowed him to minimize, unlike some of his counterparts. The poison he created and delivered by a prick of a needle, the inhalation of a tainted cigar or cigarette, or in the sweetness of a favorite confection was usually quick, efficient, and deadly.

The world was safer with the target's inevitable elimination. Anubis shook his head. Yes, he fit in with the scum of the earth, but ask him to live among good people? He physically shuddered at the thought. His assassin's nature teemed just under his skin like an electrical current. He was not at ease with anything that had happened in the last seventy-two hours. He was too exposed, and so was his family... no... he had to stop thinking of them as family. They needed to stay simply Sky and Kadey.

That had to be why his gut was telling him there was something off about Cross. Hell, the last time Anubis had spent any time being 'normal' he'd met Sky. Hiding in plain sight and recovering from his injuries, he'd laid low for three months before he'd met Sky. The two months that followed were the brightest, warmest memories he owned and he cherished them. Perhaps Kadey would look back on the next few weeks and remember him fondly. He rolled his shoulders and glanced around before starting the engine.

His feelings for his daughter and her mother were a hindrance to the situation but something he should factor into the equation. He'd be careful to avoid complicating their life unnecessarily. He glanced at his watch noting the time. The bank was on the way, so he'd make a quick stop before he picked up Sky and Kadey. He needed to set up two accounts. Just because he couldn't be with his girls didn't mean he couldn't provide for them. Besides, he had no need for the abundance of money he'd accrued. It floated somewhere in cyberspace growing in interest-bearing accounts. It was about time he put the money to good use.

"She's asleep." Sky dropped into the loveseat with him but stayed at the far end, closing her eyes as her head dropped back.

"You've been pulling quite a load for a while now, haven't you?" His hand rested on the back of the small couch within inches of her brown hair. He extended his fingers and ran them through the soft, dark fall.

Sky's eyes opened, and she turned her head to look at him. Her eyes traveled over him, assessing and familiar. "I'm so damn tired, but stopping isn't an option."

"You're going to be fired." He'd read the dossier, he knew the DA was dragging his feet, but she'd violated the trust of the office, and she was all but formally terminated.

"Yeah, I am. I tried to find you every way a normal person would look—social media, the telephone directory. I even called the landlord where you used to live. It was as if you'd dropped off the face of the earth. When none of that worked, I used the tools I had available. Was it illegal? Yes, but it was necessary to find you, and I'd do it again."

"How bad is your situation?" He wondered if she'd sugar coat the truth.

"How bad can bad get? I'm a month away from losing the house. I'm surprised they haven't repossessed the car. I pay utilities on a rotating basis, so they don't get so far behind that they get turned off. But, none of that matters. Kadey is the only thing that matters." Sky reached out and took his hand, clasping it in hers. "And she has that chance now, thanks to you."

Anubis ran his thumb up and down the top of her hand. "If I could have stayed, I'd like to think I would have."

Sky smiled and then chuckled. "We were good together, weren't we?"

Anubis tugged at her hand bringing her attention to him. "No, we were amazing. Every time."

Sky stared at him for a moment and then smiled sadly before she deflected his words with a weak, "Awww... I bet you say that to all your baby-mommas."

"I'm not that man." He wasn't going to let her believe that of him.

"What man?"

"The type to have a woman at every port. After you, there hasn't been anyone." He had to make sure she understood that she was more than a fling to him.

"Excuse me? You mean you haven't had sex since we hooked up two years ago?" Her shoulders moved with suppressed laughter before she pointed a finger at him. "You are insatiable! Nope, not buying that line, mister."

Anubis laughed and tugged her to his side. She fell willingly against him. "No, I've had sex. What I haven't had is a relationship. There has been no one who meant anything either before you or since you."

Sky tipped her chin up so he could see those expressive brown eyes. "Why?"

Anubis traced her jaw with his index finger. "Before, because I never met the right person, and after... well, after was because what we had was special to me."

"But not special enough to stay." Her flat tones held no accusation. She just stated a fact.

"Sky..." She'd never know it ripped his fucking guts out every single time he got dressed in the dark hours of the morning and left her. It was the least he could do for her. "I couldn't."

"Right." She nodded and patted his thigh with a resolved sigh. "But you're here now." Sky licked her lips before she leaned forward and kissed him.

Anubis fell into the warmth of her lips for a moment before he pulled away. "What are you doing?" He wanted to make sure he wasn't reading anything into her kiss, because once he let his desire for this woman loose, there would be no way to stop.

"Dang, I must be out of practice. I was trying to come on to you."

"Are you sure you want to do that? I won't stay, and you are in a relationship, or were until recently." Anubis hated reminding her of the fact, but he wouldn't take advantage of her, not again.

Sky leaned into him. The press of her full breasts against his chest sent an urgent wake-up call to his cock. "I'm tired, not stupid. Of course, I'm sure. And that thing with Trey wasn't a relationship. That was me looking for something I couldn't find."

Anubis pulled away as she moved forward. "Sky…"

She groaned and dropped her head back and sighed. "After you left me alone in that hotel room the last time, I made some hard decisions. I got my life on track, and I decided I would find the exact opposite of you."

"And that would be?"

"Ahhh… I wanted someone solid and dependable, a man who would stay, someone entrenched in the community, someone people knew."

Anubis's fingers continued to move up and down Sky's wrist and hand. He'd own that hit, but fuck… he wished she could know just how solid and dependable he actually was. "I understand." He did, but he didn't like it. That bastard Trey had done a number on Sky. Anyone who knew her before could attest to that. He took a mental step back. He'd played a part in her decisions so he couldn't excuse himself from blame, but, fuck, he hated being lumped together with that waste of sperm.

Sky stared out into the dark, focusing somewhere near the doorway. "Yeah, well it didn't work out too well. I tried hard to feel for him what I used to feel for you. I never could. Did we hook up over the course of the last two years? Yeah. Was it good?" Sky sat up and turned, so she was facing Anubis. "No. He couldn't hold a candle to the way you made me feel. He never once waited for me to finish before he… you know, but I thought maybe that was the norm and you were the exception." Sky shrugged and folded in on herself once again, sinking into the sofa, making herself small. "I tried. I mean I really tried to be what he thought I should be, what I thought he wanted, but once Kadey got sick, I couldn't deal with his needs any longer. God, that made him so mad. He was always angry at me for one thing or another, but he was always here, too. We haven't been together, sexually, in a long time—not since Kadey started getting sick. He was there when I needed to talk, and he stuck around when everyone else bailed."

"Bailed?" Anubis tried to understand why people would leave her without a support system.

"I guess most people didn't have a problem at first. However, when she got sicker, and everything got out of hand with… you know… finding you, they all started falling by the wayside. I can't blame them. Who wants to be associated with a criminal?"

"You're not a criminal."

"Not yet, but when the DA completes his investigation, I'll be brought up on charges."

"No, you won't." Anubis had connections. He would make sure things were taken care of for Sky.

"What are you going to do? Get your people to make it go away?" Sky snorted and shook her head.

"I am." Anubis was damn sure going to make all her problems go away.

"You can't, but thank you for being upset on my behalf. I don't deserve it."

"You don't deserve to be prosecuted for trying to save your daughter." *His daughter.*

"Necessity isn't a valid defense in most cases. Maybe the District Attorney won't bring charges, but I know he'll fire me and make sure I never work with a law enforcement agency again."

Anubis pulled her into his side. "I know you don't believe me, but I will ensure your decisions to save our daughter won't be held against you."

Sky gave him a quick grin and shrugged. "Yeah, you're right, I don't believe it. Most people don't believe in fairy tales and happily ever afters. You've given us hope and that… God, Kaeden—that is everything."

"I'd give you the world if I could."

"And yet you won't stay."

"It isn't an option." He had to make sure she understood that fact.

"Yeah, I know. But I can't help wanting what we used to have. I've tried to forget how good it was between us. It was impossible to do that, though. God, I loved you so much."

"I'm sorry I hurt you." He'd saw off his right arm with a pocket knife if he could take back the pain his actions had caused her.

"I know. You're not a bad man, Kaeden."

Oh, but he was. He was the God of Death, and he was damn good at his job. Anubis lowered his chin to the top of her head. She pushed closer to him. "Can I ask a favor?"

He nodded, his chin moving against her silky hair.

"I want to feel you again."

"I don't want to take advantage of you."

"I want you, and I know it would just be sex. I'm not asking for a commitment."

Kaeden drew a deep breath. God, he was a bastard because he was going to make love to her.

SKY PUSHED INTO HIS SOLID, WARM BODY. SHE needed this… him. She couldn't recall the last time she felt desire flow through her veins. That was a lie. It was two years ago in that horrid little hotel in Davis. She raised her chin and zeroed in on Kaeden's lips. She longed to feel the connection they once had. Yeah, she knew it was a bad idea, and yeah, she knew he was leaving. However, she wanted just a little something for herself—something to prove she was still a desirable woman. A few recent memories to help her through the rest of her life. Was it too much to ask?

His strong, rough hand smoothed over her arm and cupped the back of her neck. *Yes, sweet heavens above, yes!* The feel of his lips against hers transported her back to that stupid one bedroom apartment in Fresno and a full-sized bed that was too cramped and yet so perfect.

The familiar sweep of his tongue against her bottom lip triggered a full body shudder. She opened for him but didn't meet his searching tongue. He pulled back. "Did you change your mind?" His voice had lowered and roughened with desire.

Sky backed away and looked up at him. "No, why?"

"You weren't kissing me." Kaeden's thumb pulled against her bottom lip, his eyes searched her face when he spoke.

"I ah…" Sky blinked and tried to find a way to explain. "He ah… he didn't like it when I ah… so I… I'm sorry." She pulled away from Kaeden, embarrassed that she'd basically admitted Trey thought she was too aggressive in bed. "I should go check on Kadey." But he forestalled her exit with a warm hand on her arm.

"I'm not him." Kaeden stood and extended his hand to her. "Let's go check on Kadey, and then take this into the bedroom." Sky grasped his hand, and he pulled her up and against his rock hard body. He stared down at her for a long moment before he spoke, "We don't have to do this, not tonight, not ever."

"There won't be very many more nights like this for me. The surgery and afterward will be hectic. I'm being selfish, but I want one more night with you."

"You are the least selfish person I know." Kaeden dropped a feather-light kiss on her lips and stepped back. Sky's eyes dropped to his very prominent erection pushing against the denim of his jeans. She reached out and traced the thickness with her finger. His almost subliminal groan brought her eyes back to his face.

"Kadey..."

Sky nodded but palmed his cock into her hand.

He rocked into her and then with a soft curse pulled away. "Sky, I'm walking a thin line, it won't take much to push me over it. Go."

God, she was walking that thin line, too. Her lust sank her like a lead weight, submerging her further and further. She remembered how good this man was in bed. She nodded and stepped back one small step. Kaeden's chest rose and fell at a quickened pace, his hooded golden eyes swept over her as he watched her take another small step backward.

Sky smiled, suddenly happier and lighter than she'd been in... well, in a very long time. She spun on her heel and headed down the small hallway. A soft illumination filtered through the hall into Kadey's room. Kadey had kicked off her blankets. Sky crept in and pulled them up over her daughter. She dropped her head for a moment and whispered a prayer of thanks. Sky leaned over and brushed a kiss on Kadey's forehead before she backed out of the room. She almost closed the door but left it open enough that Kadey could see the hallway nightlight.

The old hardwood floor in the hall creaked and moaned when she and Kadey walked down it, but Kaeden's step hadn't made a sound. Sky had no idea how Kaeden walked so softly.

Sky paused at her bedroom door. Kaeden lay on her bed wearing only black briefs. She let her eyes feast on his body. Wide shoulders, thick arms, a muscled chest and tight cut abs.

A dark happy trail ran from the hair on his chest to below his waistband. His cock pushed the material of his briefs out in an obvious statement of arousal. His thick muscled legs flexed as he lifted one knee. "Is she sleeping?"

His words broke Sky's trance-like observation of his body. She smiled and pushed her door closed. "She is."

Kaeden extended his hand and Sky took it. She gave a small laugh. "Is it strange that I'm nervous?"

Kaeden rose to his knees. Even with him kneeling on the bed, he was taller than she was. He pulled her to his chest and took control of her mouth. This time she met his tongue and let herself explore the man she once knew so well. She luxuriated in the feel of his hands against her. He broke the kiss and slid her t-shirt over her head.

Immediate embarrassment flooded her. The old bra she wore was ugly and utilitarian at best—a cheap knock-off brand that had long outlived its purpose. Kaeden dropped the straps from her shoulders and kissed her collarbone as he deftly unhooked the fasteners, dropping the material to the floor. He leaned back on his heels and raked his gaze over her. "My God, you are so beautiful."

Sky lowered her eyes. She wasn't. She was average on her best day. Kaeden reached out and tipped up her chin with his fingers. She met his gaze—barely. His eyes softened as if he understood her reticence. He lowered into another all-encompassing kiss. Sky pushed into his body. He controlled the descent onto the bed and rolled her under him. She arched into every touch. His lips traced the most sensitive spots as he mapped her body, first by touch, then by kisses. Her jeans and panties disappeared, as did his briefs. Their combined need built into a heat that would not be denied, a flashpoint turning the smoldering embers that had lain banked for two years into a blazing inferno. Kaeden moved away and reached toward the nightstand where he'd left his wallet. Sky heard the crinkle of the package and put her hand on his arm. "I'm sterile. When Kadey was born, there were complications, and the doctors had to take everything. I had a complete hysterectomy. Then I was tested for everything under the sun when they assumed I could donate blood to Kadey. I haven't been with anyone since."

"You didn't say anything when we met in Davis." He held himself over her, his eyes searching her face.

"Yeah, well, not sure how I could tell you without telling you about Kadey." Kaeden would never have known about their daughter...

Kaeden dropped lower and kissed her before he spoke, "Our time together cost you so much."

Sky heard the emotion in his voice even though he dropped his gaze and denied her a view into his soul.

"No, our time together gave me everything. Kadey is my world." Sky reached up and wound her fingers through the hair at the back of his neck.

Kaeden moved slightly and centered himself between her legs. She loved the feel of his weight against her. His big frame dwarfed her. She could feel the heat of his cockhead at her core. She arched her hips to encourage him to move. He held his body over hers, and their eyes locked as his girth split and entered her. Sky's eyes rolled back in her head, or at least she thought they did. The heat and size of his cock as he slowly entered her was just as good, no... better... than her memories.

He stopped once he'd thrust as deep as he could, their bodies merged as close together as humanly possible. He wrapped his arms under her shoulders and cradled her into his chest. "I'm not going to last. You feel too good." He lowered into a slow kiss, his tongue mimicking the movements of his cock. Sky wrapped her arms and legs around him, absorbing the blissful feeling that permeated every cell in her body. He leaned to one side and slid his arm down from her shoulder to her waist, and then to her thigh. He gripped it gently and lifted her leg. The change in position sent a shower of sparks cascading through her like an arc of light in an abyss that had been dark for far too long.

"Yes. There!" Sky's eyes popped open, and her hushed whisper was instinctual and unstoppable.

"Yeah, you like that, babe?"

Kaeden's hips moved again as he thrust and Sky gasped. "Yes! Oh, God, please don't stop."

"Not stopping," Kaeden repeated the move and Sky bit his shoulder instead of screaming. That cascade of sparks morphed into a consuming explosion of white-hot heat. She bucked against him, her limbs tightened and her core clenched against the intensity of her orgasm.

She held on as he lost control and slammed into her, chasing his own release. He arched and with his mouth opened in a silent shout reached his climax. The taut muscles of his neck, shoulders, and chest were flush from his effort. Sky wrapped her arms around him and pulled him down on top of her. She couldn't let him see the emotions that were running through her. She wouldn't let him know how much being with him again meant to her. She'd promised him it was just sex. Only it had never been 'just sex' with Kaeden. It was so much more. It always had been… at least for her.

He hefted his weight off her and rolled to his side pulling her against his heated skin. She allowed herself a moment to snuggle into his strength, to pretend that tonight would last forever. Besides, the only person she was hurting was herself. Right?

CHAPTER SIX

KADEY YAWNED WIDELY AND CUDDLED INTO HIS SHOULDER. Her eyes drooped and closed but didn't stay shut. "One more story?"

Anubis pulled the sweet, just bathed scent of his little girl into his lungs and locked its memory into the vault of things he wanted to remember forever. He sat on her twin bed with his legs stretched out over the pink satin comforter as he read a second bedtime story to her. They'd had a quiet day, which Anubis assumed was the norm. Kadey tired easily, and her short bursts of energy were followed by naps. Sky had been on the phone off and on all day working with the hospital to schedule the surgery. The credit card he'd provided for her to use for medical expenses not covered by her insurance had paved the arduous, twisting road that Sky had to traverse through the hospital's accounting department.

Anubis pulled Kadey into a hug and kissed her hair. "Only one more." He heard the house telephone ring and glanced out the window at the darkness. It was too late for the hospital's office workers to be calling. Kadey yawned again and pointed to another *Dr. Seuss* book stacked beside the bed. "That one, Daddy."

He never wanted to forget the feeling that went through him every time Kadey called him 'Daddy'—another remembrance to be locked away in his memory vault. "You got it." He removed her book out of the middle of the pile as Sky appeared at the door.

"There is a Mr. Ben Gall on the phone for you?" Sky walked in and held out her hand for the book. "He said it was important. I'll get her settled."

Anubis handed off the book and leaned down, giving Kadey a kiss on the forehead. "Goodnight, squirt."

"Goodnight, Daddy."

He watched as Sky slid into his space and opened the book. She started quoting the words without looking at the page. Instead, her eyes traveled to him. Worry and fear were easy to read in her expression. Anubis winked at her and gave her a smile, hoping to relieve some of her concerns.

He checked his cell phone to make sure the house was secure before he picked up the phone. "Go ahead."

"We have a problem." Bengal's voice grated across the connection. "Standby for Alpha."

Anubis listened to the distant clicks before Jacob King's voice came across the line. "Alpha."

"The phone is unsecure, sir. We have one minute left before triangulation is possible."

"Copy all. Asset Six Four Nine, the medical office you went to this morning was destroyed. Arson. The employees in the facility when you were processed are dead. Intel tells us one was tortured."

"They did not have my identity." Anubis ran scenarios through his head, but more questions than answers appeared.

"They have the patient's information." Bengal's woman came over the line. "Someone accessed the hospital's medical system from the clinic's IP address five minutes before the fire alarms went off. They know. On the receiving end, the clinic used the patient's name to flag the file on the blood workup for her doctor. Anyone with a browser and half a brain can figure out your blood types are a match. Her identity was compromised, that means you're all in jeopardy." Jewell's fast explanation turned Anubis's blood into ice. He glanced up when he heard Sky walk down the hall.

"When was she compromised?"

"Forty-seven minutes ago." Bengal's voice announced.

"Orders?" Anubis snapped the question.

Alpha responded, "Safeguard your family. Get clear of there and then access the Gateway at Fairfield."

"Affirmative." Fuck. Forty-seven minutes. The fuckers could be outside now.

"A familiar will make contact." Alpha's comment registered a second before Anubis heard Alpha click off. He dropped the landline into its cradle. He snapped his head to meet Sky's worried look. "Is she asleep?"

"Yeah, within seconds of you walking out here. She was exhausted. Why?"

"You need to get a bag for you and for Kadey. We need to leave. Now."

"What? Why? What's wrong?" Sky moved only when he grabbed her arm and pulled her into her bedroom.

"The people who drew my blood yesterday were murdered, and the clinic was torched. They don't have my information, but whoever killed them have accessed the file with Kadey's name on it. They are either on their way here, or they are outside as we speak. Now, move!"

"She needs the operation. We can't leave! Why would someone murder those people? Who would do that? Why would they do that?" Sky's face turned an ashy white, and she grabbed his arm.

Anubis palmed her cheek in his hand. "Listen to me, Sky. Kadey will have the best care my agency can provide her, but first, we have to get out of here. You have three minutes." Anubis pulled her in and kissed her hard before he turned off the lights in the front room. To her credit, Sky flew down the hallway as he waited for his eyes to adjust to the darkness. He pulled back the blinds enough to see outside the house. There were no new cars on the street, but that didn't mean a damn thing. He checked his phone again. The security measures he'd placed around the house hadn't been compromised.

Anubis headed down the hall and watched as Sky grabbed several changes of clothes for herself. She threw her clothes in a large duffle bag along with a quick swipe of her and Kadey's toiletries off the bathroom vanity. Sky stopped at a cabinet and pulled out a large sheath of papers. Glancing over at Kaden she whispered, "A copy of her medical records."

She slowed down after shoving the documents into the bottom of the duffle. Sky walked into Kadey's room quietly and carefully opened Kadey's dresser drawers, pulling out clothes for the little girl. Once done, she stuffed a stack of books from Kadey's nightstand into the bag and grabbed the teddy bear she'd been holding last night and a ragged looking cat he'd seen Kadey hug when she was tired. She headed out of the room into the hall where she grabbed Kadey's jacket and hers. Sky turned in a complete circle and scanned the area. Finally, she looked up at him, "I'm ready." She dropped the bag at the foot of Kadey's bed.

"Where is your phone?"

Sky patted her back pocket and pulled out the pay as you go phone. Anubis dropped it to the floor and put the heel of his boot through the device.

KAEDEN'S PHONE VIBRATED IN HIS HAND. "FUCK. SKY, listen to me. Stay in here and do not open that door unless you hear my voice. Take this. When someone answers, tell them six-four-nine has made contact and then hang up." Kaeden's urgent whisper fell around her, heavy and uncomfortable.

"What? Why?" Fear climbed her spine like a fat spider—one slow hairy leg at a time.

"Repeat it for me, Sky."

"Six-four-nine has made contact."

"And then you hang up."

Sky swallowed heavily and nodded her understanding.

In a practiced fashion that made her think he'd done it many times, Kaeden unhooked his belt buckle and pulled a long multi-strand wire from the wrong side of the belt. The ends were plastic coated. He wrapped the coil around his hand, tucking the ends, so they stayed in place. After buckling his belt back in place, he reached down into his boot and pulled out a wicked looking knife.

"Kaeden? What's going on?" Sky shivered and glanced back at Kadey.

He entered a number into the phone and handed it to her. "Stay here. Don't come out."

Sky opened her mouth to object but snapped her mouth shut before she uttered a sound. He left the room and silently shut the door.

"Operator Two-Five-Two." *What was it with the numbers?*

"Six-four-nine has made contact." Sky hung up as directed and leaned against the thick wood of the door. She pressed her ear to the crack where the wood met the doorjamb ,hoping to hear what was going on. She heard a muffled scuffle that lasted for far too long, and then nothing for what seemed like an eternity. Sky turned around and slid down the door.

A loud thud resounded and then the sound of glass crashing to the floor. She looked over her shoulder, but Kadey slept soundly. Sky pressed closer to the door. She heard the low rumble of male voices, then nothing.

THE INDICATORS FOR THE FRONT DOOR CHANGED FROM green to red. They hadn't made it inside by the time he eased down the hall. He avoided the middle floorboard that squeaked and stepped over another that popped and rubbed. He glanced at his phone again and pocketed it. If they were coming in any other venue than the front door, he'd deal with it later.

He stood behind the door, watched, and listened as someone manipulated the lock. A final twist freed the mechanism, but Anubis knew from experience the front door stuck. He moved just as someone shouldered the heavy oak door. The first person through the door stumbled, and Anubis flew into action. He grabbed the man by the neck and pulled him forward, sending him to the floor. He slammed his fist into the second man's throat, pulled him forward into the first man and kicked the door shut. The second man lunged at Anubis's legs, but a sharp kick to the nose dropped him into a heap. The first man raised a gun. The coiled garrote snaked from his hand, and Anubis whipped the wire, wrapping it around the barrel of the weapon. He pulled back, bringing the gun and man toward him. His knee and the man's head met. Anubis wrapped the garrote around the second man's throat. "Who sent you?" He hissed the words out and tightened the wire. The man clawed at his throat, gasping for air. Anubis felt rather than saw the first man move. A flash of silver was his only indication. He spun and yanked his human body armor directly in front of the knife that flew his direction. The knife buried itself to the hilt in the man's chest. Anubis dropped, bringing the dead man with him. He raised his knife and flung it back at the man who didn't have the intelligence to take cover. At such close quarters, there was no way he could miss. The motherfucker died before his head hit the floor.

Fucking bastard, now he had no answers. Anubis pushed the heavy son of a bitch off him and started to stand. A rush of heavy footsteps dropped him down again. The new attacker flew over him. Anubis grabbed his foot and yanked him back, pulling him off balance. Diving onto the man's back, Anubis grappled, using the newest assailant's momentum against him. The man stumbled forward, pushing the couch with him. Anubis used that moment to whip his garrote around the man's neck and power him to his knees. "I don't need to fucking kill you, you son of a bitch, but I really, really want to. Who the fuck sent you?"

Sky looked at the phone she held in her hand. She could call 911. Whoever was out there with Kaeden was trespassing… or breaking and entering. The cops should be able to arrest them. "Sky, it's me."

She jumped up and unlocked the door. She gasped at the blood splashed across his shirt. "Are you hurt?" She reached out to him, but he grabbed her arm and spun her around.

Kaeden gestured toward the bed. "I need you to carry her, so my hands are free." Sky glanced at the stuffed bag at the foot of the bed. He wrapped the fluffy pink comforter around Kadey and lifted her out of the bed before he handed her to Sky. He picked up the duffle, shouldered the bag and pulled a handgun from a concealed holster on his calf. Sky blanched at the sight of the weapon and hugged Kadey closer to her.

"What exactly do you do for that agency?" She hissed as she followed him out of the bedroom and down the hall.

Anubis cast her a quick look. He had to give her credit, she must be scared, but the woman was not falling apart. He led her to the back door and motioned for her to still. The bodies were behind the couch. Three stupid men. The third had a bit more intelligence than his contemporaries did and Kaeden needed information. The accent and the fact his garrote was around the man's throat made it hard for Anubis to understand his words, but obvious answers emerged. The intruders weren't local hired muscle. Muscle squealed like a pig at the butcher's begging for mercy. This man knew he was going to die and he still took pleasure in telling Anubis what was supposed to happen to Sky before they took the little girl. *The girl is bait.* The heavy accent and strained voice from the garrote that wrapped tightly around his throat still echoed in his mind. The bastard had no remorse. Neither did Anubis. He'd listened to the crunch of cartilage snapping and the whistling gurgle of a windpipe severing with immense satisfaction. The fucker.

He made certain he shielded Sky's line of sight from the carnage that lay a few feet away. The stench of blood curled in his nose as he herded Sky through the living room into the kitchen. While confident the three dead in the living room were the only ones sent to the house, Anubis wasn't going to take any chances. He carefully surveyed the exterior through the kitchen window while he palmed the latest version of his cell phone. Accessing the phone app again, he ensured nothing else had disturbed the sensors around the house. All were green. He glanced out the window again before he slowly opened the door and motioned for Sky to follow.

They headed through the back door and into her neighbor's side yard. Sky made a move to go toward her car. Anubis placed his hand on her arm stilling her. He shook his head and then motioned toward the neighbor's backyard. He tossed the bags over and then vaulted the four-foot fence easily. He reached back for Kadey and waited while Sky scrambled over the chain link. He handed Kadey back to Sky and silently beckoned her to follow him. They worked their way through six different yards before Anubis felt comfortable enough to approach an older model mini-van parked on a darkened side street. Sky followed closely behind him. Anubis scanned the area before he leaned against the driver's side door. His eyes continued to travel around them as he fisted his automatic and used the weapon to break the driver's side window.

Sky jumped at the breaking window, causing Kadey to stir. Anubis reached in and opened the vehicle from the inside. Obeying his silent gesture, Sky got into the back seat with Kadey cradled in her arms. Anubis climbed in, jimmied the steering column and yanked the ignition wires free of the casing. Twenty seconds later, they coasted down the side street without headlights.

"Lie down on the seat beside her. I don't want either of you visible." Anubis waited until Sky lay down before he turned on the headlights and headed out of town. The vehicle had two-thirds of a tank of gas. If they were lucky, the owner wouldn't realize the van was missing until morning. He palmed his burner phone and sent a text. *649 out w/family heading to Gateway. Rabbit hole for familiar. ETA 2 hr.*

Anubis merged onto Interstate 80 heading east. The traffic in his rear view gave him no cause for concern, but he kept his eyes on his six. He'd have to find a crowded rest stop, steal a set of plates and switch them out with the minivan, but until then he needed distance.

"Kaeden?"

Sky's voice drifted to the front seat. He turned his head and caught her eye for a second before he returned his focus to the road. "You can sit up."

He heard Sky moving around and a seatbelt clicking. There were a few awkward moments as she clambered into the front passenger seat. He was damn glad he had good reflexes. He somehow managed to dodge elbows, knees, and feet, so he didn't end up with a black eye.

"Okay." Sky pulled her jacket down, tugged her seatbelt across her chest, and secured it. She turned and angled her chin defiantly. "You *will* tell me what is going on. *Now.*"

Anubis sent her a sideways glance. His gaze flicked to his daughter.

"She's asleep. Now start talking."

Anubis scratched his chin with his thumb and tried to formulate some semblance of the truth she'd be able to understand.

"Who was at the house? I heard you talking to someone. I heard you fighting."

He shot her another quick look and shrugged. "I don't know who they were. There isn't any need for concern. I ensured they won't follow us."

"Why did they come at all?"

"I believe it had something to do with my job." Anubis couldn't place the accent of the man he'd convinced to talk. It was familiar but not quiet Suriname. It was, but...

"The job where you have 'people'?"

He snapped his head toward her and focused on the conversation at hand. "Yes. The same one. Overseas."

"Yeah, we've established the place and the fact that you have *people.*" Sky turned even farther in her seat to face him. "Why are we running? Who is after us?"

"I don't know."

"Not good enough." Sky snapped.

He understood the fear running through her and the need to

take care of her daughter. He felt the need and desire to protect both of them, but it wasn't fear that fueled him, it was unadulterated rage toward the bastard who'd try to take them from him. He couldn't let her see any of that, so he answered her questions as calmly as possible. "It is the truth. I'll tell you what I think, but I'm making huge assumptions, something I am not comfortable doing."

"Oh, by all means, please leave your comfort zone." Sky crossed her arms over her chest and glared at him.

Anubis wanted to smile at the attitude but figured the fact he thought she was amusing wouldn't be well received. "I believe someone, perhaps an enemy of mine, has somehow obtained a sample of my blood. They were alerted to my presence yesterday here in California when my blood sample was loaded into the healthcare system. I don't know any concrete specifics other than we are in danger."

"That. That right there. Explain that. How are we in danger? *Why* are we in danger? What do you do that put not only you but Kadey and me in harm's way?"

"I eliminate difficult problems for my company."

"Like what, a corporate hatchet man?"

Anubis nodded. Close enough.

"What company?"

"Guardian Security."

"Guardian?" She'd heard of them. Sky put her thumb into her mouth and chewed on her nail. "Overseas." She mumbled the word around her finger.

Anubis nodded again.

"So... you're like some kind of mercenary." There was a distinct hesitancy in her question.

He nodded. He'd let her believe that was the worst of it. She could probably understand the concept of that role. The danger the public associated with mercenaries would explain the urgency of their flight into the night. Anubis reached over and pulled her hand down, keeping her from chewing her nail to the quick.

She glared at him and popped the other thumb into her mouth, speaking around it, "Who would be after you? What did you do?"

Anubis slowed and hit the turn signal, pulling into a heavily populated rest stop just east of Davis. "I did my job."

"Which was?"

God, the woman clamped onto the subject like a pit bull. Couldn't blame her, though. He pulled into a vacant slot at the very back of the parking lot. He turned off the lights and performed a scan of the lot before he turned and looked at her. "I eliminate problems, Sky. People don't like it when I do my job. Organizations and people that terrorize the world do not take kindly to being thwarted, and I'm damn good at what I do. I have made enemies. As long as I remain anonymous, I travel the world without any problem."

"Except for now."

"Right. There is always a chance people in my line of work will be… exposed. When that happens, the vipers slither out of the cracks and come hunting. My enemies will exploit any perceived vulnerability—like those close to me. I'm solitary for a reason. Those are the reasons I left you in Fresno, why I didn't want to come back and bring my world into yours, and those same reasons are why I'm leaving as soon as both of you are safe and Kadey is recovering." Anubis pulled the cheap, plastic light cover off the interior light and pulled the bulb out. "I'm going to take care of some business. Don't get out. I'll keep the vehicle in view at all times."

Anubis opened the door and slipped out, shutting it without a sound. He dropped back out of the dim cast of the ancient light illuminating the parking lot and moved behind the van. A rear license plate would be easy to remove from a parked vehicle. The front would take some ingenuity. Anubis carefully removed the tags from the vehicle he'd stolen and put them inside his half-zipped jacket. He watched for several minutes until he saw his target. A large ten-passenger van pulled up toward the far end of the parking lot. A troop of six kids and two very bedraggled parents exited the vehicle. The children were arguing with each other, and the parents were following numbly behind the hoard. He waited until the contingent made it to the bathroom facilities before he walked to the far side of the target van, dropped down and rolled under the vehicle. He slid to the front and quickly dropped the plate, replacing it just as quickly. He shimmied to the side to catch a look at Sky. She was chewing her thumbnail watching the cars come and go. He pushed to the rear of the vehicle and exchanged plates.

Anubis rolled to the far side of the target van and did a quick sweep of the parking lot. He stood and casually strolled through the open space back to where Sky waited. He watched as the worry on her face lessened. He raised a finger when she started to open the door and dropped to the front of the van screwing on the new plate. The rear plate took less than a minute to affix.

"You stole someone's license plate?" Sky hissed.

"Yes. If the owner of this vehicle reports it was stolen, we need different tags, so the police don't stop us."

"But… even if you are a mercenary, you're a good guy. Right? Shouldn't we be going *to* the police, not running *away* from them?"

Anubis started the vehicle and turned on the headlights, pulling out of the parking lot.

"Right now, I don't trust anyone except the people my handlers tell me to trust."

"Handlers?"

"The ones who give me my assignments."

"They know about Kadey, right? They know she needs this operation?"

"They were the ones who told me about her and allowed me to come to you."

"Allowed you? Do you trust them?" Sky put her thumbnail in her mouth again.

"With our lives."

"Where are we going?"

"Not far. Just outside Fairfield. We'll need to get a hotel room and wait until my people make contact. It won't be nice, but it will be safe." He couldn't risk using one of the Kaeden Lang credit cards if the identity the architect had engineered for him had been compromised, so an hourly rate hotel would keep them safe until his contact arrived and gave him the necessary documentation to access the Gateway and the security and medical facilities it provided.

"Kaeden, I'm scared." Sky's voice trembled. She drew an audible breath and continued, "I think we should go to the police."

Anubis reached over and grabbed her cold hand, giving it a gentle squeeze. "I know you're afraid, and it is a perfectly normal reaction. Give me twenty-four hours. If you don't believe that you and Kadey are safe and that she is getting quality care, I'll drive you to the nearest police station myself." He'd never risk Sky or Kadey to the inadequate protection of the local police, but he felt no guilt in telling her that lie as it would never be an issue. The Gateway was the perfect place to hide in plain sight.

Sky's hand remained unmoving in his. Anubis squeezed it again and released it, realizing the trust he asked her to give him came at a price—one he wasn't sure Sky was willing to pay. "Kadey will have the best care. I promise you."

"I want to believe you." Sky's voice drifted over to him, faint as if she'd said it to herself.

CHAPTER SEVEN

KAEDEN WALKED OUT OF THE OFFICE OF THE rundown strip motel and headed across the cracked asphalt toward the van. Sky watched him approach, not knowing how to settle the fear that threatened to choke her. She felt like she'd woken up in the middle of a Jason Bourne movie. The frenzied way they shot the action scenes that made you cling to the edge of your seat while praying everything would work out and fighting a sick feeling in the pit of your stomach, duplicated her current feelings— afraid, nervous, and sick to her stomach. Kaeden opened the side door, unbuckled the seatbelt and reached in, lifting Kadey from the first-row bench seat. Sky got out and retrieved the bag she'd packed. The thing felt as if she'd thrown in a ton of bricks. Strange, when she was loading it a few hours ago, she hadn't noticed how heavy it was. She closed the van and turned toward the long row of rooms that spread out from the main office like a line of linked ants.

Kaeden dangled the key to the room from his hand. "146." He motioned for Sky to lead so she turned on her heel and headed to the small covered walkway that connected all the units. At the door to the room, she stopped and inserted the key before flipping the light switch. It was a basic room. Two queen beds, one chair, and a low dresser with a box type television sitting on top of the laminated wood. Sky had been in worse rooms... maybe.

She moved in, dropped her bag on the chair and pulled the old, faded bedspread down off the bed closest to the bathroom. Kaeden laid Kadey down, waking her up.

"Where are we?" Kadey yawned, sleep still heavy upon her.

"We are going on an adventure, but you have to go back to sleep first." Sky pushed Kadey's curls back from her face and pulled the fluffy pink blanket that Kaeden had wrapped around her back up over her shoulders. "Momma's right here."

Kaeden tapped her shoulder gaining her attention. He mouthed "Be right back. Don't go out."

Sky nodded her head. There was no way she'd leave Kadey. Taking her out of the room in the middle of the night, in questionable surroundings? So not going to happen.

Sky waited until she was sure Kadey had settled back into a comfortable sleep and then inspected the bathroom, turned up the heat to take the chill off the room and moved the bag out of the chair. She sat down and gazed at her sleeping daughter, wondering how she went from desperate to find Kaeden to being on the run with him as if she was some type of criminal. She leaned forward and placed her head in her hands. She needed to think, but she knew next to nothing. Everything that had happened was because Kaden had said they were in danger. The clinic where he'd had his blood taken was burned to the ground, and two people were killed. Wait. Sky glanced at the red numbers of the digital clock on the nightstand. In a small city like Sacramento, something like that would be headline news. The eleven o'clock news would be on in ten minutes.

Sky turned on the television and quickly muted it. She scrolled through the channels until she found Sacramento's local station and dropped the remote on the chair beside her. Sky pulled her legs up, hugging them, and stared sightlessly at the images that flashed across the screen. Kaeden Lang, a person who didn't exist, a mercenary that eliminated problems for Guardian Security, had driven her into the middle of nowhere in a stolen van, with stolen plates and she had just… let him.

Her stomach sank at that thought. How many ax-murderer movies had she watched? Never get into the car with the guy who didn't exist. Never go away without telling someone where you are…

Sky glanced at the telephone beside the bed. She could call someone and let them know where she was… but who? Who did she have to call? Trey? Sky stuck her mangled thumbnail in her mouth and bit down repeatedly. If she called Trey, what would he do? Sky glanced at the door as she lifted her thumbnail to her teeth and thought. She could call her dad back in Arizona. But he wasn't really an option… She heard two voices lowered in conversation pass by the front of the room. The voices disappeared when she heard another door open and close. Another late-night check-in.

The television news flashed on the screen. Sky watched through the first story, a mug shot of a man filled the back screen; the bottom stated he was an escaped felon. She watched as the news continued. Nothing about the fire. Her ravaged nerves throbbed just under her skin, raw and painfully present. She pushed down the fear that threatened to overtake her. When the newscast came back on, she unmuted the television and turned the volume to the lowest level possible. The commentator detailed a fire in old Sacramento at a medical clinic. The graphic behind the woman held the words Suspected Arson. Sky leaned forward as the woman ended the story. "The fire is under investigation as arson and is suspected as the cause of death for

Doctor Patrick Shipley and his employee Debbie McComb. We will keep you informed as details develop."

Sky clicked off the television and wrapped her arms around herself. *Okay. Okay... no, not okay.* She spun around while standing in the middle of the small hotel room. The air in the room disappeared, and it became hard to pull oxygen into her lungs. Everything that had happened tonight was real. Someone was after Kaeden. They could use Kadey to get to him. No... no... no! Sky ran her hands through her hair and pulled. Think, think, damn it! What should she do?

The door opened, freezing her movements. Kaeden slipped in and closed the door behind him. Sky launched into him. He caught her with a muffled, 'oomph.'

"Hey, what happened?" he whispered as he pulled her into his body and wrapped her in those thick solid arms.

Sky buried her head in his chest. "It's true, the clinic was burned down. They suspect arson. Two people are dead. A doctor and some lady who worked for him." Kaeden's hand stroked her hair as his other arm wrapped securely around her. "I'm terrified for Kadey."

"Hey." Kaeden tried to put space between them but Sky linked around him like steel bands, and she wasn't going to let go. Not now. He finally settled for tipping her head up. "What's happening here?"

"I saw the news! How can you be sure they won't find you? Find us? We need to go to the police—"

Kaeden's finger landed on her lips. He threw a glance over her shoulder towards Kadey. "Okay, I know all about the murders. I know about the arson. My people are coming to meet us and give me the credentials I need to get us to the safest place we can go. We are waiting for them here. The bad guys don't know we're here. I've cleaned and disposed of the van. We paid cash for the room, and there is no camera system in this motel. There is no way anyone will be able to find us here. We *are* safe. I promise I won't let anything happen to you, but you need to settle down."

Sky pulled her head back removing his finger from her lips. "Settle down? *Settle down*? How can you say that? Someone is looking for you and has Kadey's information! Someone who has murdered… *as in killed*… two people! I won't settle down!" Kaeden glanced over at Kadey again. She tossed in her bed. Sky snapped her mouth shut and pushed away from Kaeden.

Kaeden took a step toward her. "I won't let anything happen to you."

Sky shook her head and pinched her mouth shut before she snapped, "You can't say that. You have no idea what those people could do!"

Kaeden looked at the ceiling and rubbed the back of his neck. He blew a huff of air through his nose and sat down on the edge of the bed. He patted the mattress beside him. "Sit down with me, Sky."

She didn't want to sit down. She wanted to run, to find the police, and to get help to flee from the criminals that were targeting them.

"Please."

His plea cut through the thoughts spinning around her brain. She ran her hands up and down her arms trying to warm herself before she stepped toward him and perched on the end of the bed. "We have to get help."

"I don't need any help taking care of you, Sky."

The calm tone he used brushed against her ragged nerves and made her bristle even more. "How can you say that?"

"Because I know what *I'm* capable of doing… *to them*." He turned to face her. Sky pushed her hands up and held them out as she tried to talk sense into Kaeden. "Wait, look I know you have a gun, and yeah, that freaks me out, but you told me that you don't know who is after you. They could have a gang or a cult or an army of people."

Kaeden stood up and paced the small floor of the hotel room. He looked at her several times before he spoke again. "Sky, what I do for Guardian is very specialized. I guarantee you there isn't a threat out there that I can't handle. You *are* safe here as long as you do what I tell you. You'll just have to trust me on that. I can't tell you any more, and I've probably already overshared, but know I will kill anyone who comes through that door without an explicit invitation."

Sky blinked up at him. The venom in his voice turned his grandiose statement into a believable threat.

"I am a dangerous man. Deadly. I won't sugarcoat that truth. I am everything you and Kadey don't need in your life, but I can protect you, and I will. You can believe me or not. Frankly, that doesn't matter in this situation. What matters right now is that you are safe. Now, you need to get some sleep, so when Kadey wakes up, you'll be able to take care of her and the events of the day."

Sky stared at the man in front of her. It was as if he'd shed another layer of skin and become another version of Kaeden, one she hadn't seen before, but one that had been under the veneer the entire time. Sky swallowed hard and nodded. She doubted she'd sleep, but she'd lay down with Kadey. Taking off her shoes and jacket, she slipped into the bed beside her daughter. She wasn't going to lay down beside Kaeden. Not tonight. The man she'd made love to in her home last night wasn't the same man who stood in this hotel room.

Kaeden turned off the light and Sky rolled onto her back as she listened to him stretch out on the bed. His words echoed around her brain in a swirl. He was dangerous. Deadly. He'd told her again the exact reasons why he would not stay with them, and why he would leave as soon as Kadey was through her surgery and recovering. Her last fragile hope for a normal relationship with Kaeden died, marked by a silent tear that slid down her cheek. She heard his phone vibrate. The pale green shadow of his display momentarily illuminated his features. Sky watched as he thumbed a text and dropped the phone on his chest, rendering the room dark again. She had no idea what tomorrow would bring, but Kaeden was right. She needed rest because she would need to deal with events as they unfolded. Carefully she reached out and placed her hand on Kadey's before she closed her eyes and said a silent prayer—a prayer for protection for all of them.

CHAPTER EIGHT

> **Credentials in route. Contact in a.m.**

Anubis read the text and acknowledged the input. > **Fix required.**

>**Sacramento location?**

> **Affirmative. X3**

> **Confirmed.**

Anubis hit the power button on his phone and dropped it on his chest. It was a burner phone, and it couldn't be traced, yet he itched to take out the SIM card and break the piece of plastic in half—and automatic reaction after so many years in the field.

He didn't enjoy scaring Sky, but she needed to understand what he was capable of. Hell, he probably should have made that point clear before they became physical again. As much as he knew it revealed him as a selfish bastard, he couldn't regret being with her. His body yearned for any contact she'd allow. Fuck, the woman lit him up like a load of chaff out of the ass end of an AC-130 Hercules. Brilliant, hot and sparkling for a short duration, but doomed to fall away and burn out, leaving nothing but the conjured memory of the moment floating in front of your eyes.

He knew the moment she drifted to sleep. Her breaths lengthened, and the rhythm relaxed. Anubis started constructing the events of tomorrow, adding a never-ending loop of possibilities that he may have to deal with. The actions that were mandatory were simple. Meet the contact, secure his credentials and make his way into the Gateway. He'd make contact with Guardian via secure lines at that point and find out what the fuck was going on.

Kadey mumbled something in her sleep. Anubis turned his head toward the bed where the two most important people in his world slept. He didn't know how Guardian was going to arrange the surgery, but he trusted the organization to get it done. They'd never let him down before.

Anubis allowed himself to doze, trusting years of training and living one-step from death to alert him if anything went amiss. At six, he shifted off the bed and eased out of the room. The motel was quiet as he made his way across the street to a small mom and pop restaurant. Anubis sat down at the counter. He could see the door to his unit from where he sat. There was no reason to fear they'd been followed. The van was clean and parked behind the local sheriff's office, co-located with the small fire department. Anubis grinned to himself. He'd wondered how many shift changes it would take before they checked out the van parked in the back corner of the lot.

"What can I getcha?" A disembodied voice called out of the kitchen.

"Coffee and a to-go order," Anubis called back.

"Damn waitress is late." A haggard man pushed the silver doors open and grabbed a mug and the coffee pot as he walked past. The cup plopped down, and the coffee poured with efficiency. "Name's Ernie. What do you want in that to go order?"

Anubis nodded at the introduction and deliberately answered the question without returning the favor of an introduction. "Two orders of pancakes, scrambled eggs and bacon." Anubis couldn't eat, not unless he'd cooked it, or trusted the person who was cooking, and Ernie wasn't on that very short list. "Can I get two cups of this to go and a large milk?"

"No problem. Give me a minute to get this made up. If you want a refill, the pots are over here. Holler if anyone else shows up, will ya?"

Anubis arched an eyebrow but nodded. Damn, living in a small town had to be a kick. He listened to Ernie clanging around in the kitchen. The coffee smelled good, so Anubis stood and walked behind the counter, dumped the cup Ernie gave him and grabbed another out of the middle rack. He pulled the orange tab on the coffee machine and rinsed the cup with steaming hot water. Three times. The coffee that was brewing when he entered the restaurant sat in the machine. Anubis pulled the filter holder out of the machine and examined the paper. No unexpected discolorations or odors. He filled the clean cup and went back to his stool before he took his first sip. It was worth the effort; the coffee was damn good.

A sheriff's car pulled up in front of the establishment partially blocking Anubis's view of his unit. He slid to the adjacent stool clearing his field of view. The deputy stretched his long, lanky body as soon as he got out of his vehicle. He ambled in and looked around, his eyes landing on Anubis. "Where's Iris?"

"She's late again." Anubis pursed his lips and whistled then bellowed, "Yo! Ernie! You got another customer."

Ernie pushed his head far enough around the door to see who it was. "Hey, Dean. Breakfast sandwich and orange juice?"

The deputy stretched again. "Nah, I need coffee this morning. The baby is teething and ain't nobody sleeping."

"Grab yer own. I'll bring out the sandwich in a minute." Ernie ducked back into the kitchen, and the deputy filled his cup and then took a seat next to Anubis.

"Dean Potter. You new around here?"

"Yep. You lived here long?"

"Hell, seems like forever, but shoot... it has only been just over a year. Once I get enough experience, I'll apply to bigger departments. What about you? What do you do?"

"I work for the Air Force." Anubis took another drink of his coffee.

"Yeah? Normally all the people coming in to work at Taylor Air Force Base stay over in Fairfield. Why are you all the way out here?"

Anubis smiled and winked at the sheriff. "Surprise inspection. The new wing commander called in a favor from the Inspector General. They sprinkled us all around the area so there would be no notice."

"Damn, I pity them. The Air Force is always doing exercises and inspections." Deputy Dean took a drink of his coffee and yawned hard, cracking his jaw in the process. They sat in comfortable silence while they drank their coffee.

Ernie came out with two foam containers and two paper bags. "Your total's fifteen even." He spoke to Anubis and then placed the small bag in front of Dean. The deputy picked up the bag and stood. "Put this on my tab will ya, Ernie?"

"You got it." Ernie went to the old cash register and pulled out a tattered spiral notebook.

"Take care, man." Dean headed for the door.

Anubis looked up from his wallet and nodded at the deputy. "You, too." He pulled a twenty from his wallet and dropped it to the counter.

"Damn it, the delivery truck is early." Ernie watched the food service truck make the turn into the drive. "Go ahead and grab two to-go cups and fix them up any way you want. Flip that sign to 'closed' when you leave? I'll switch it back when I get done putting this delivery away." Ernie didn't wait for Anubis to respond but hit the silver door and headed to the back of the building.

Anubisfelthisphonevibrateandpalmeditreadingthenewtext.
>**Cobalt**

He glanced out the window. His contact had found him. He didn't make it hard. He was in the only pay by the hour motel in the area they knew he'd be heading toward. He typed in his countersign. >**Azure** and hit send.

Anubis moved away from the counter, rinsed out the take-out cups, three times, prepped two cups of coffee and gathered the sack containing the breakfast he'd ordered. The person making contact would wait until they were sure the area was secure before showing themselves. In the meantime, Sky and Kadey needed to eat.

He strolled back across the street and unlocked the motel unit. Anubis knew immediately that someone else was in the room. The chills that ran up his spine settled quickly. Kadey and Sky still slept in the far bed oblivious to the intruder. He set down the food but picked up both coffee cups as he turned.

"You want cream or sugar?" He whispered the question.

"Depends. Have I done anything to piss you off recently?" Asp's deep voice scratched through as a whisper.

Anubis motioned out the door, and both men departed silently. Anubis handed the coffee to Asp. Asp looked at him and reached out, taking the cup from the hand that Anubis was lifting to his lips. He chuckled at Asp's caution. "It has been quite some time since I've poisoned anyone on our side."

"But you admit you have." They strolled to the end of the small units.

"I can neither confirm nor deny…"

Asp's deep laughter pulled a genuine smile from Anubis. It had been almost three years since he'd seen his friend.

"What are you doing back in the States?" Anubis leaned against a post and kept his eyes trained on the unit where Sky and Kadey slept.

"Had a mission go south. The back-office hacks seem to think I need a break to regain my strength and heal, and I need to do a re-eval on the go/no go. Seems I was a bit too angry for the shrink's liking." Asp's arm curled, exposing a line of pink and red scars from his wrist to where his leather jacket hid the freshly healed wounds.

"Had that happen. About six years ago. Laid up for five months until the powers-that-be called me back." Anubis took a drink of his coffee.

"I see you were busy during that time." Asp waggled his eyebrows.

Anubis sneered a semi-smile and shook his head. Asp on assignment was silent and deadly, but outside the time he was working in his profession, the man talked a mile a minute and was as subtle as a ton of bricks falling in the middle of a freeway during rush hour traffic. Anubis had no idea how the man managed to meld the two sides of his personality, but he was one of the elite in Guardian's Shadow World, so he obviously managed it well.

"She's raised the little one by herself. I had no idea." Anubis shrugged off the guilt. He'd had no knowledge of the little girl. If he had, maybe… hell, he still didn't know what he would have done. *Yes, you do*. He swatted the small inner voice out of his thoughts

Asp reached into his jacket and pulled out a manila envelope. "Credentials to access the Gateway. Bengal relayed that your medical authorization is already in the system. You won't have any problems accessing the medical facility with the identity the architect gave you."

"New name?" Anubis put the envelope into his jacket not bothering to look at the information. He'd read the brief when Asp left.

"Beats the fuck out of me, I didn't look. That's information I didn't need to have." Asp leaned against the grey siding of the last unit. He fished out a set of keys from his pocket. "Burgundy Cadillac STS with luggage for all three of you in the trunk. Alpha told me to put a field kit for you in the spare tire compartment."

That meant he had another weapon and ammunition plus a clean, secure phone.

"I figured you'd need some grub. Groceries are in the trunk. I stopped in Sacramento and picked some stuff up for you. Nobody but me has touched it or had the keys to access it. It's safe."

Anubis dipped his head and cleared his throat. His phobia about food wasn't well known, but a few did know. "Thank you." He hadn't eaten since he'd made pancakes with Kadey two days ago. The only reason he could eat the pancakes was *he'd* opened the sealed pancake mix. *He'd* inspected the container of milk and broke the seal on the jug. Eggs were damn near tamper-proof, but he checked each one before he broke them into the batter.

"Meh…you'd have done the same for me. I was instructed to tell you the clean-up is done." Asp hefted his large frame off the side of the building. "Take care of yourself, my man. If you need me, reach out. I'm not on assignment, and I kinda like the area. Whatever it takes, brother." Asp extended his hand.

Anubis once again noticed the new scars. He wondered what had gone down, but knew not to ask. If Asp needed to confide in him, he would. He grasped Asp's proffered hand and shook it finishing the motto they lived by, "Thank you, and I'm here for you too, as long as it takes, brother."

Asp spun around the corner onto the gravel. The lack of noise as he walked away wasn't a surprise. For a big man, Asp was damn near silent. Anubis peeled himself off the post he was holding up and headed back to the room.

Sky was up and in the bathroom, but Kadey was still asleep. Anubis moved their breakfasts and the large milk to the small table. He'd go across the street to get her another cup of coffee if she didn't want to share his.

He set his cup down and pulled out the envelope. Three DoD identification cards fell into his lap. Kaeden had a Common Access Card with an encrypted chip. Sky and Kadey had been issued DD Forms 1173, dependent ID cards. Kaeden picked his up and looked at the civilian rank he'd been assigned. *Holy fuck.* The architect had engineered him a Senior Executive Service employee, Level II cover. Shit that was a four-star general equivalent. Level I and II's could actually be presidential appointments. Kaeden, Sky and Kadey Long. Not much of a difference, but enough to negate a search of any system for the surname of Lang and it was vastly different from Meyers, not that it would matter once the Rh-null bloodwork was determined. However, Guardian had a way to suppress that information within the military channels. No, he wouldn't have any problem accessing the installation or getting medical attention for Kadey. Guardian gave him the golden ticket, and he held the golden ID in his hand.

Sky quietly opened the bathroom door and came out as Anubis pulled two more documents out of the envelope. "What is that?" She sat down opposite of him.

He pushed the take-out containers toward her. "Breakfast for you and Kadey."

"No, I mean that." She nodded towards the identification cards and grabbed his coffee from in front of him.

"Our ID's to access our gateway to safety, Taylor Air Force Base, and to the medical facilities on the base." He passed her the ID cards.

"Long? What if they figure out these are forgeries? We could go to jail." Both of Sky's hands shook when she put down the coffee to take the identification cards.

He reached over and moved the coffee cup before she spilled it and burned herself. "They aren't fake."

"Are you in the Air Force?" Sky's question was more of an accusation.

"I am today." He raised his ID card.

"But…"

"Sky, I assure you Guardian has cleared us through this process. We work with all kinds of agencies, the FBI, CIA, DEA and the DoD. Hell, we work with Mossad, MI6 and every other intelligence agency out there. If they need our specialties, we respond. If we need their resources, it's reciprocal, legal and above all else… safe."

"So we are going to the Air Force base, now?"

"After Kadey wakes up. I'll go out to the car my company provided and get your luggage."

"What luggage?"

"They provided an appropriate wardrobe for our time at the base." Anubis rose from where he sat.

"Wait, Kaeden…" Sky looked back at Kadey who rolled over and flung off the covers, still asleep but waking. She motioned toward the door, and he followed her out. When the door closed, she put her hand on his forearm. "I wanted to apologize."

Anubis kept a carefully blank face. "For what, exactly?"

"Well for getting so upset last night and for doubting you

were trying to take care of us. It's just that…" She pulled her hand through her hair and then leaned into his chest resting her forehead on it. He instinctively curled his arms around her. "I've never done anything like this before. I'm major-league freaked out about the doctor and that other person being killed and there are so many questions I have that you won't—"

"Can't." He interrupted.

She nodded. "Right… can't answer. I'm overwhelmed, and I need to do what is right for my baby. Can you promise me we won't get into any trouble for using those IDs?"

Kaeden smiled and tugged at her hair until she looked up at him. "I swear that the IDs are legitimate. You and Kadey are my dependents as far as the Air Force is concerned. Guardian has laid the groundwork, so you don't need to worry any longer. We will access the base, get Kadey to the hospital, and take it from there. As soon as we drive through those gates, we are safe. I'm going to go get you your luggage. You can keep whatever has been provided or replace it with what you've brought. You eat, get a shower, and get Kadey ready to go." Anubis leaned down and kissed her forehead before he turned her around and all but pushed her through the door. He pulled the door shut behind him and glanced at the car Asp had dropped off. They were going first class, and for that, he'd make sure he thanked Alpha. The man was all about family.

CHAPTER NINE

SKY SAT IN THE FRONT SEAT OF THE new vehicle. She glanced back at Kadey who was leaning over and staring out of the window at the front gate of Taylor Air Force Base. Kaeden queued up in the line of traffic and rolled down the driver's side window. His employer had provided the clothes they all wore. The expensive silk blouse, linen slacks and high heels she wore cost more than her entire monthly salary working for the District Attorney. She didn't tell Kaeden, but the fact that someone knew their sizes freaked her out. Kadey chose to wear a beautiful pink dress complete with pink patent leather shoes. Whoever purchased the outfit also included pink barrettes for her hair. To say Kadey was excited to be on the 'adventure' would be the understatement of the year.

"Momma! Look, he has a gun!" Kadey pointed to the uniformed guard standing at the gate. Indeed, he had a handgun strapped low against his thigh. The holster was grey and blended with the camouflage uniform he wore. "Yes, I see. That is so he can protect everyone. Just like a policeman, but he's a soldier."

"Airman," Kaeden spoke for the first time since they left the little motel.

"What?" Sky had no idea what that meant.

"He isn't a soldier. He is a Staff Sergeant in the Air Force. He's an airman, but he's also an NCO, so calling him sergeant is more appropriate."

Sky blinked at the information dump. She looked back at Kadey and made big bug eyes at her. The little girl laughed and waved at the 'sergeant' when they pulled up to his location beside the gate. He smiled and gave Kadey a small wave. Kaeden handed over all three IDs, and Sky held her breath.

"Mr. Long, we've been expecting you. If you would pull over to the right please, sir?" He handed the ID cards back and grabbed the microphone that was attached to his lapel. "Taylor, this is Gate One, notify Eagle One that the primary is on base." Kaeden waited for the second lane of traffic to clear and pulled over as directed.

Sky grabbed Kaeden's hand and squeezed it. She glanced back at Kadey who was almost standing on her head looking at the huge overhang covering the gate. She hissed at Kaeden, "Why does he want us to pull over? Who is the Eagle guy? Are we in trouble?"

Kaeden parked the car and turned to her. "No, I'm assuming the 'Eagle Guy' is either their squadron or the Support Group Commander. For an installation this size, I'd wager the Wing Commander is a Brigadier General, so probably a minion detailed to make sure we make it to our quarters and that we have everything we need."

"Are there always so many guards at the gate?" Sky looked back. There were two other airmen or sergeants that she could see. One of them had not only a handgun but a machine gun.

"I don't know. Manning depends on a lot of different things."

Sky watched the sergeant as he walked over from the gate shack. He wasn't looking at them, but at the outbound traffic. He kneeled down beside the driver's side door. "Sir, our Support

Group Commander, Colonel Cologne is approaching. We will stop traffic and allow his driver to cross over and come into this lane. Please follow his vehicle to the DV quarters."

A dark blue vehicle approached, and Sky watched as the people at the gate stopped traffic with an effortless command and allowed the other vehicle to swing around the gate shack. The car pulled up beside the new Cadillac. The passenger window rolled down, and a middle-aged man in a uniform spoke, "Mr. Long, Mrs. Long, welcome to Taylor Air Force Base. Please follow me; I'll escort you to quarters."

Kaeden started the car and pulled into traffic after the dark blue sedan. "Just like that?" Sky marveled.

"I told you to trust me." Kaeden grabbed her hand and squeezed it once before he dropped it.

Sky gaped out the window. The base was incredible. Even in the fall, the grass was green and mowed to within an inch of its life. The bushes were all trimmed and neat. Everything was so clean and well maintained. Nothing was out of place. The fastidiousness of the installation had a calming sense of order, and it seemed to surround everything. Cars stopped for people in crosswalks without any prompting, which was baffling and altogether awesome. Brown signs with letters and numbers, not really words, made no sense to her and pointed in different directions, but even those were all the same size, uniform with clean lines and unobtrusive.

"Momma! Look!" Sky whipped her head around to see what had Kadey excited. A row of huge planes sat right off the road where they were driving. "Can we ride in one?"

"Oh honey, I don't think so. Right?" Sky handed that loaded question over to Kaeden for support.

"Those planes are used to take people and equipment all over the world. They make sure all the military people have what they need to do their jobs. If we rode in one someone might not get what they need, when they needed it."

"Oh. Okay. That would be mean." Kadey craned her neck to see the planes as they passed.

They followed the dark blue car through the installation until they pulled up to a small series of buildings tucked under a canopy of old, beautiful trees. The two people in the lead vehicle exited and immediately put on hats. Kaeden put the vehicle in park and glanced at Sky. "Let me do all the talking."

Oh, heck yes, please. "Absolutely." She sure as heck wasn't going to open her mouth and insert her foot. She'd gladly put this all on Kaeden.

They got out of the car as the men approached. Sky busied herself getting Kadey out of the car as the men introduced themselves. When she turned to them all eyes were on her. She squeezed Kadey's hand and glanced over at Kaeden.

"Honey, the Colonel asked if you wanted a tour of base housing and to meet with some of the other wives at the Officer's Wives' Club after Kadey's appointment."

Sky drew a deep breath; obviously, Kaeden was pushed into a corner if she already had to talk. "I really appreciate the opportunity, but we've had a rough couple of weeks. If we could just relax tonight?"

"Of course, ma'am. General Hewitt's protocol office developed a possible itinerary for your stay, but of course, your family comes first." He turned to Kaeden, "Mr. Long, my executive officer, Captain Munson, will bring your luggage inside."

Instead of handing over his keys, Kaeden popped the trunk and pointed out what he wanted the other man to bring in. Once the trunk closed, he put his hand on the small of Sky's back. They strolled down the sidewalk and into the fancy apartment. There was a small kitchen, a living room, an office and two bedrooms, each with their own attached bathroom. Sky and Kadey explored the rooms while Kaeden dealt with the officers.

"Momma, when we go to the hospital, I get to come back here to sleep, right?"

"That's right, baby. We are just going to meet your doctor and maybe do some tests." Sky had to break that to the little girl.

Kadey looked up at her with sad eyes. "But I don't like tests." Kadey associated tests with blood draws and needles.

"I know, but if we have to do tests, we'll ask your daddy if we can get a special treat afterward, okay?" Sky had no idea if that was possible, but there had to be a place where they could get ice cream on the base. God, she hoped there was.

"Chocolate?" Kadey pulled her hand out of Sky's and climbed up on the bed. She sat down and fluffed out her skirt around her.

"If that's what you want, you bet." Sky sat down beside her and gave her a sideways hug.

"Am I going to get my operation here?"

"Yes, I think so, baby."

"Why?"

"Because they can take better care of you here."

"Why?"

"I don't know, maybe the doctors are smarter here?" Sky made bug eyes at Kadey again diverting the little girl's worry. Sky glanced up when a soft knock on the door sounded. "Come in."

Kaeden walked in and sat down on the other side of Kadey. "We are free until our appointment at two. The chief cardiologist will be overseeing Kadey's care. We're clear."

∼

SKY WATCHED AS KAEDEN PICKED UP A SLEEPING Kadey out of the back seat of the car. She shut the door and locked the vehicle with the key fob. The appointment at the medical facility had lasted three hours. Not because of any wait, because there was absolutely no waiting for them. They'd been assigned an escort as soon as they arrived at the huge medical facility. Sky didn't have a clue what rank the woman was, but there were a lot of stripes on that sergeant's arm. The woman was professional and courteous while taking them from one spot to the next. By the time they walked out of the facility, they had been to the laboratory to have blood drawn for both Kaeden and Kadey, an EKG done on Kadey and then one final stop for an MRI. That is where they met the chief cardiologist. They called in an anesthetist who gave Kadey a light sedative so she could once again sleep through the entire procedure. For that, Sky was thankful. The loud banging and clanking of the MRI would have terrified Kadey, not to mention the little girl would not have been able to lay still for the extended period of time it took to run the image.

Sky had to acknowledge that Kadey's Air Force doctor was amazing. She'd given him the only copy of Kadey's medical records as soon as they met. Nobody asked about the little girl's last name being different on the records, which was yet another thing that had been weighing on Sky's mind. By the time they left, the doctor's staff had made a copy of all the records and returned the originals to her.

"We will review all the tests and information from the previous doctors, but as I am sure you know, the biggest stumbling block to Kadey's operation is her blood type. Are either of you a suitable donor?" The doctor spoke to them in a darkened room as they watched Kadey in the MRI machine.

"Yes, I am Rh-null." Kaeden's eyes didn't move from Kadey's small form.

"Sir, I'm sure you realize how rare your blood is. I know our leadership would like to encourage you to register with the…"

Kaeden put up his hand and shook his head. "Not possible due to the nature of my position and the risk it could cause to the security of my work."

The doctor let out a sigh. "Figured it was something like that. Otherwise, you two would be registered as a national treasure."

Sky shook herself out of her thoughts and hurried ahead of Kaeden to open the door to the apartment where they were staying. She unlocked the door, pushed it open and switched on the light. Kaeden made his way to Kadey's room and laid her down on the bed. Sky took off her pretty, new shoes, pulled a blanket up over her, and tucked her in. The little girl was exhausted.

Sky followed Kaeden out of the room and shut the door, leaving it open enough so Kadey could see the hall light which she flicked on as she walked past it. Kaeden spoke over his shoulder as he exited the front door, "I'll be right back." She watched out the window as Kaeden walked to the car and opened the trunk. He returned with a small black bag and two big canvas totes.

He placed the black bag on the top of the refrigerator and sat the two canvas bags on the kitchen counter. Sky drifted his direction and watched as he unloaded… groceries?

"There is a ton of food already in the refrigerator." Sky opened the door and pointed to the stocked shelves.

Kaeden shrugged. He carefully inspected each seal on the items he took out of the bag. "Habit. I won't eat anything I don't buy or prepare."

Sky pulled out one of the dinette chairs and sat down thinking back over her association with Kaeden. The stark truth of his words hit her. When they'd been dating, they cooked at home and went out after they ate or he'd pick her up after dinner, and they'd go dancing. Later, during their hook-ups, they barely got out of bed, let alone worried about food.

"Why?"

"Paranoia brought about by a profession that places me in potentially dangerous environments. I'm acutely aware of what can happen if you aren't careful."

"What? You mean like food poisoning?" She could see where that would be a problem if he didn't always have proper refrigeration or cooking facilities.

Kaeden stopped unloading the bag and turned his head toward her. His eyes filled with mirth and he laughed. "Yes, exactly like food poisoning."

He opened a can of smoked almonds and pulled out a tin of crackers. Sky had never seen crackers in a tin before. Kaeden popped the lid and put them on the table with the almonds. He opened several more tins and cans making an impromptu feast out of nuts, crackers, dried fruits, preserved meat spreads and several canisters of chocolate. He opened the second bag and smiled. Kaeden revealed a bottle of dark amber liquid. "Would you like a drink?" He held up the bottle toward her.

"What is it?"

"Irish Whiskey." Kaeden turned on the hot water and let it run. He rummaged in the cabinets and pulled out plates and glasses. Sky watched as he washed, re-washed and then rinsed the dishware.

"I think they're clean." She picked up a macadamia nut and popped it into her mouth.

"Another habit." Kaeden fished the glasses out, poured a small amount of whiskey into each glass, and then put the glasses in the freezer. He pulled out a couple of bottles of water from the bag and opened one for her and one for him.

"Are you ever going to be able to tell me what you do?" Sky scooped up a handful of a dried fruit combo and picked out the mango pieces to eat first.

"Probably not." Kaeden pulled out his phone and frowned at the face of the device.

"Issues?" Sky was immediately on alert.

"No. But my scheduled phone call has been pushed back." Kaeden spread some canned meat spread on his cracker and downed it in one bite. He made and ate six more crackers slathered in meat spread before he started on the nuts and fruit. The man demolished most of the food in record time.

Sky tipped her head and watched him. When was the last time she actually saw him eat anything? The other morning when he'd made pancakes with Kadey. "When was the last time you ate?"

Kaeden shrugged and got up to retrieve the whiskey. He extended one glass to her and took his seat again. "It doesn't matter. I eat when I can. I've learned to deal."

"Why didn't you say something?" Sky took a sip of her whiskey. The strong liquor burned all the way down her throat, and she gasped a breath in surprise.

"Smooth, huh?" Kaeden smiled and winked at her.

"Yeah…totally smooth." Sky sat the liquor back and grabbed the water bottle hoping to quench the fire currently roasting her esophagus.

She elevated the bottle to her lips and drank down half of it. When she lowered the bottle, Kaeden was watching her, and she saw the darkening look of desire in his eyes. She gulped down the last swallow of water. "Want something, big boy?"

He took a drink of his whiskey. "I somehow always want you."

Sky set her water bottle down and picked up a piece of chocolate. "What would you do with me if you had me?"

Kaeden's gaze traveled over her. He shifted in his seat and leaned forward. "Everything. If I had you, and you were mine…" He reached out and drew her hand from the table turning it palm up. He traced his finger across the palm of her hand sending a full body shiver through her. "I've spent so many nights imagining how I'd tease your body, the way I'd take you to the point of losing your mind only to leave you at the edge, teetering until you begged me for release. I'd worship your body, Sky. You'd never doubt that you were the amazing, beautiful woman I see."

Sky pulled her hand back.

His eyes flashed to hers.

"But you won't stay."

"If it was possible?" He shrugged and shook his head not answering his question. "I want you. Both of you, but my life is…"

Sky held up her hand. They'd done this bit before. "Right, I know. Complicated. Look, Kaeden, I get it. I'm a side thing, and Kadey is a child you never wanted. I appreciate you stepping out of whatever spy-thriller movie set your life exists on to help us. Let's just leave it at that. Kadey is having surgery in two days. The doctor said we could go back to our own physician after he sees her at the two-week point post op. So, in sixteen days, you'll be free to do whatever it is you do. I'll go back to the house before the bank repossesses it, pack up and figure life out. We'll be fine."

Kaeden leaned back and diverted his attention out the picture window at the front of the apartment. "If I could change what I am… what I do…"

Sky could feel the pain and regret in his voice, it was that palpable. Whatever kept him from… no. She wouldn't do that to herself again. She stood up and walked around the small table dropping to her knees in front of Kaeden. But she *would* take her pleasure where she could, and she would try to take away some of the pain that seemed to swamp Kaeden.

≈

FOR THE FIRST TIME SINCE HE JOINED GUARDIAN, Anubis seriously questioned whether or not he wanted to retain his position within the organization. He glanced up as Sky rounded the table. When she lowered to her knees in front of him, she held his full attention.

"Kadey is asleep." Sky rubbed her small hands up and down his thighs. Her head tipped to the side as she searched his face, appearing deep in thought.

Anubis nodded at her comment, not sure he deserved where her words were leading.

"Come to the bedroom with me, Kaeden." Sky stood and extended her hand to him.

Kaeden stood and glanced at the door. "Let me lock up. I'll be there in a moment."

Sky glanced at the door and then back toward the bedroom. "Don't make me wait too long." She stood up, putting her hand on the back of his neck and pulled him down to her. She'd taken off her heels. Her head barely made it to his pecs. Kaeden leaned down. Before he met her lips, she whispered, "We both deserve a few moments in time. The ones we can look back on and remember."

Kaeden let her lead the kiss. She was the one initiating the intimacy, and he'd willingly let her lead after the mind fuck Arnie had laid on her. He remembered a confident woman who wasn't afraid to take what she wanted. Her hesitancy was Arnold T. Cross's fault, and Anubis hated the man for it. Sky's tongue swept his bottom lip, and he opened for her, giving her access and meeting her tentative caress of his tongue. When she pulled away her eyes remained shut; her lips were full and red, and her cheeks were flushed. If there was a way to commit every line of her face to memory, he prayed to be able to do it—and he wasn't a praying man. He didn't have the right to ask God to be forgiven for something he was going to keep doing.

Slowly her eyelids rose. Her pupils were wide, almost consuming the dark brown of her irises. "Don't take too long." She slipped out of his grasp and headed to the bedroom. Anubis made quick work of closing up his remaining food, placing an almost unperceivable mark on each can in an exact location. If anyone were to tamper with his food, he'd know. He locked up and pulled the drapes so no one could see inside. He checked all the windows before he peeked in on Kadey.

Kaeden stepped across the hall and pushed open the door. The shower was running, and the bathroom door was ajar. Kaeden pushed the door open and leaned against the wooden frame. The frosted glass of the shower muted Sky's naked form, but it couldn't take away from the beauty he witnessed. She leaned her head back sending her dark brown hair down her back in a silken fall. She turned to him, opened the door and smiled. He lost his clothes in as much time as it took to cross the bathroom floor. He'd secured his automatic and secondary weapon in the trunk of the car when he retrieved his food.

Sky held the glass door ajar and boldly looked at him from head to toe. He cupped his shaft and stroked it. His desire for her hardened his cock into granite within seconds of seeing her naked and waiting for him.

She backed away, and he stalked forward. "I need you, Kaeden." Sky ran her hands up his chest, the spray of the shower darkening the hair on his chest where her hands roamed.

"Tell me what you need, babe." Kaeden pulled her to him and lowered his lips to hers.

She leaned back in his arms and ran her hands up his biceps to his shoulders. "I want you to lift me up and fuck me against the shower wall. Hard and fast. I want to feel your cock inside me tomorrow morning."

It was a favorite position for both of them, but oh damn, her words. She ramped his need up into the red when she spoke with such bold assurance. She hadn't been this outspoken since he'd left her in Fresno. He was happy to have the old Sky back, if even for the little while he pushed her against the wall.

"Fuck yeah, there's the woman I used to know." Kaeden reached down and grabbed her thighs, pulling her up to his waist. Her small body was easy to lift. Her legs wrapped around him and he felt it as she crossed her ankles at the small of his back. He pinned her back against the wall and lowered to fuck her mouth with his tongue. She met his kiss with a force and desire that activated every memory he had of her. She bit his bottom lip. He pulled away and laughed at the challenge that shone clearly from her eyes.

Sky wrapped her arms around his neck and pulled herself up until she was even with his eyes. "I want you inside me."

"You're not ready." His cock wasn't small, and he'd be damned if he was going to hurt her. Foreplay, in his case, was a necessity, not a nicety.

"Feel me, big boy. I'm wetter than this shower. I'm ready."

Anubis slid his hand down her hip and swept the outer lips of her sex before he entered her with two fingers. He felt her slick heat. Fuck, she was ready.

Sky gasped and threw her head back exposing her neck. She bucked her hips against his hand. "God, yes. Please. Now."

Fuck, the way the woman wanted him, even after all the shit he'd drug her through, it was a miracle given to a sinner. One he'd cherish and protect. "Hang on to me, babe." Anubis waited until she tightened her grasp and reached down to position himself at her core. He cupped her thigh with the other hand holding her up. "Loosen your hold." He leaned forward placing her back against the wall and dropped his head to her shoulder. The tight heat of her sex wrapped around the head of his cock. He thrust up into her. They both moaned at the pleasure of the sensation. Anubis wrapped one arm around her waist, and the other gripped her thigh supporting her on his cock. "So fucking good, Sky. So good." His hips thrust deep of their own accord.

Sky's breath punched out with each collision of their bodies. She used the muscles of her legs to lift and drop, meeting his animalistic rutting of her in a frantic, frenzied climb toward release. Anubis covered her mouth with his when her gasps became words, and the words became too loud. She clawed at his back, and he drove deeper and faster. Sky's body tightened like a bow, seconds before she shattered.

Anubis crushed her to him as he chased his release. Her tight, hot body wrapped around him, depending on him to keep her aloft, safe and satisfied, fed his buried desires, stoking the flames until they were all consuming.

Sky was his, damn it! His and he was fucking claiming her. He thrust as far inside her as he could and lost himself.

The sensation of Sky's hand stroking his back broke through the euphoria of orgasm. He loosened his arms slightly and lifted his head. Sky's eyes searched his. He dropped a soft kiss to her lips. "I think I've become addicted to my daughter's mother." Anubis pressed his forehead against hers. "I want you."

Sky's hand stopped its up and down motion. Anubis didn't open his eyes, he couldn't look at her, wouldn't acknowledge that she might not return his feelings.

She unhooked her legs, and he let her down. "Kaeden, look at me."

Anubis squeezed his eyes shut and shook his head. Her voice was so… resolute, he'd fucked up by admitting his feelings.

"Kaeden." Sky's hand cupped his cheek. "I've always wanted you."

Anubis opened his eyes. She had a sad smile on her face.

"I don't know how to do this." Anubis hated admitting his confusion and his weakness, but she deserved to know.

"Neither do I. Relationships don't come with a manual, or if they do, we sure as fruck missed it when they passed them out."

An unexpected bubble of laughter burst out of him. "Fruck?"

She slapped his shoulder and stuck out her tongue at him. "*We* have a daughter who is a parrot."

Anubis cupped the back of her neck and waited until she looked up at him. "I need to talk to my people. I don't know who is after me." He motioned his head toward the door, "Outside there is a threat against me. They've proven they will kill to get to me. I couldn't live with myself if I put either of you in jeopardy. I'll have to leave you, to make sure the threat is pulled away from you until my company can handle the situation."

Sky leaned into him and wrapped her arms around him. "I'm not going to lie. I don't want you to leave, but I understand."

"You—"

"Momma! I'm hungry!"

Anubis spun, putting Sky between his very naked self and his five-year-old daughter, who was obviously at the bathroom door, or… fuck, *inside* the room.

Sky laughed and grabbed his arm, steadying herself. "Okay, baby! Let me get out, and I'll get your dinner."

"Is Daddy in there with you?"

Anubis could see the muted form of Kadey's pink dress and her dark brown curls as she walked toward the shower. *Fuck, fuck, fuck!* He cupped his cock and balls trying to hide them as he crouched behind Sky's tiny form. His eyes scanned the shower enclosure...looking for an escape hatch. Something... anything! *Fuck, he was trapped*!

"Ummm... yeah, he's helping me wash my hair." Sky made a face and shrugged at him. It might have been funny if his dick wasn't hanging out in the open with his daughter coming closer.

"Okay. Can I turn on Dora?"

"Sure, baby." Sky opened the door and peeked around the frosted, and steam laden glass. Anubis shuffled as far into the corner of the shower stall as he could and prayed for the power of invisibility. He now understood the definition of complete and total mortification. He heard Sky talking. "You know the rules. Don't answer the door. I'll be out in just a minute."

"Don't forget to tell Daddy I get a treat because of the tests!"

Anubis inhaled and pushed back into the corner praying to every deity he'd ever heard of or imagined that somehow the tile wall of the shower would consume him.

"I won't, and I promise we'll find something special. Now pop on out to the front room. I'll be right there." Sky remained at the door for at least fifteen long seconds before she pulled it shut and spun around. "Well, that was exciting." She blinked before she burst out laughing. "Oh my goodness! You are as red as a lobster!"

Anubis dropped his cock and balls and damn near collapsed against the wall. "That shit *isn't* funny."

"Yeah, it kinda is." Sky laughed and grabbed the soap.

"No, it isn't!" Anubis snapped up the shampoo and poured a portion into his hand spinning Sky and working the suds through her hair as she washed her body.

"Oh, that's where you're so wrong. It was hilarious! Besides, she didn't see anything." Sky laughed out loud. "The big bad man was hiding in a corner, behind me!" Sky spun and put her soapy hands on his chest as she leaned back into the jets, rinsing her hair and body at the same time.

Anubis watched the suds slide down her skin. Her too thin frame was still unbelievably beautiful. He held the small of her back as she worked the clean water through her hair. When she moved forward, her smiling eyes opened and found him. "That is something I'll need to work on, though. I've never shut a door or locked it."

Anubis shifted her, so he was under the jets. He soaped up as he regarded her. He would love to be the one to cause her to shut her doors, but he had no idea how to make it happen. He needed to talk to Bengal or Alpha, probably both, but that needed to wait until they dealt with the current threat against him and his family. He turned off the water and wiped an area of the frosted glass clean of steam. He peeked out into the bathroom looking for Kadey.

"Is the coast clear?" Sky laughed as she reached around him and pushed opened the door. Anubis jumped back from the open area and retreated into the back corner. It was instinctive self-preservation. Sky grabbed a towel and wrapped it around her as she padded across the tile to the door. She shut the bathroom door and spun around. "You can come out now, it's safe."

Anubis grabbed a towel and wrapped it around his waist. "I don't think you should be enjoying this as much as you are." It had been one hell of a long time since he'd been the butt of a joke and he wasn't sure if he was alright with it. "How are you going to explain me in the shower with you?"

Sky bent over, wrapping a towel around her hair. She stood up and tucked in the end of the towel. "I don't intend to explain a thing unless she asks a question. If she asks, I'll handle it." Sky stopped and blinked staring at the steam covered mirrors above the vanity.

"What is it?" Anubis scanned the room suddenly on alert.

Sky cocked her head at him and gave him a puzzled look. "When Trey wanted to spend the night, I refused to let him. I didn't want to have to explain his presence to Kadey. I just realized what a line of bull puckey I fed him. I just didn't want him to stay because the only one I've ever wanted to have to explain to Kadey... was you."

CHAPTER TEN

KAEDEN SLID OUT OF THE POCKET DOOR AND closed the desk area off from the living room where Kadey and Sky were engrossed in a movie they'd pulled up on *Netflix*. When he received the message indicating the scheduled check-in was pushed back, he didn't have time to wonder if the causality for the delay was related to the events of the previous day. To say he'd been distracted wouldn't even scratch the surface of the mindset he'd been working through while the doctors examined Kadey.

He couldn't imagine how Sky had managed to stay sane. By the time they left the hospital yesterday, he wanted to wrap Kadey in bubble wrap and eliminate anyone who caused her any discomfort. He may have even developed a plan or two... especially the phlebotomist that failed to find her vein the first time. Sky handled it like a champ and found ways to distract their daughter. The heartfelt sobs from his baby girl ate away at his self-control faster than a flame through flash paper. If Sky hadn't been there to settle them both down, the phlebotomist would have been sucking his meals through a straw for the next month.

His phone vibrated in his hands, and he accessed the call. "Six-four-nine."

"I pass you Cobalt." He recognized Bengal's voice immediately.

"Azure. What do you have for me?"

"The line is secure. Standby. We need to bring in Alpha and Archangel." The line went dead. Anubis sat down in the desk chair and closed his eyes. Fuck. Archangel was now *the* big man, the one in charge of all of Guardian. He'd seen him once at a gathering that he'd dropped into, uninvited. Archangel and Asp could damn near be identical bookends they were built that much alike.

Bengal came back on the line. "Archangel, Alpha, you have Six-four-nine, and CCS on a secure line." Bengal identified the cyber intelligence office from which his woman, and now he, worked.

"How is your daughter?" The raspy voice wasn't Alpha and sure as fuck wasn't Bengal, so Anubis assumed it was Archangel's.

"She is getting the care she needs, sir. Surgery is scheduled."

"Roger that. We've asked the Secretary of the Air Force to authorize the base to temporarily elevate the security at Taylor Air Force Base."

Anubis leaned forward and propped his elbows on the desk. "The rationale?"

"Alpha, fill him in." Archangel's voice grated against his ear.

"We have verified through several sources that there has been a hit issued on your alias, your daughter, and her mother." Alpha's words dropped like lead.

Anubis drew in a breath and released it. He repeated the action two more times before he spoke. "The identity of the entity that funded the hit?"

"At this time, we've followed the money trail back to Suriname."

Anubis collapsed back into the leather chair and stared at the ceiling. "Fuck me. They obtained blood samples from the room where they held me."

"Probably. The man who was your target, Haghen, was Satan incarnate, but his nephew, Faas? That fucker makes his uncle look like Santa Clause." Bengal added the information.

"Faas?" Anubis had no idea who succeeded Haghen. That mission had been fucked up from the start. When the security team cornered the entire kitchen staff, Anubis bided his time, but the fuckers never gave him a chance to make a break for it. Hell, he didn't recall most of the torture sessions. The fuckers who worked him over were nothing but brutes. If they knew what they were doing Anubis would have remembered every excruciating second of the time he was held.

"Haghen's nephew."

Anubis closed his eyes against the memory of the incident. Haghen moved through the country in erratic fits and starts. Anubis managed to work his way on as kitchen staff at one of the compounds the man frequented. The compound security strip-searched everyone who worked in the house, so Anubis procured his chemicals from within the compound in order to complete his mission. The ad hoc poison he'd used worked too quickly. Hagen's security team corralled the kitchen staff, himself included when the man collapsed. Days later, Bengal arrived and wiped out what remained of Haghen's security team to get to him. From what he'd been told and read about the operation, there had been a security contingent assigned to the compound. The belief was that they were to finish the interrogations. Anubis didn't remember the rescue. He'd been too fucked up. Bengal told him he'd died twice on the short airplane ride back to the states. However, Guardian's docs started his heart pounding again, twice, and patched him up before they sent him north. He spent about a month at a secure facility in South Dakota undergoing medical and psychological exams before he was released to recover. If he'd been a normal member of Guardian, he would have finished his rehab at the complex in South Dakota, but to minimize his exposure, they segregated him and let him leave as soon as he was able to care for himself. Anubis stuck a pin in the map and chose Fresno. The rest was history.

"Faas is a medical doctor. From what we can extrapolate, he is the one that directed your blood be gathered and tested, and from the condition you were brought back in, there is no doubt they had more than enough to process. Our hypothesis is that he was waiting for you to surface. The logic behind the trap was sound. Revenge for his uncle's death is obviously the motivation here." Alpha cleared his throat and continued, "CCS correct me if I get this wrong, but when the mother had her cousin enter your daughter's blood into CODIS, it triggered our alarms and must have also somehow alerted Faas's people. The DNA was a partial match. That meant they had family they could leverage. Only the trail ended at the Merced County Sheriff's office. Faas's people knew you had a relative in the state, so they began the search. When your blood was logged in at the hospital, they were able to trace it back from where it originated. Obviously, they had someone who was monitoring for anything that indicated an Rh-null blood test."

"When they found it, they backtracked to the clinic, to find me." Anubis acknowledged the correlation between the deaths and his blood tests.

"Yes, but the doctor and nurse didn't have any information about you," Bengal interjected the comment.

"Which is why they followed the test back to the healthcare system, broke through the flimsy ass firewalls and found your daughter's information." That was from Bengal's woman.

"That information brings us up to this morning." Alpha stepped back into the conversation.

"The contracts that are out on us." Anubis's skin prickled against the adrenaline that was coursing through his veins. He had the name, Faas, and a reason, revenge for a job. One that had almost killed him. "I need a dossier on Faas," Anubis added.

"We can get you background on what the fucker's been doing, but he's been below everyone's radar. The more we dig into this guy, the more he becomes a person of interest." Archangel's voice rasped across the line.

"He's taken a contract out on my family and me." Anubis left the rest unsaid. Anyone who had the balls to take a hit out on a Shadow deserved the hellfire and brimstone that would rain down on his ass.

"The contract has been posted on the dark web. Unfortunately, we've been down this road before. We are better prepared to monitor the traffic on that side of the ether world. From what we've discovered Faas has put big money on you. However; there is very little chatter about the hit. From what we can discern Faas doesn't have the juice to get anyone to accept the hit, especially since Guardian's assets have started chatter stating this contract was tainted."

"So, you're convinced there isn't a threat?"

"Convinced but cautious, hence the increased security at the installation where you're staying."

"Where is that bastard now?" Anubis growled the question. He could hear the rustle of paper in the background before Alpha continued, "According to our human intelligence sources, Faas hasn't been seen at his compound in Suriname for two days. The assumption is he is traveling to California."

"What is that assumption based on?" The jump was a big one to take. Normally when dealing with hits ordered by the private sector, the entity initiating the contract wanted layers or buffers between them and the instrument. Coming to California would remove several layers of plausible deniability that Faas could claim.

"The son of a bitch is a sadistic bastard. Again, according to local human intelligence assets, Faas has a god complex. If someone takes the contract, he'll want to be on hand. We can't validate part of this information, but the contacts have been used in the past and were found reliable," Alpha relayed the information.

It was a risk to make a decision based solely on human intelligence unless the organization could validate it by other means. If they had any confirmation, such as documentation, physical movement, financial, communication, cyber trail or even an independent third-party verification they could make better plans.

Alpha's voice cut into his thoughts, "But even without verification, we aren't taking any chances. We have every resource available monitoring arrivals at commercial ports of entry, and we are processing all private flight plans, but in effect, this is a needle in a haystack search."

Archangel's gravelly voice scratched across the phone, "We are flying in a doctor to follow Kadey through the medical process. When she is stable enough to move, we are recommending your daughter and her mother be transferred to the complex in South Dakota. We can provide care and ensure protection in case anyone is stupid enough to accept the hit."

"And I'd be free to take care of the situation with Faas," Anubis said what everyone was thinking.

"As a reminder, Faas *has not* been coded or sanctioned," Archangel stated emphatically. "I have another meeting I need to attend. Alpha I need you to join me. Bengal. Take care of this. Do I make myself clear?" The raspy question released a smile on Anubis's face.

"Crystal, sir," Bengal replied quickly.

"Take care of your family, Six Four Nine," Archangel commanded before Anubis heard two distinct clicks on the line.

"We have two assets in the area. Asp and Moriah. They've received Air Force credentials. Moriah will shadow you at the hospital. Your daughter's operation is the most important thing for the next forty-eight hours. Let Moriah keep you safe. You concentrate on your family. You know how to contact Asp and if needed Thanatos. I'll paraphrase Archangel. You know how to take care of your family. Take care of them. Whatever it takes."

"As long as it takes." Anubis hung up and replayed the conversation in his head. A Guardian doctor would be present for the operation. He walked to the window and looked out. He was grateful for the oversight on his daughter's behalf. Having someone watch his six, even while on the military base, meant Guardian wasn't taking any chances with his family's security.

Moriah, hell that was some firepower. She was an urban legend of sorts—the only female assassin who worked for Guardian and one of only three in the world of her caliber—if one was to believe the whispers. Of course, there weren't calling cards or a list of "Who's Who" for people in his profession, but they were a small community. You knew of your contemporaries. Not by sight, but by reputation. Anubis knew the specialties of the elite that drifted in the shadows outside the reach of the rest of the world. Moriah killed at close quarters, she wielded a stiletto knife that had become legendary. Thanatos also killed at close quarter, the weapon wasn't specific, but the method was always up close and personal. It was rumored he looked in the eyes of each person he killed as they died. Asp was lethal with any type of firearm, from just about any distance, but rumor had it he preferred to use his hands. Which might explain the scars that Anubis had noticed when they'd last met.

Having any of them holding his six when Kadey was in surgery was a relief. Moriah would watch over them, and he had Asp at his disposal. Anubis nodded his head. If necessary, he'd use their talents to track his prey and to keep his family safe, but Faas was his. Although Guardian hadn't officially sanctioned the hit, they were doing nothing to stop him from going after the bastard himself. In fact, they gave him every tool he needed. Three elite assassins working the same case, four if you counted Bengal, and that man could never be counted out. Anubis smiled to himself as a saying from his long-forgotten childhood in New Orleans popped into his head. The creole in him sang the phrase, *Laissez les bons temps rouler*. Let the good times roll. Faas had no idea what was coming his way.

He pulled the blinds shut and headed back into the front room. Sky sat alone on the couch. She smiled at him and patted the seat next to her. "She conked out right after the first song. I knew you were busy, but I hoped we'd have a little mommy and daddy time tonight." Anubis sat down, and she leaned into him.

"You sure you want to risk it? We may get busted again."

"She rarely gets out of bed once she goes to sleep for the night. I'm willing to risk it if you are."

Fortunately, Kadey hadn't given the shower incident a second thought, or at least not that Sky had told him. Fuck yeah, he was willing to risk it. Hell, he was learning he was willing to risk just about anything when it came to Sky and Kadey. He lowered his lips to hers, gradually deepening the kiss. He leaned back and pulled her on top of him. She pulled away from his kiss and glanced down the hallway. He followed her eyes before he brought his focus back to her.

Sky smiled and arched an eyebrow. "You stay right there. That way you can see if Kadey comes out of her room."

"Say what?" Anubis gave a furtive glance toward the hallway but his attention snapped back to the happenings on the couch when Sky unbuttoned his jeans and pulled the zipper down. His cock pushed against the cotton fabric of his briefs. Sky looked up at him and smiled. "I've been waiting almost two years to do this again." She lowered herself to his cock and mouthed it. Her hot breath and wet lips dampened the material that encased his dick. He lowered his hand and ran it through her hair, pulling it back, so he was able to see what she was doing. Fuck, his hips pushed forward in an automatic bid to get closer to the delicious lips that were teasing him. "I need more of your mouth. Take me out."

Sky looked up at him. Her big brown eyes shone with excitement. She rose up onto her knees before she glanced down the hallway. She stood, shimmied out of her pajama shorts and straddled his thighs again. "I'm going to let you fuck my mouth, but don't come. I want you to fuck me."

He may have stopped breathing. In fact, he was pretty damn sure his heart stopped beating for a couple of seconds. The way Sky talked was as much foreplay to him as the dainty hands and fingers that currently roamed his chest. She knew how to rev all his fucking engines, and the woman had his cock pegging the red zone without putting him in her mouth. She pulled his waistband down and released his rock-hard dick. He grabbed the base and squeezed it to stem the looming orgasm rolling down his spine. "I'm not going to last if you suck me, babe. As much as I want your mouth, I need to be inside you."

Sky smiled and dropped down, licking a stripe from his fingers that still held the base of his cock up the underside. She circled the sensitive head with her tongue before sucking it in. Anubis hissed and stroked up on his shaft as she lowered. Her tight, hot suction pulled him closer to the edge. "Sky, if you don't stop, I'm going to come."

She smiled and popped off his cock and sat up. Her legs were on either side of his thighs on the couch cushion. She drew her fingers to her mouth and obscenely swirled her tongue around them before she sat down on his thighs and dropped her hand to her sex.

"Holy fuck... you're trying to fucking kill me." He watched as she spread herself open and rubbed her clit. A soft gasp from her snapped his eyes from her hands to her face. "I want to watch you make yourself come." Sky reached up and pinched her taut nipple through her pajama top. A sharp inhale of air brought him out of his stupor. He reached down and cupped his balls pulling them away from his body as he stroked. Fuck, her eyes followed his hands. Anubis moved his legs up sliding her closer to his cock. Her hand continued to hold back the folds of skin around her sex as she slid right up to his cock. Anubis pushed his hips up, driving his shaft into his cupped fist and across her exposed clit. Sky gasped and ground her hips forward. His fist sped up, working only on the head of his dick as he used his cock to stimulate Sky. They found an awkward, fantastic, stilted rhythm and chased their release. Every time Sky ground down it put pressure on his balls, and white hot jolts of electricity slammed through his lower extremities. He reached up and cupped one of her breasts, finding the hardened nipple. He pinched it and she jerked forward, landing both hands on his shoulders as she continued to grind against his hard-as-fuck cock. He cupped her neck and pulled her down for a kiss. Sky's hips stuttered, and she cried out into his mouth. He gripped his shaft hard and rammed it through his fist without any pretense. His orgasm raced through him and blinded him with a white-hot intensity that left him shaking. Sky fell on his chest, lying in his cum. He could feel the dampness of her completion on his balls.

He worked on catching his breath while he ran his hand through her dark brown hair. "Fuck, babe. That was so good." He kissed the top of her head.

"Yeah, we fit. I missed you so damn much." Sky snuggled into his chest.

Shit, he needed to tell her what was in store for her and Kadey. Damn it, he hated to ruin the moment, but she needed to know. "Tomorrow we need to talk about what's going to happen after the surgery is done." Anubis continued to stroke her hair as he spoke.

Sky tensed in his arms. "Is it bad?"

"No. Nothing to worry about. I just want to give you as much information as I can."

Sky sighed and nodded her head, which tucked her closer to his chin. "Thank you. For everything."

Anubis closed his eyes and let her drift to sleep. She should never have to thank anyone for caring for her. He'd really done a number on her. That was something he wished he could rectify.

CHAPTER ELEVEN

SKY PACED THE SMALL WAITING AREA. THE NURSE had explained the television monitor had a number-coded system that told Sky each time Kadey was moved from one area to the next. According to the number they assigned her, Kadey was still in the operating theater. Sky paced the fourteen steps to the window, turned, glanced at the computer screen and walked the same fourteen steps back. Kaeden leaned motionless against the doorframe. She could feel his eyes track her, but there was no way she could stop pacing. If she stopped, she'd start chewing her fingernails again. She'd already bloodied her fingers, and Kaeden had literally pulled her thumb from her mouth and forced her to notice what she was doing. Sky glanced at the clock and then at the screen. Three hours. Her baby had been out of her sight for *three hours*.

"Sky, come sit down, just for a little bit." Kaeden's voice broke into her mental hysteria.

She shook her head and walked to the window, glanced at the screen and turned around to collide with Kaeden's chest.

His hands cupped her upper arms. "Please, you're exhausting me. Come over here and sit down, just a minute.

Kaeden guided her to the bank of plastic chairs that were connected to each other by chrome tubing. He sat down and pulled her into his lap. Sky tucked into his chest and hid her face in the curve of his neck. He didn't wear cologne, but he didn't need it because the man's scent was simultaneously arousing and a balm that soothed her frayed nerves. He rubbed her back and lifted away to kiss the top of her head.

"She'll be okay. We'll get you both out to the ranch in South Dakota where you can relax, and she can recover."

"You're sure they will be able to take care of us?" She repeated the questions that they had gone over yesterday. They'd replayed this exact conversation many times since he told her the plan. Guardian had the facilities to take care of Kadey, and the care would be free. Kaeden had paid all her bills in California. She didn't have to worry about the bank repossessing her car or her house or about suffocating under a mountain of medical bills.

Kaeden needed to go back overseas to wrap up some loose ends. He never waivered on the fact that he wouldn't stay. Sky sighed, resigned to never having the closeness she needed from the man. She closed her eyes and melted into his warm strength for just a moment. She had him for now.

"Mr. and Mrs. Long?" Sky spun around at a man's voice and then sent a wild glance back at the monitor. Kadey was still in the operating room.

"What is it?" Sky shouted the question. Kaeden grabbed her arm steadying her when she jumped up, and thank God he did. She didn't know if she could keep herself upright. The man wore scrubs and an eye patch. He removed his surgical cap exposing a wave of blonde hair.

"Kadey is fine. I'm Doctor Adam Cassidy. I'm sorry we didn't meet sooner, but Guardian sent me to monitor Kadey's case and to ensure she gets the best care possible. I arrived this morning and have been with her team. I'll also be the one who will take care of her follow-up when we get back to South Dakota. The repair of the defect and the valve went straight along textbook lines. Kadey is strong, and her heart is now working the way the doctors were anticipating."

Sky clasped her hand over her heart and closed her eyes saying an immediate prayer of thanks. She popped her eyes open and asked, "When can I see her?"

"She'll be out of the operating suite soon, then in post-op until she comes out of anesthesia before we take her to ICU."

"ICU?" Sky gasped.

"Standard procedure for a surgery of this nature. They can monitor her better there. I anticipate she'll be in a normal room by this time tomorrow. I'm sure we will take you back as soon as possible, so she doesn't get scared when she starts to wake up. I'll come get you as soon as the staff here authorizes it."

"Thank you." Sky whispered and collapsed into Kaeden's hold. She swiped at the tears that trailed down her cheek.

"Hey, that was good news. No tears are authorized." Kaeden pulled her into his chest.

She nodded but cried all the harder. "I'm just so relieved." Sky wrapped her arms around Kaeden's waist.

"I know." Kaeden held her until the tall blonde pirate-slash doctor came back for them. Sky clung tightly to Kaeden's arm until she saw her baby. The nurse standing beside her bed smiled at Sky. "She's waking up. She'll be groggy and sleepy, but she did very well."

Sky smiled and wiped at her wet cheeks again. She picked up Kadey's small hand careful not to touch the IV or any of the cords that attached her daughter to the machines monitoring her. "Oh, my God! Kaeden, her hand is warm." Sky reached down and touched Kadey's feet. They were pink and toasty. "Her feet are warm, too!"

She smiled back at Kaeden and the pirate doctor. She'd have to ask the man's name again, but later. She was so happy to touch her baby right now that nothing else really mattered. Sky leaned down and spoke to Kadey, "Hey baby. You did it. The doctors fixed you all up. Pretty soon you're going be able to run as much as you want."

Kadey's eyes blinked open, and she smiled. Just a small smile, but Sky felt her eyes well up with tears again. Kaeden brought a chair up, and she sat down, still holding Kadey's hand. He leaned over and kissed Kadey on the forehead. "You did good, sweetheart." Kadey mumbled something that made Kaeden smile.

"What did she say?"

Kaeden stood up and blinked back what seemed suspiciously close to tears. "She said she wants her treat."

Sky laughed and kissed Kadey's hand. "As soon as the doctor says it's okay, we will get you all the ice cream you can eat."

KAEDEN SQUEEZED SKY'S SHOULDER AND BACKED AWAY GIVING mother and daughter a few moments. He saw Doctor Cassidy out of his peripheral vision and spoke to him. "Thank you for being here." He was able to breathe, finally. He'd masked his emotion all day to remain strong for Sky, but the thought of his little girl under the knife eviscerated him. The inside of his cheek was bloody because he'd stopped himself from asking all the questions Sky had already asked. He was walking a tightrope without a net. He wanted to know the answers, but to let Sky know he was so emotionally invested... fuck, that wouldn't be fair to her.

"I've got a little girl. Elizabeth. We call her Lizzy. She's four. If anything ever happened to her, I'd want to make sure she had the best care possible. You never have to thank me for taking care of anyone in the Guardian family."

Anubis nodded. He'd spent so much time on the fringes of the organization, the outpouring of help was overwhelming. "Thank you for taking care of my..." Kaeden swallowed hard and cleared his throat, "...my daughter." The words were no more than a whisper. Sky couldn't have heard him.

"Oh, and I have a message for you. Fury says your family will be safe with him. Take care of your business. I'm going to add my two cents. Whatever it takes, brother."

Anubis turned his head to look at the doctor. The man concentrated on the tablet he held. Thank God, because the tightrope just got a fuck-ton thinner. Anubis nodded and cleared his throat again before he spoke, "For as long as it takes, brother." Anubis extended his palm and shook the hand of a fellow warrior.

Damn near twenty-four hours later, Anubis finally convinced Sky to go to the cafeteria to get something to eat. Kadey had been placed in a private room, and Doctor Cassidy had assured him Kadey was doing well. He sat down in one of the oversized chairs that came with the private room. He saw the door open and watched as a woman slipped in. She wore scrubs and had a tablet in her hand, but she didn't move toward Kadey. Instead, she leaned against the wall. She was average height and average build and of oriental descent. She'd pulled her thick black hair back into a ponytail. The assassin he knew as Moriah jacked up her foot and propped it against the wall as she fished out something from her pocket. "Your woman met up with Cassidy. She's in good hands." She tossed the object at Anubis.

He caught it as it flew toward him, and lowered his gaze to it before lifting his eyes and raising his eyebrows. Moriah shrugged. "Asp told me to give that to you as soon as I could. This is the first time I've had the opportunity to make contact."

Anubis lowered his chin once in acknowledgement. "Thank you." He examined the tin of peanut butter crackers as he spoke. "Are you following us back to the complex?"

Moriah nodded. "I have orders to make sure your woman and child remain safe. I'll travel as a nurse. Cassidy knows. I would appreciate it if you didn't tell your woman."

"She knows nothing about us." Anubis opened the tin and devoured the first cracker sandwich in one bite.

Moriah scratched her arm in a lazy fashion as they watched each other. "She will find out eventually. When she does, wouldn't you rather that you were the one to control the information?"

Anubis shrugged and popped another sandwich. Asp sending him food was a new trend, but one he would not object to. "The only thing she needs to know now is that her daughter is safe and receiving the care she needs."

Moriah swung her steady gaze from Anubis to Kadey. "Children deserve to be healthy and happy."

"They do." Anubis's mind flitted back to his sister and the horror of her death.

"Do you believe we will ever be happy?" The question drew his eyes from his daughter.

"Bengal is happy." He knew Fury was happy too, but that was one secret he'd take to his grave. Bengal was open about walking into the light. Fury had "died" in order to escape the Shadows. Each had a different path and different circumstances. Anubis wondered if they would be the only two who would escape.

Moriah nodded. "I heard. I'll keep the three of you safe tonight. Get some sleep. I have a feeling you're going to need it."

Anubis inclined his chin in acknowledgement as she slipped from the room. He closed his eyes momentarily, committing the woman's facial features to memory. She'd given him her trust. The gift was rare, and he understood how much it took to lift the veil they lived behind. He'd revealed himself to Bengal, Thanatos, Asp, Lycos and now Moriah—five of the deadliest people in the world with whom he shared an alliance only they could understand. Moriah's revelation of her appearance was a binding gesture not easily given, and it was coupled with respect that came from an acknowledgement of his years of succeeding where others had failed. Their Shadow World lives were interwoven and yet solitary. He opened his eyes and stood up; stretching before walking the few steps required to stand at the bedside of his baby girl.

Anubis pushed her dark brown curls off her forehead and leaned down to kiss her mop of brown hair. Somehow, he had to find a way to merge his world and Sky's. He needed a way forward, a way he could walk toward the light, but not be exposed by it. He needed a path where Sky and Kadey could walk near the shadow but not be consumed by it. Anubis took his little girl's hand in his, careful not to move any of the tubes or wires that ran to the machines. "I'll figure it out, princess. I promise. Somehow."

CHAPTER TWELVE

SKY HUGGED THE NURSES THAT FOLLOWED KADEY'S GURNEY down to the ambulance bay. Her sincere, exhausted 'thank yous' weren't nearly enough for the loving care they provided. She watched as her daughter was carefully loaded into a waiting vehicle. Kaeden helped her into the back with him as Doctor Cassidy joined the driver in the front of the ambulance. It was still dark when they parked a short time later.

"Where is the plane?" Sky yawned and leaned her head back against the hard, interior wall of the vehicle.

"It isn't due for about ten minutes." Kaeden put his arm around her and tugged her into his warmth.

She nodded and gazed at her daughter. They were through the worst of it now, or at least that what the doctors were saying. She closed her tired, burning eyes.

Sky's head lolled to the right and rolled, waking her with a jerk. She blinked rapidly and whipped her head up checking on Kadey. How could she have fallen asleep? Rolling her shoulders, she yawned and shifted in her seat.

"You could have slept. You haven't had more than a couple hours sleep in days." Kaeden's arm dropped around her.

"Neither have you." Sky shook her head trying to clear the cobwebs out of her brain.

"I'm used to it." Kaeden glanced at the watch on his wrist. "The plane should be here shortly."

Sky sighed and dropped her head on his shoulder. She glanced at the pirate doctor's profile. The man was attentive and kind. He'd showed her pictures of his daughter. She liked the man even though the eye patch made him look sinister. The biggest thing was Kaeden trusted him and knowing that made this transport a little easier.

"I'm going to miss you." She whispered the words. They'd been with Kadey almost non-stop since her surgery without any privacy. Sky wanted Kaeden to know before she and Kadey flew away.

He pulled her tighter against his side. The comfort and warmth of his big frame filled her tired body. A loud roar drew her eyes out the window towards the flight line. A shiny black jet taxied toward where they waited. Gold lettering and insignia adorned the nose and tail of the aircraft. She'd seen private aircraft on television, but this one made the ones the movies depicted look like children's toys.

"That would be our ride." Doctor Cassidy and the medical technician who was driving the Air Force Ambulance exited the vehicle.

Kaeden turned her toward him. "I need you to take care of yourself and Kadey. Stay at the compound while I take care of the situation here."

"You are going after the people who killed the doctor and the other person, aren't you?" Kaeden had told her that he was a mercenary. Mercenaries killed people… or at least they did in the movies.

"I'm going to make sure you and Kadey are safe." The non-answer didn't escape her attention. Kaeden's lips dropped to hers. "Don't worry about me. You focus on Kadey's recovery. I'll take care of things here."

Sky lifted her hand to his jaw and stared into his eyes. She still felt the same insane attraction to him even though she knew that this could be their final goodbye. "Promise me you'll stay safe."

"I promise I'll be careful."

"Not the same."

"Best I can do."

Sky smiled and rose up on her toes to reach him. He lowered his lips and brushed a soft, sweet kiss on them. The back door opened up pulling them apart. "Okay, let's get this angel onto the plane." Doctor Cassidy helped the medical technician... airman... sergeant... whoever, with the gurney. Sky and Kaeden followed them out of the ambulance. She walked close beside her daughter as they approached the aircraft. Two identical men in black flight suits walked around the outside of the plane. Sky glanced from one to the other. No, she wasn't seeing double.

"Ma'am, I'm Dixon, this is Drake. We'll be taking you and the little one back home." The man smiled at her and extended his hand.

"I'm Sky, and that is Kadey." She shook his hand before she motioned toward where Doctor Cassidy, the attendant, and Kaeden worked to get Kadey moved into the aircraft.

"It's a pleasure to meet you. We want to get you back in time to get you settled in and comfortable before dinner. Why don't you go ahead and follow them onboard? We're going to finish our flight inspection and get going." The man extended his arm toward the open doorway. While he was polite, Sky knew the request was more of an order, not a suggestion. She nodded and headed up the stairs after her daughter.

Kadey was awake and smiling when Sky walked through the door. Doctor Cassidy had quickly become Kadey's favorite, especially after telling her all about the dogs, cats, horses, and cows that awaited her in South Dakota.

Kaeden lowered and gave Kadey a kiss. He whispered something in her ear. Kadey smiled wide and nodded her head. She carefully lifted her arms and hugged her daddy. Sky's eyes pricked with tears again. She never thought she'd see the day where Kadey knew her father, let alone hug him and share whispered words with him. Kaeden kissed her cheek one more time before he stood and moved away.

Doctor Cassidy slid in where Kaeden had been standing. He showed Kadey the safety belt he was going to use and was answering the first of hundreds of questions the little girl would undoubtedly have for him. Kaeden grabbed Sky's hand and moved her toward the door. He waited until the medical technician deplaned before he spoke. "There are so many things I can't tell you, but I want you to know the things that I can share. I will always regret leaving you when you were pregnant—"

"You—"

Kaeden slid a finger over her lips with a gentle touch.

"I didn't know I was going to be called back, but it is a regret that I have, and it will always live with me. I also regret that you didn't think you could tell me about Kadey." He shook his head as she started to speak again. "I understand why you didn't. You are a wonderful mother to her. I'm sorry you've been touched by the danger that surrounds my job, but I'm not sorry for the time I spent with you, and I'm not sorry about Kadey."

The emotion in his eyes told her that the words he spoke were true. A certainty settled in her heart that knitted together a few of the fractured pieces of her soul. The scattered remains of their past were held together with a precarious bond and absolutely no promise of a future. His kiss lingered light upon her lips.

"Kaeden," His name left her lips on a sigh as he pulled away.

He leaned down and whispered in her ear. "Take care of my little princess." A breath of a kiss touched her cheek before he turned and walked out of the aircraft.

One of the pilots entered and announced they were ready to start the engines. The other followed him in within minutes and closed the cabin door. Sky moved to a seat near Kadey and buckled in. She smiled nervously at the Doctor Cassidy who sat next to her and the stand-offish nurse that had been working with him.

The doctor returned her smile. "I know telling you not to worry would be pointless, but that man is one of the best at what he does." Sky's head whipped toward the doctor. "And what exactly *does* he do, Doctor Cassidy?"

The man turned and leveled a one-eyed gaze at her. "He makes the world a safer place. Most of the world's population is ignorant of the horrendous evil that exists. He is a weapon against that evil."

Sky opened her mouth and then closed it before she finally asked, "What does that mean? How is he a weapon?"

Doctor Cassidy glanced over at Kadey who was once again napping thanks to the mild sedative he had given her at the hospital before they loaded her into the ambulance for the ride to the flight line.

"Weapons can be defensive or offensive. You can use a weapon, in this case a person, to remove the threat before it becomes a danger to the innocent—or you don't and the countries of the world play janitor and are stuck mopping up the mayhem and destruction left behind. He and a few others are tasked with ensuring the evil in this world stays in the shadows." The doctor turned in his seat, leaned back and closed his eye.

Sky glanced from him to her daughter. Kaeden was a mercenary, he'd told her that. He'd never told her what the job entailed. She rolled her head and looked out the window sightlessly. The last days were a blur of emotion and adrenaline.

She'd prayed for salvation for Kadey, and it was dropped into her lap when Kaeden appeared in her kitchen.

Sky glanced back at her daughter, then took in the rich appointments of the private aircraft rocketing her to some complex where free healthcare and safety awaited. Her reality had morphed into something she didn't recognize, all because of Kaeden.

"You don't have to solve the problem today. Relax and grab some sleep while you can." The doctor didn't move or open his eyes when he spoke.

"Will I ever know the answers to the questions?" Sky spoke to herself.

Doctor Cassidy rolled his head toward her and opened his eye. "I believe the question you should be asking yourself is: in the grand scheme of things does it really matter he can't discuss the specifics of his job?"

CHAPTER THIRTEEN

ANUBIS STALKED TO THE WAITING VEHICLE PARKED NEXT to the ambulance on the ramp of the flight line.

"Where to?" Asp's question pulled his attention away from the aircraft that was powering up.

"Nowhere until that plane takes off." Anubis kept his eyes on the plane as it powered up and then exited the parking apron where it had stopped. The two men sat in silence until the rev of the engines at the end of the flight line rattled the windows in the vehicle. The bird screamed down the runway and took off in a high arc. Anubis felt his heart leave his body and go with his women, and the physical separation felt as if it snapped his humanity from his body. He turned to Asp and an evil sneer threaded its way across his face. "It's time I go after this son of a bitch."

"Awesome. Where are we going?" Asp started the Air Force vehicle and drove off the parking ramp through one of the side gates that meandered through the various maintenance areas by the flight line.

"We?" Anubis shook his head. "You're still on the sideline."

"That's bullshit, and you know it. Besides, you could be walking into your death. This guy is hunting you. He made a mistake going after your woman with three men. I'd bet my offshore account that he sends a fucking army after you next time."

Or an assassin or two. "Not taking that bet. Head back to my DV quarters. They have a secure landline in the office. I need to contact Bengal and find out what he knows about Faas."

"Didn't you get that information when you went against his uncle?" Asp signaled his left-hand turn and waited for a push-back tug to pass in front of them.

"I got enough to know Haghen had been coded and that he was the scum of the earth. Beyond that, I don't give a shit." Anubis stared out the window watching the trees and buildings pass.

"Huh."

"What the fuck is that supposed to mean?" Anubis knew he was wound tight and tried to rein in his attitude, but he wasn't sure he managed it.

"In order for me to do an assignment, I demand the entire brief. I want to know the exact type of scum I'm working against, down to the body count and where he buried them."

"Why the fuck do you need to know that?" Honestly, Anubis was surprised Asp would be given the information.

"I used to work for another agency. I completed a mission where my handler told me the man was a traitor and that he was selling national secrets to the enemy. I found out six months later he was innocent. He'd been a pawn in the handler's political climb up the agency's ladder. That's when I punched my exit ticket."

Anubis snapped his head toward Asp. "Holy fuck." He had complete and total faith in his handlers at Guardian. He knew when they handed him an assignment the targeted individual was guilty and evil. He couldn't imagine being placed in the same position as Asp. "How did you end up with Guardian?" Anubis tossed the question out as they pulled up in front of the DV quarters he'd been assigned.

"Long story."

Obviously, Asp was done sharing for the day. Anubis closed the conversation, "Roger that."

They made their way to the small apartment, and Anubis headed for the office. Asp stopped in the kitchen. "I'm going to eat. You want your food?" Asp asked with his head buried in the refrigerator.

"No." He'd eaten before he'd met up with Sky at the hospital. Moriah was watching his family, so he was able to come back to the apartment, shower and eat. He dialed Bengal's number and put the phone on speaker.

"Reynolds."

"Still not used to that name, man." To Anubis, he would always be Bengal.

"Takes a hot minute, that's for sure." Bengal's voice sounded distracted. "Give me a minute to secure the connection and get Alpha on the line."

"Roger that." Anubis put the phone on mute. He could hear cutlery rattling in the kitchen and the refrigerator opening and closing. Asp strode into the office with five inches of meat and cheese stacked between two half inch slices of bread.

"How the fuck are you going to eat that?"

"One bite at a time, my man. One bite at a time." Asp put the plate on his lap, hunched over, and smashed the sandwich between his fingers before his mouth took massive chunks out of the whole. Anubis chuckled to himself at the sight. The man was the exact opposite of what Anubis thought of when he thought of an assassin. He stuck out in a crowd, like a flashing neon night light in a pitch-black cave.

"Alright, Alpha's on the call, and I've pulled up the files on Haghen and Faas."

Anubis unmuted the speaker. "Affirmative. I have another with me."

"Six-six-eight." Asp managed to confirm his identity around the pile of food in his mouth.

"Six-four-nine, I pass you, Cobalt." Alpha's voice rang out in the room.

"Azure, sir."

"Six-Six-eight, I pass you, tackle."

Asp moved the food in his mouth to the side and barely managed. "Bait, sir."

"What the fuck are you eating this time?" Alpha laughed the question out.

"A sandwich the size of my head," Anubis answered for Asp because he'd just taken another massive bite.

"Figures. Alright, let's run this down. CCS, the floor is yours."

"Haghen's nephew Faas has flown under the radar because his transgressions haven't affected us or our allies. It seems Faas has a penchant for killing his compatriots and raining terror down on the good citizens of Suriname, but he's very careful to only target those who can't fight back. Until he went after you and your family."

The information about Faas was superfluous to Anubis's objective. He really didn't give a flying fuck what Faas had done in the past. "Where is he now?"

"San Francisco. At the Apogee, he's—"

"And there is where we have the problem." Alpha's voice interrupted Bengal. "He's in the United States. As of this time, he is not coded. The evidence we have tying him to this situation is circumstantial. We have no live witnesses, and for obvious reasons, six-four-nine will not be making any witness statements." *Yeah, there was no way an assassin would make a good witness.* Alpha continued, "Faas is a bastard of the highest order, but as of this time, Guardian is not authorizing you to go after him."

Asp looked up from his sandwich, his questioning gaze met Anubis's stare. Anubis lowered his eyes and waited. He had infinite patience and right now he needed to amass as much information about Faas as possible. "I copy."

"I understand your family is enroute to the complex. Perhaps you should take some time to tie up some loose ends and figure out what your future looks like. When you're ready to talk, I have an option I'd like you to consider. Until then, check in with CCS as required. I'll deactivate you until you've finished what you need to do. Take all the time you need, six-four-nine."

Anubis read between the lines. His automatic "Yes, sir" acknowledged the non-command. Alpha couldn't authorize the hit, but he was giving Anubis the time to take the matter into his own hands.

"CCS, make sure six-four-nine gets the documentation he needs to complete his leave of absence. We want to make sure the HR people don't have a cow."

Anubis shot his eyes to Asp who wore stupid ass grin. As far as humanity knew, the Shadows didn't exist so HR was a smokescreen. Alpha was instructing CCS to give Anubis the information he needed to take care of Faas.

"Roger that, sir. I've already dropped it." Bengal confirmed the order.

"How did I guess that? Alpha out."

They waited for Bengal to confirm Alpha was off the line. "Take note of those HR forms I sent you. That department is in a state of flux right now. There is a telephone number you'll need to call if you have any issues while you're on vacation.

"Got it." Anubis lifted the receiver and set it back down. He leaned back in his chair and steepled his fingers together staring out the window at the few cars driving down the boulevard.

"They didn't sanction the hit, and the man is in the US." Asp leaned back after putting his empty plate on the desk.

"Correct." Anubis continued to stare out the window. The Apogee, if he recalled correctly, was a grand old hotel in the heart of San Francisco. He needed a blueprint of the facility. Hopefully, Bengal had included one in the documentation he dropped into Anubis's Shadow World email account. If not, well, he'd had missions where he'd flown by the seat of his pants. He could do it again.

"What are you going to do?" "Nothing." Anubis turned his head toward his friend. He wasn't sanctioned on this operation. His company wouldn't extend themselves further, he knew they couldn't without crossing lines they would never cross. The Shadows were different. They operated in a transient state, not quite of the world, and yet in the world and answerable to the rules and regulations Guardian put in place to police their profession. If they went rogue, they would be no better than the people they put down. The cold, calculating way he was plotting the death of a man who had paid to have Sky killed and planned on using his daughter to lure him to his death proved he was already rogue on this case. If anything went wrong... Anubis shook his head. If his actions brought any inquiry into the death of Faas, if he missed a camera and his picture revealed his past identity, if his method of assassination led the international community to Guardian's door, he'd be cut off from the tether of sanity that was Guardian.

"Bullshit. I can read your intent from here." Asp dropped his head back onto the high backed chair and raised his eyebrow. The expression mocked his statement as much as his words.

"No. I'm going to do exactly what Alpha said. If I want my family to be safe, I need to decide a few things. I can't remain a Shadow, but I don't know how to walk in the light anymore. I'm fucked up and I'm the worst of all possible situations for them. I need to figure out a way forward."

"Right, and the yellow brick road is actually made of twenty-four carat gold, and it starts right outside this door. I heard the same thing you did. Don't lie to me." Asp kept his gaze locked on Anubis.

"Then stop asking me stupid questions." Anubis pulled the secure phone Guardian had sent him out of his pocket and hit up the email account where Bengal had dropped the information he needed. He stood and looked at Asp. "I'm doing this one alone, brother. I can't ask you to step into my destiny."

"I don't recall you asking." Asp stood and looked at Anubis.

"You're right. I'm telling. I'm not letting you, or anyone else, buy into this hand. The cards that have been dealt are mine to play." Anubis held out his hand.

Asp stared at his hand and then, slowly, reached out to grasp it. "I'll lay it on the line for you, brother... I'd have a problem being involved anyway, but... you need to take a breath and think about what you're going to lose if you take action." Asp swallowed hard and continued, "You take care of you. I'm a phone call away when this becomes a sanctioned dossier."

"I know it, and I appreciate it." Anubis shook the big man's hand and released it. After what Asp had confided not thirty minutes ago, he understood how an off the books operation would be damn near impossible for him to support. That the man was still willing to be called in for backup spoke volumes. He watched as Asp spun on his heel and left the apartment without another word. Anubis glanced down at his phone and hit the draft folder where the documentation was waiting. He had one evil mother to put down. He needed facts, and he needed them now.

CHAPTER FOURTEEN

FINALLY, THAT MOTHER FUCKER, FAAS, HAD RETURNED. THE bastard and his guards had ghosted from the Apogee. Anubis worked what information he had and leveraged a few favors from Bengal using the HR number he'd supplied. Faas had taken a whirl-wind trip to three different cities in the United States. Baltimore, Chicago, and Dallas. Unofficially, Guardian was tracking his movements because he'd been placed on Shadow's scope of vision. Officially, Bengal's woman along with all the other assets Guardian could muster were working to build a case against the bastard and bring him down. There was no chatter on the contract out on him, Sky and Kadey. It seemed the word had spread taking Faas's business would be a mistake a person wouldn't live through. He'd used the time Faas was out of town to visit Arnie, old buddy, old pal. A smile tugged at his lips. The memory of the man pissing his bed when Anubis woke him up in the middle of the night was something neither of them would soon forget. Good ole Trey. What a joke. The bastard was walking the straight and narrow now, and Anubis planned to make sure he didn't stray an inch. Sky would never have to worry about that fucker coming back into her life.

Anubis looked up at the old limestone façade. He'd cased the hotel five times with five different disguises, and spent countless hours over the last two days watching, waiting and learning. It took perseverance, but Anubis finally tracked down the limo company that Faas had contracted. Hacking the company's database to ascertain Faas's schedule was child's play for someone like Bengal's woman, but Anubis wasn't a computer expert, so he went after the information the old fashioned way.

He waited outside the limo company in his very ordinary later model Nissan. Parked across the street, he watched the expensive cars come and go. The car he waited for pulled into the fenced lot as the sun was setting. A telephoto lens aimed at the driver identified his mark. Anubis positioned an audio enhancer and turned on the device. He'd bought it online and had delivered overnight. The power of the American consumer who wanted access to everything, right now, and oh, by the way, screw the fact that what you were buying was made for only one thing—to breach a person's privacy. The small warning on the manufactures website that cautioned a person to use the listening devices, trackers, and other equipment on sale within the confines of the law *really* worked. Placing the cheap earbud into his ear, he zeroed in on his target—Faas's limo driver.

Another driver came up beside his target. "Hey man. Good day?"

"No, the fucker I pulled is a total ass." That was Faas's driver. Well, good to know the man was a decent judge of character. There was static every time a car idled by in front of his vehicle, and he lost the conversation for a hot second when a semi pulled past.

"Hector's for a cold one?" Anubis sat up and pushed the ear bud in trying to hear more.

"I don't know man. I'm beat." Faas's driver said.

"…only one…forget the asshole…"

Anubis lost the comms but saw his man nod and pulled the

small parabolic dish down. He palmed his phone and did what anyone else in the world would do. GTS baby. He Googled That Shit. Finding the most likely establishment in the local area with Hector's in the name, Anubis headed out.

The bar wasn't a dive, but it wasn't a high class joint either. Anubis reached into the back seat and grabbed a ratty old San Francisco 49er's hat, a beaten up leather coat and his cash stash. He filled his wallet and locked the car after grabbing the equipment he needed.

He opened the thick wooden door and ambled into the dark interior. He straddled a stool and waited for the bartender. She made her way down to him and smiled. "Hiya. You're new. What can I get you?"

One glance behind the bar, and a real smile lit his face. "I'd like a bottle of your best IPA and give me a can of pistachios and a can of trail mix." The little display held a prominent position behind the bartender.

"You know you can have our bar mix, no charge?" She reached into the cooler and grabbed a local IPA. Anubis watched carefully as she opened the bottle and sat it in front of him.

"Yeah, but I'm kinda addicted to that brand." Anubis tipped his head toward the display again.

"Hey, it's your dime." She turned around, and Anubis wiped the mouth of the bottle with a napkin he pulled from the middle of one of the small stacks that sat at intervals down the dark wood of the bar.

She dropped down the two cans. "That will be seven dollars each for the nuts. The beer is six. So twenty."

Anubis pulled his wallet out and fished out a fifty. "Start a tab for me?"

"You got it, sweets." The bartender took his money folded it lengthwise and laid it on a ticket where she annotated his order.

Talk about old school. No computer inventory or point of sale system. Anubis studied the cans, and satisfied they hadn't been tampered with, he opened them and popped a handful into his mouth washing it down with the surprisingly strong and slightly bitter IPA. It was damn near perfect.

He'd almost finished his snack when Faas's driver and another man walked into the establishment.

"Hey, Karen." Faas's driver called out as they sat down a couple stools over from Anubis.

"The usual, guys?" The bartender called from the far end of the bar.

Regulars. That would mean they would know he wasn't.

"Yeah and a bowl of bar mix."

"Like I don't keep you two fed." Karen quipped from the far end of the bar.

"I'm telling you, Massey was a dick to stick me with this guy, man. He knows I can't handle cigarette smoke." Faas's driver sat with his elbows on the bar and ran his fingers through his hair. "I picked him up this morning and did what we always do, ya know? I trot around to the door to open it and introduce myself. I'll give you ten bucks if you can guess what the fucker said."

Karen placed a large bowl of bar mix down in front of the men along with two domestic brews. She popped the top and grabbed their credit cards.

"Tab?"

"No."

"Yes."

They spoke at the same time and then looked at each other and laughed. "Okay, yes. I need to forget today." Faas's driver was a young kid. Maybe mid twenties and Karen winked at him making him blush.

"That's my man, Jamie."

Karen shook her head and placed the cards, number side down on two tickets jotting down what they'd purchased. Anubis filed the driver's name away. Jamie.

"Seriously, guess what the fucker said?" Jamie downed half his bottle in a single draw.

"Ummm… Good morning?"

"No. Try, 'I don't give a fuck who you are. You are being paid to drive this car. My bodyguards will open my doors. Now get the fuck out of my face.'"

"You're shitting me?"

"Nah man, I'm not. And like I told you on the way over, the fucker's smoking in the car even after I told him it was against company policy."

"Did you tell Massey?"

"Yeah, he's giving me the Lincoln tomorrow."

"The one with the separate rear ventilation system?"

"Yeah, I can at least breathe. I had to shower at work because I smelled like a fucking ashtray. I guess this guy is somebody with enough scratch that the company won't mind the cleaning charges."

"Do you have him again tomorrow?"

"Yep."

"You need another beer, or twenty."

Anubis turned in his seat. "Sorry, couldn't help but overhear. Let me buy the next round. Call it a sympathetic gesture. I'm in sales and dicks like the guy you describe make my life miserable."

"Fuckin'-A, man. We're just trying to make a living." That came from the other driver. Jamie nodded his head in agreement.

"Karen, a round for all of us, on my tab." Anubis gestured toward Jamie and…

"Name's Rick." Anubis held out his hand as Jamie introduced them.

"Jamie and this here is Don."

"Pleased to meet you."

"You from around here?" Jamie glanced at the Niner's hat.

"Nah, love the team, though. Grew up watching Montana and Young."

"The glory days." Dan held up the beer Karen had placed in front of him.

"Amen." Anubis echoed and handed Karen another fifty as she placed his beer in front of him. She raised her eyebrow at him and dropped the money on top of the fifty he'd already ponied up.

Anubis had most of the information he needed, except what time Jamie was picking up Faas tomorrow. They discussed football, politics and made their way through three more rounds before Jamie pushed his empty away. "Guys, it's been real, but I have to pick up the douche bag at two sharp," He cleared his throat and mimicked Faas's accent, albeit poorly, as he spoke, "I will be at the west side entrance at exactly two p.m. If you are not there, I will have your job." Jamie groaned as Don and Anubis laughed at his mimicry. "Fuck, *and* I have to detail the Mercedes for Jenkins because I lost a bet... so as much as I would like to have another one, I'm tapping out."

Don threw in the towel, too, leaving with his friend. Anubis said goodnight and watched as they left. He leaned on the bar and took a drink of his beer. Jamie was a good kid. He hoped that rear ventilation system worked well.

ANUBIS WALKED DOWN THE BUSY SAN FRANCISCO SIDEWALK. The normal hum of the city ebbed and flowed around him. He kept his eyes forward as he shuffled past the entrance to the hotel. His hair was now auburn, and he'd fashioned a disheveled Mohawk with some cheap gel. His ripped jeans displayed the stains he'd engineered. The chains that hung from his belt slapped his thighs and made a distinct counter sound to the stumbling step of his unlaced combat boots. The old, tattered leather bomber jacket he wore kept the cold, wet San Francisco weather from reaching him. The lead lining of the *right* pocket also kept his own weapon from killing him. Anubis shrugged the filthy backpack he carried by one strap back up onto his shoulder.

He turned the corner and walked down to the middle of the block. A side entrance to the hotel was located about five feet from where he took up residency. Anubis leaned against the building pulling one leg up and resting it against the wall. A half smoked cigarette from his *left* pocket made its way to his lips. His eyes roamed up and down the block, casually taking in every scrap of information revealed to him. Housed in an old building, Apogee appeared to be an easy mark, but the security installed by the new owners was impressive

He watched as Jamie drove by. The long grey Lincoln pulled up to the curb and parked. Anubis ran the gambit of what events could transpire in the next three hundred and sixty seconds. Granted, Anubis's preferred method of assassination was poison, but he was deadly with any weapon and today he hid that weaponry in plain sight. His garrote looped from his belt amongst the chains, and he'd tucked his three guns in his clothing, one behind his back, one inside his unlaced combat boot, and one under his arm in a shoulder holster. If he was lucky, he wouldn't have to use them today. He hated counting on luck, but for this bastard, only the worst kind of death would suffice. If this event didn't work, he'd find the son of a bitch again and slit his throat.

His nose burned with the smell of alcohol. He glanced at his watch and lit the half-smoked cigarette. The stench of the alcohol he'd splashed on himself this morning swirled with the smoke that he exhaled from his lungs. He hadn't showered or brushed his teeth. He'd calculated his bedraggled appearance to project an intentional misrepresentation of his economic status and physical condition. He prayed the fucker, Faas, was the sadistic, greedy bastard his dossier and Jamie depicted.

Anubis reached into his lead lined pocket and palmed the pack of cigarettes with his lead lined glove. Faas was a chain smoker, and he was addicted to a cheap brand of American cigarettes. You'd think that a person with a medical degree would know better. Obviously, some people felt they could defy the odds.

The door beside him opened and Anubis made his move. He bounced off the wall and stumbled down the sidewalk colliding with Faas's bodyguards.

"Fuck, man... why don't you watch where you're going? Do you think you own the fucking sidewalk?" Anubis pushed one of Faas's bodyguards off him dropping his pack of cigarettes as he did. The bodyguard shoved him backward into the limo. Anubis made a showing of sliding down the side of the car. "Fuckers made me drop my smokes." He leaned forward and reached for his cigarettes. A foot stepped on his hand, grinding it under an expensive Italian leather shoe. Anubis hissed and reached for the foot in a pathetic attempt to move it off his hand. He watched Faas bend down and retrieve the pack of cigarettes.

"Hey... give me back my smokes, man. You can't take them, they're expensive! I ain't got any money to get more."

Anubis watched as Faas shook out a cigarette and put it to his lips. "Fucking gutter scum." Faas spoke the words in his native Dutch. Anubis moved his hand in a futile attempt to get to the cigarette pack. The bastard brought out a gold lighter from his pocket and lit the cigarette inhaling deeply. Anubis ceased his struggling and swallowed a triumphant smile. It was the hardest thing he'd ever done. As soon as Faas took a pull off that cigarette, he'd killed himself. The bastard just ingested a lung full of Polonium 210 and that radioactive shit sealed the fucker's fate. Faas was dead. He just didn't know it yet.

The bastard pocketed the rest of the pack and purposefully used all his weight to tread over Anubis's hand. The position of his hand under the fucker's weight was awkward, and the pressure pulled a true grimace from him. "Asshole, you broke my hand!" Anubis let spittle hang from his lips, hopefully enhancing his already disgusting appearance. Faas laughed at his anguished outcry and took another deep pull from the cigarette as he waited for the first bodyguard to open the limo door for him. The second bodyguard kicked Anubis in the ribs as Faas entered the limo and once again attempted to kick him in the head, but Anubis rolled just in time to cause the fucker to miss. The man spat on him. Anubis let it run down his cheek as he laid on the sidewalk and grinned as he watched the limo pull out into traffic.

"Hey, I'm calling the cops if you don't get up and get out of here. We don't want any trouble. Go get your drunk on somewhere else."

Anubis glanced over at the uniformed door attendant. He raised an eyebrow at the man and vaulted to his feet, wiping the fucker's spit off his face as he did. "Not a problem, I'm done here." Anubis's cultured voice accompanied a jaunty salute in the attendant's direction. He tucked his right hand into his pocket and headed down the sidewalk. Now to get to Suriname, because he was going to have a conversation with a dead man.

Anubis stopped long enough to reach into his boot and grab his cell phone. He palmed it and pressed in the numbers. Asp had called him twice in the last three days. The phone rang once before the man answered.

"Go."

"Your ass in trouble?" Anubis asked without preamble.

"Nope, going fucking stir crazy."

"I'm heading out of the country." Anubis smiled at the thought.

"Out of the country?" There was a long pause, so much so that Anubis looked at the face of the phone to ensure the call hadn't dropped.

"Where and when?"

Asp offering back up was unusual, but not unheard of, especially if the man was on medical leave. "Paramaribo, Suriname. Two days."

"Rally point?"

Anubis thought for a moment. "Café Suriname. 2100 hrs."

"Roger that."

Anubis hit the button ending the call and thumbed the back of his phone opening the battery compartment. He popped the battery out, and flipped it into the street. The sim card pulled out easily, and it snapped in half with minimal pressure. He chucked the phone in the next trashcan, scattering the sim card as he walked. The long trip back to his hourly rate hotel room was a necessary precaution. About a block away from the hotel, he ditched his modified jacket underneath several plastic bags about halfway down in a dumpster that over flowed with rancid waste. The trace amounts of radiation would dissipate quickly, but he didn't need to endanger anyone who might pick it out of the trash and put their hand in the pocket without wearing lead lined gloves. He took off his gloves and shoved them into the fetid mess with the leather jacket before he pushed his filthy, odorous hands into his jean pockets and headed to his room.

CHAPTER FIFTEEN

SKY SAT ON THE HUGE WRAPAROUND PORCH AND pushed the swing with her toe. Kadey was sitting on the porch playing Barbie Dolls with her new BFF, Lizzy. The sweet little blonde-headed girl was over the moon about having a new friend, and Kadey was just as enamored.

Sky watched the girls play. She was still paranoid and kept Kadey in her direct line of sight. According to Doctor Cassidy, Kadey's procedure was a complete success, but Sky'd been worried for so long, not worrying was... well, it was impossible. She could feel herself hovering like a helicopter parent. She knew she was doing it, but until Kadey got the all clear from the cardiologist, who was scheduled to fly in next week for her check-up, she wasn't going to allow Kadey to do a single thing that was remotely strenuous. The surgical wounds were healing well, so her sitting outside on the porch with Lizzy getting some fresh air on an unusually warm late September day wasn't too risky. Well, it wasn't risky at all, at least that is what Doctor Cassidy and two other doctors here at the ranch had told her. Sky really liked the team of doctors at the complex.

"Are they getting along?" Sky glance up as Lizzy's mom came out on the porch. The woman was strikingly handsome. Keelee Cassidy was uncharacteristically tall, with long blonde hair. She had an athlete's body, hard and toned, but she was a kind lady who doted on her daughter. Sky had learned Keelee's father owned the ranch where the hospital and training facilities were housed. He also built the log cabin mansison where she and Kadey were living. The place was a woodworking marvel.

"No problems whatsoever. They are so good together." Sky moved her legs so Keelee could sit down.

"They are. Lizzy is around adults most the time. It is wonderful that Kadey is here." Keelee pushed the swing sending them on a gentle back and forth. "How are you doing?"

"Me?" Sky blinked repeatedly and finally shook her head. Why would Keelee ask that? "I'm fine."

Keelee chuckled and turned in the swing. "If I knew you better, I'd probably call you on that lie."

Sky pulled up her legs and hugged them while still looking at her daughter. The girls were changing their dolls' clothes for the tenth or twentieth time. "How about, I'm hanging in there?"

"That, I'd buy." They sat in a compatible silence for a few minutes until Keelee cleared her throat. "So your man is a Guardian?"

Sky turned her head and gazed at Keelee. "Kaeden? I'm not sure you'd call him my man, but yeah...he is. He works for Guardian, and Guardian is taking care of Kadey, but I really have no idea what he does."

Keelee pushed the slowing swing again. "I don't really know what Adam did... and still does on occasion."

"Why don't you ask him?" Sky gave a quick glance towards the girls, but returned her attention to Keelee waiting for an answer.

"Not sure I want to know, to tell you the truth. You see, my sister works for Guardian. I've pieced together a patchwork theory of what they do. Suffice to say they are the good guys and what they do is dangerous as hell, but important."

Sky grabbed a strand of hair that blew into her face and pulled it behind her ear. "I keep thinking of Kaeden like *Jason Bourne*. I know that sounds stupid…"

"I've seen that film. That dude's the assassin with the memory problem, right?"

"Yeah, but I know Kaeden isn't an assassin, I mean… there's no way. Like I said. Stupid."

"No, it isn't stupid. Not really. The people that Guardian select to work with them are the best at what they do, kinda like that guy Bourne was. They constantly train, here and at other facilities, across the world. The men and women who work for Guardian are held to a standard not many can achieve."

"How do you know that?" Did she know more than she was letting on?

Keelee let out a small laugh. "Honestly, I don't, but I heard my husband's boss, Jason, who is actually my step-brother, say it over and over. Adam and the other doctors here on the ranch take care of those who are hurt while doing their job. I have never heard of an agency who cares for their people the way Guardian does."

"So your husband is a mercenary, too?"

"Mercenary? Where did you get the idea that Guardian hires mercenaries?"

"Kaeden said something about it." Sky vividly remembered him telling her that's what he was.

"Huh, really? I don't think I've ever heard that. From what I know about the organization, which granted, isn't a ton, Guardian doesn't hire or train mercenaries. My husband was part of a team of men who did jobs no one else could do. That was how he lost the sight in his eye."

Sky tensed and snapped her attention over to Keelee. "Then what are they if they aren't mercenaries?" Why had Kaeden let her believe he was a mercenary if Guardian didn't employ them? She brought her thumb to her mouth and nibbled on the small edge of the nail that had just started to regrow.

Keelee shrugged and looked out over the ranch buildings. Her voice was thoughtful, "In my opinion?" Keelee glanced over at her, kicked the floorboard and sent them on a gentle glide again. Sky nodded, and Keelee looked out over the property again. "They are men and women who have an incredible conviction that this world can be a better place and are willing to put their lives on the line to make it so. The teams that train here defy what I thought I knew about altruism. They are selfless, to a fault." Keelee rolled her head and looked at Sky. "Especially the men. Lord above, if I had a nickel for every time one of these men screwed up with his girlfriend or wife because he did what *he* decided was the right and selfless thing to do… Well, I wouldn't need any of those cows in the pasture for income, I can tell you that!"

"You keep mentioning teams. Kaeden doesn't work with a team." Sky watched as the girls exchanged dolls and dug through a large plastic tub looking for yet another outfit to put on them.

"Ah, well personal security officers work alone. They do protection details for people. My stepsisters all work or have worked for Guardian. One works with computers, one left the company and now heads security for her husband who's a country-western superstar, and the other is a crazy woman, but she's a kick ass personal security officer. She travels all over the States. Overseas too… sometimes."

"That must be what Kaeden is then, but he said he only worked overseas."

Keelee turned her big blue eyes to Sky and stared at her long enough to make her uncomfortable. "What?"

"He only works overseas?"

"Yeah? Is that a bad thing?"

Keelee let out a huff of air and chuckled. "Nope. I wouldn't worry too much about your guy. I'm sure he'll be fine."

Sky nodded and watched the girls play. *I wish Kaeden was out there doing that selfless and stupid thing for them.* She gave herself a stern mental shake. She wasn't Kaeden's girlfriend, and he wouldn't be coming for them.

CHAPTER SIXTEEN

ANUBIS GLANCED AT HIS REFLECTION IN THE MIRROR. He'd washed the auburn tint out of his hair. His natural dark brown hair, golden eyes, and darker complexion made blending with the native population in Suriname fairly easy. He could pass as Creole, one of the two larger demographics of the South American country. Most people in the States didn't realize those of a Creole background didn't necessarily all live in Louisiana—were not original to anywhere in the US, for that matter. Anubis had learned enough Taki-Taki, or Surinamese, to get by with the locals. His Dutch was fluent and most of the country spoke English, but he didn't want to identify himself as an American for a myriad of reasons.

The one and only direct flight from the States to Suriname had landed about an hour ago, but just as he had, Asp would find an alternate means into the country. He found a table at the back of the café facing the Garden of Palms, or the back garden of the Presidential palace. The café was small but had four entrances and exits, one of which wasn't common knowledge. He'd found the café when he worked the Haghen case. The crime rate in this portion of the city capital was minimal, so he didn't need to concern himself with anything that would draw the attention of nation's police force to him or Asp.

Anubis ordered a coffee and pretended to read a local paper, studying the people inside and outside the café, but it wasn't the population that held his interest. Not four blocks from where he sat, Faas was sequestered in his capital city residence. Anubis quickly reestablished his contacts in the country and paid handsomely for the information. He knew the minimum necessary to get into the compound, but from that point forward, he'd be playing everything by ear.

A large shadow loomed over his table. Anubis kicked out the chair next to him and lifted his finger to the waiter that hovered not far away.

"You don't need to order me a new one, you haven't touched yours." Asp's Dutch was damn near accent free.

"True, but it is the socially acceptable thing to do." Anubis hoisted his eyes up and smiled. Asp let out a bark of laughter turning just about every head in the café.

"Since when have we done anything that could be remotely considered socially acceptable?" Anubis shook his head and folded the newspaper.

The waiter arrived with the coffee. Asp smiled at the young man and asked in damn near flawless Taki-Taki if they had peanut soup with tomtom available. The man's face split into a huge grin as he answered so rapidly Anubis almost missed his affirmative reply. Asp ordered the food and turned back to Anubis.

"What? It was a long drive." Asp leaned back making the small bistro chair groan.

"Right."

Asp chuckled at Anubis's dry retort before he checked to make sure they were not within hearing distance of anyone. He lowered his voice and moved forward so there was no way anyone could overhear them. "How are you going to do it?"

"Polonium 210."

Asp drew a sharp breath and glanced around the café again. "Where the fuck will you get that shit?"

"Russia." Well, actually, it was from a contact in Vancouver who knew people, but the man across from him didn't need to know that. Asp leaned back and crossed his arms, staring at Anubis. Hell, Anubis could almost see the wheels in his companion's head turning.

"When will you administer it?"

"I already have."

"Already administered?"

Anubis nodded and gave a slight motion toward the kitchen where the waiter emerged with a huge bowl of peanut soup. The fragrance of the Madame Janette peppers and the size of the mashed-up plantain balls, or tomtoms was mouthwatering. Nevertheless, Anubis would settle for the aroma as eating something someone else had prepared wasn't going to happen.

"Then why the fuck are you here?" Asp breathed the question as he took a bite of the soup. He rolled his eyes and moaned in some kind of food-induced orgasmic shudder.

Anubis shrugged, "He should be starting to feel the effects."

"Again, I ask, why are you here?"

"I want him to know who killed him and why."

Asp glanced up from the soup he was shoveling into his mouth. He held Anubis's gaze for a long moment before dropping his regard to the thick broth under his spoon. Asp carefully sat the spoon down and straightened in his chair. He crossed his arms and spoke with concise, clipped words. "I've never known you to be careless, but this idea is ludicrous. Hell, it could even get you killed. Then where would your family be?"

Anubis leaned forward, and he nailed the table with his index finger, stabbing the paper. Asp's eyes followed and widened. There was an article accounting the mass murder that occurred in a small town in the rainforest not twenty miles away. The entire town slaughtered for no other reason than for Faas's people to move in and take over a profitable gold-mining operation owned by the village co-op. "You said you wanted to know everything there was to know about your assignments. I followed suit. Not only has this bastard tried to kill my daughter's mother and use that little girl as bait to lure me out and kill me, but he has also killed hundreds, if not thousands, of men, women and children in this country to fill his accounts. The political structure here is so damn corrupt they turn a blind eye as long as revenue to their bank accounts grows. At his direction, his men wiped out this village. He's taken young women out of their homes, away from their families to *service him*. They never go home, Asp. He runs a human trafficking ring taking street children from the cities in Brazil and ships them out to rich first-world countries. He is responsible for the major drug routes through the country and is profiting from selling it not only in Suriname, but in Guiana in the west and French Guiana in the east. He is sadistic; he is relentless, *and he is mine*."

Asp leaned forward and met Anubis's anger with his own. "Was yours. He's already dead."

"But he doesn't know why."

"He doesn't need to know."

"I disagree."

"You're not an avenging angel. That isn't what we do."

"What are you? An ethical assassin?"

"It *is not* what we do at Guardian."

"Maybe it should be." Anubis met his stone-cold stare with one of his own. This wasn't a dossier driven assignment or an imperative mission. Faas had tried to kill Sky. The same monster had been willing to kidnap his little girl to get to him. Asp said he needed background when he hunted. Anubis had *provided* him ample background.

Anubis shook his head and spread out his hands. "What the fuck am I missing here? You needed background, and I gave it to you. I could use your assistance. Watch my back while I get in that compound. He has a small army guarding him. What more information do you need? I'll get it for you."

Asp sighed. "The only information I needed, you already gave me. The man is already dead. You have your vengeance, and the scales are level. Facing him down isn't necessary, or smart."

"*I* need it." Anubis ground the reply out between clenched teeth. He did. He had to see Faas. He needed to see the man's face when he realized *why* he was dying.

"No, I'm sorry, Ani. I can never go there again. Sanctioned dossiers only. Take it from someone who has innocent blood on their hands... don't go there, my friend. You may not be able to find your way back."

"He tried to kill *my* woman, and he would have killed *my* daughter once they lured me out. They deserve justice." Anubis leaned back in his chair and stared at his friend.

Asp picked up his spoon and stirred the soup without really paying attention to the food in front of him. He glanced up at Anubis. "If you need my help on this, I'll give it, but if you cash in that chip you can consider our association over. You'll lose my contact information. I can't cross that line, not for you... not for anyone." He put the spoon down, crossed his arms over his chest and held Anubis with an unblinking stare. "Answer something for me?"

Anubis moved his eyebrow up in response, too pissed to reply.

"If you go in there tonight and shit goes south. You die… what do you want Guardian to tell your daughter? What are they supposed to tell Sky? That you'd tied up all the loose ends but wanted to prove a point, *and it killed you*? Stop thinking about yourself, Ani. You have the miraculous gift of a family now, something the rest of us will never have. Go after them, not some selfish sense of revenge." Asp stood and dropped a business card and stack of money on the table. "You let me know what you decide. That's my contact information here in Suriname." The big man turned around and left.

Anubis watched as he slipped out the door and disappeared into the darkness of the night. Plucking up the contact information, he pocketed the valuable card. In Suriname, there wasn't reliable cell service so knowing where to locate Asp was important.

He pushed the newspaper away from him and glanced out the window. Everything that Asp said was true. *Everything*. Why couldn't he just walk away, knowing that Faas would die a slow, torturous death? He knew exactly how the radiation would kill the man's organs, the way his body would shut down and slowly cease to exist. Hell, the entire world would know that he'd been assassinated if the hospital diagnosed the symptoms correctly. That the hospital in Suriname would be able to make that diagnosis was a stretch. There would be no reason to check for radiation poisoning.

Fuck… why wasn't it enough? Anubis knew, deep down, he knew why it would never be enough. For the first time in his Shadow life, *he* had something to lose. *Someone* to lose and they were precious to him. He needed the absolute certainty that Faas would never be able to reach out and hurt his family. He needed to look at Faas and see the sickness working its way through his body. *He* needed the closure.

Anubis got up, dropped another bill on the table for his untouched coffee, and left through the back of the facility. He was literally ten minutes walk from where Faas lived. Anubis paused outside the café to let his eyes adjust to the darkness. He leaned against the side of the building and surveyed his surroundings, noting the couple making out across the street. They were oblivious to the world, only involved with each other. An old man and woman strolled toward him as they chatted in low melodic voices. Their gnarled hands interweaved between them. There was a couple desperately trying to placate a tired toddler at the corner. Their low gentle hushes finally worked, settling the child. The couple looked at each other as the baby grabbed the bottle the husband was able to dig out of the diaper bag. He could see the connection between them. He could see all the aspects of humanity that he'd walked away from, ignored, and avoided since he started work with Guardian.

Anubis pushed away from the wall and headed west towards Faas's compound. He should have put a bullet in the man's brain when he had the chance in San Francisco. Fucking hindsight… it was always 20/20.

CHAPTER SEVENTEEN

"ARE YOU SURE?" SKY WASN'T, SO SHE ASKED again.

"Yeah, we'll be fine. Look at them; they're sleepy already. I'll get them into pajamas before we settle down to watch Dora. Come on, when was the last time you took a nice, long, hot bath? Had a glass of wine or read a book?" Keelee stood beside her in the expansive living area of the main ranch house. A fire roared in the massive fireplace making cheery popping and hissing noises and coating the room in a golden hue.

"I can do you one better. Ask me when was the last time I shaved my legs." Sky gave Keelee a wide-eyed face, crossing her eyes briefly.

Keelee laughed so hard she almost choked. "Oh my God, way too much information!" She glanced at her watch. "Adam will be home in thirty minutes. You know Kadey will be fine. I promise we won't run around the house fifty times or teach her how to become a bull rider. Well, at least I won't until she gets older."

Sky stuck her index finger in her mouth and nibbled on her nail. She pulled it out and offered another option, "I could watch them both so you and your husband could get some alone time." She really didn't want to let Kadey out of her sight. Like, at all.

"Excuse me? Have you met my dad and stepmom? Girl, we are lucky to get Lizzy three nights out of the week." Keelee turned to face Sky and dropped a hand on her shoulder. "Look, I know you've been through some serious shi… stuff." Keelee glanced over her shoulder at the girls who were still playing with their Barbie dolls. "Give yourself one night. Get out the tree trimmer and hack down the forest growing on your legs, grab a bottle of wine out of the chiller," Keelee motioned to the impressive, well stocked bar at the other end of the living room, "…and get some quality sleep. Kadey will be okay, she's under a doctor's roof, and I promise I'll come get you if anything happens, but you and I both know she's going to be fine."

Sky glanced back at her daughter and nodded. "Alright, let me go pack her a bag."

"No need. Lizzy may be a year younger, but she's got some height on Kadey. I know I have pajamas and clothes to fit her. Just go hug her goodnight and we'll be on our way."

Sky cocked her head up at the tall blonde and arched an eyebrow. "You're afraid I'm going to change my mind in the time it takes to pack a bag."

"Yup, nailed it in one, and I'm not giving you a chance." Keelee spun on the heel of her cowboy boot and literally hopped over to the girls, bringing a barrage of giggles from all three of them. "Surprise! Kadey you get to spend the night with Lizzy! I'll make cookies after dinner, and we can decorate them tomorrow morning!"

"Yeah!" Lizzy jumped up and down with her mom, but Kadey stood still and looked back at Sky. She walked over to her mom and motioned for her to bend down. "Are you going to be afraid if I go to Lizzy's?" Kadey's golden eyes held hers.

"No…" Sky made her face as serious as she could. "I know where you are and if I do get afraid or lonely, I can come get you.

It's okay to have fun with Lizzy and Miss Keelee tonight."

"But what are you going to do?"

"Probably read a story and go to bed."

Kadey put her hands on her hips and tilted her head at Sky. "That doesn't sound like much fun, Mommy. You should come spend the night with us!"

"Ah, well I was kinda looking forward to reading my story. Maybe I'll come over next time." She winked at Lizzy who now stood beside Kadey. The two girls were joined at the hip.

"Okay, but if you get scared or lonely, you can come over, too." Lizzy grabbed Kadey's hand after her proclamation. "'mon Kadey. Let's go!"

Kadey turned to leave, but Sky called her back. "Hey, what am I, chopped liver? Where is my goodnight hug and kiss?"

Both girls giggled and in unison ran back to her for a hug. Sky swallowed a lump in her throat as she watched her baby grab Keelee's hand and leave without a backward glance. She'd been singularly dedicated to making sure Kadey was alright for so long, she had no idea what to do with an evening without her. The last time she'd left Kadey alone was over two years ago... the last time Kaeden had called and asked her to meet him in that ratty-ass hotel.

Sky drew a shaky breath and glanced over at the bar. She hadn't had a drink since the sip of whiskey Kaeden had given her prior to Kadey's surgery. God that seemed like ages ago. Sky walked behind the bar and searched through the wine selection. A huge glass faced refrigerator held the wine. Blue lights illuminated the sections telling her to what degree the bottles were chilled.

"I'd recommend the chardonnay."

Sky jumped and spun around. Her hand clutched at her chest. The man that stood behind her was huge.

"I'm sorry, I didn't mean to scare you."

"I didn't hear you." Sky pulled in a lungful of air and let it out slowly, trying to still the hammering of her heart.

"I have a habit of walking softly. Training, I guess." The man rested his forearms on the bar. He was blonde and heavily muscled. The suit he wore emphasized his physique instead of disguising it. He held out his hand. "I'm Zane Reynolds. I work with Kaeden."

"Oh." Sky reached for the man's hand and shook it. "I'm Sky, but you probably knew that since you said you work with Kaeden. He didn't mention you, but then again, he hasn't said much about his work. Wow, that sounded bad, didn't it? Yeah, it did. And, I'll just shut up now." Score one for her, she was babbling like an idiot and in front of one of Kaeden's co-workers.

The man laughed and rounded the end of the bar. He was really big... like huge. Sky backed away, uncomfortable for no reason other than she didn't know this man. He stopped and pulled out two glasses filling them with ice. "I'm making a drink for myself and my fiancée. May I make you one?"

Oh. Fiancée. Here? Sky turned her head around looking for another person.

"Jewell will be here in a minute. She's in the kitchen with her mom and stepdad catching up. We don't make it out here too often."

"You don't live here? Well, obviously you don't..." Sky felt her face flame up. Goodness, what was the matter with her tonight?

"We live and work in D.C., but we have some business to attend to out here within the next week or so. We can telecommute until then, so to speak." He lifted an empty glass and an eyebrow.

"Yes, thank you." She had no idea what the man was going to pour, but anything at this point would work. A dark amber liquid splashed two thirds of the way up the ice before he poured a clear soda into the glasses and stirred.

"Hey, what's taking you so long?"

Sky spun around at the sound of the woman's voice. Wow. Did they not grow normal sized humans at this place? The woman wasn't as tall as Keelee, but she was way taller than Sky's five foot four inches. And she was beautiful, like model-type beautiful.

"Sky, this is my fiancée Jewell King. Jewell this is Sky Meyers."

Sky waved from behind the bar and kept her mouth shut. God only knew what would come out of her mouth if she opened it now.

"Oh! Sky! Hi! It is so good to finally meet you!" The woman came around the bar and wrapped her up in a hug.

Sky's hands stayed suspended in mid-air, one holding her drink and the other frozen by the shock of a person she didn't know hugging her.

"Sorry, she's a hugger," Zane commented when his fiancée pulled back.

"True. I am. But hey, where's your daughter? I read that everything went perfectly and that she's doing amazing." Jewell took her drink from her fiancé and gave him a sweet kiss as a thank you.

Sky put down the drink and clasped her hands together to stop her hands from shaking. The woman's comments reverberated in her head. "How did you read anything about Kadey?"

"Huh? Oh, I run the computer systems for Guardian, and we've been helping with your situation from the beginning." The woman's smile faltered, and she glanced over at her man. "He didn't tell her?"

"Obviously not."

"No."

Sky and the big guy spoke at the same time.

"Well, this isn't awkward, is it?"

A smile grew on Jewell's face until she started laughing. "Let's start over. Hi, I'm Jewell King. Our section was the one that identified your attempts to find…" She looked over at Zane. "Kaeden."

"Right, Kaeden."

Sky cocked her head and glanced from one to the other. "You need to explain why you don't know his name."

"Oh, that's easy. I've never met him. He's a case file number to me, nothing more. Zane here, he used to work with him, and they're friends. Besides, if it isn't coding, I'm not likely to remember a damn thing." The woman took a sip of her drink and closed her eyes. She let out a small whimper. "I so needed this after today."

"You did one hell of a job. Consider this unhealthy indulgence a reward." Zane wrapped his arm around Jewell's waist and pulled her in, kissing her on the forehead.

Sky looked away from the intimate moment. Dang it, she was kinda stuck. She couldn't get past them to leave them alone.

"So where is Kadey?"

Sky popped her attention back up to the couple as Jewell looked at her expectantly. "Ummm… she's spending the night with Lizzy at the Cassidys." Sky cast a glance toward the twenty-foot front doors where they'd left not ten minutes ago.

"Awesome, that means you're free to come to girls night. My sister Jasmine, my mom, my sister-in-law Ember usually drink some cocktails, well, they drink wine, and we binge watch *Supernatural* and talk girl talk. Keelee usually comes, and now I know why she begged off."

"Ahh…" Sky's eyes darted around the room looking for an escape or an excuse to decline the invitation.

"I think you might be piling just a little too much on Sky right now, hon." Zane's comment had Sky's head nodding north and south in a nanosecond,

"Oh." Jewell glanced down at her drink. Zane leaned down and whispered in her ear. The woman smiled and nodded before she cast her glance over toward Sky. "I'm sorry. I'm not the best at social interactions. If you want to come, that would be cool, but if not, I understand."

Sky felt the release valve activate and the pressure that had descended on her started to evaporate. "I'm actually looking forward to going up to my room, taking a nice long bath and reading a book."

"I get that." Jewell grabbed Zane's hand and pulled him out from behind the bar.

Another wave of relief washed over her. The man was big and having him block her exit was intimidating.

Halfway to the door, Jewell threw over her shoulder, "Tell Kaeden we said hi."

Sky looked down at her drink. She wished he'd call, but with each day that passed she grew more certain Kaeden wasn't coming back—not for her, and not for Kadey. She'd figure out a way to get her life back. Being dumped in the middle of nowhere with a bunch of strangers was an absolutely dick move on Kaeden's part… except for the free medical care. And room and board… so maybe not a dick move…

"He hasn't called, has he?" Zane's question pulled her from her muddled thoughts.

Sky shook her head. "No, I haven't talked to him since the day we left California. He said he was tying up loose ends, but I honestly don't expect him to call or come back." As far as Sky knew, Kaeden hadn't so much as called or texted to check up on them. His concern for Kadey seemed real. *No, stop it!* Dang it, she *knew* he cared. He'd protected them from the thugs who murdered the two people in Sacramento. He'd contacted his people and taken them to the safety of the Air Force base. Kadey had world-class care both there and here at Guardian's facility. Kaeden cared, she didn't doubt it, but…

Zane and Jewell looked at each other before Zane turned back to her. "I'll reach out and see what's up. I know there is no reason to worry. Good night."

"I'm not worried about Kaeden. Enjoy your evening." Sky spoke as they walked hand and hand out of the room.

She set the drink down in the sink and nibbled on her thumbnail. Her nerves were shot. Sky rubbed her eyes before tears could form. She wished things were different. She wished Kaeden could be the permanent fixture in their lives that they both yearned for. But his reality and hers were never meant to mesh. She knew that and still… she wished the ending to the story would change, even though she knew it couldn't. Sky headed up the stairs to her room. Why did she think this time would be different? Because Kadey was involved, obviously. Sky headed upstairs. She needed to grow a spine when it came to Kaeden. Or armor. Yes, armor would be better. Especially now that she wasn't the only one he could hurt.

CHAPTER EIGHTEEN

ANUBIS OPENED THE FIRE DOOR AND WALKED DOWN the long hallway. The antiseptic smell assaulted his nose. The light blue scrubs and doctor's ID pinned to his pocket kept all but the most cursory glances to a minimum. He'd stopped at the entry point to wash and put on his isolation ward garb. Faas and his bodyguards lay in the rooms beyond in the isolation ward. A quick look at the man's chart revealed the doctors were currently testing them all for typhoid fever and malaria plus a host of other diseases found in the rainforest climate of Suriname.

Anubis flashed his badge at the door where a bodyguard for Faas stood. The man nodded and turned his head down the hall, dismissing Anubis without a second thought.

He entered Faas's room, pulled up the one and only chair in the area, so he could examine Faas as he lay there, asleep or unconscious. The man's skin held an ashen pallor. His lungs labored, the deep rattle foretold the failure of his respiratory system. Nothing could forestall the inevitable. Anubis pulled a vial of adrenaline from his pocket and pulled a few CCs into a syringe. He'd made a compromise based on Asp's concerns. He waited and watched Faas's compound. He saw them take Faas to the hospital. The bodyguards followed in a separate ambulance, and the medical personnel wore masks, but no suits that would protect them if they suspected radiation poisoning. The likelihood that the guards would be able to infect anyone was very slim. Exposed to secondhand smoke from a Polonium 210 inhalation wasn't necessarily deadly. The damage done to them would be slower, less traumatic, but if Faas had smoked the entire pack in their presence? Their deaths would be a sure thing.

He sat watching Faas for several minutes. All the hate and rage that filled him fueled his urge to fill the syringe and shoot Faas straight to hell with an exploded heart.

Anubis glanced at the closed door as he pushed the few CC's of adrenaline into Faas's IV. It took about thirty-five seconds before Faas's eyelids fluttered open, his heart monitor chirped a faster tempo.

The man's eyes searched the room, landing on Anubis. "Who are you?" His native Dutch language slurred as Faas reached for his chest. "I don't feel well."

Anubis crossed his arms. "You're dying."

"No, they said malaria, maybe typhoid." The fact that Anubis spoke English with an American accent must have registered. Faas licked his lips, and his eyes searched the room wildly. "Guard!" His voice didn't carry far enough for the guard to hear.

"Don't you recognize me?" Anubis asked. "You stepped on my hand."

"The cigarettes? You came here because I took your cigarettes?"

Anubis let a sinister smile spread across his lips. "No, you dared come after my woman and my child."

"Ah… you are him. The one I've been waiting for. The one who killed my uncle."

"From what I hear, I beat you to the punch. I made it easier for you to take over."

"He was old. He wouldn't have lasted."

"Then why did you come after me?"

Faas coughed and spit up blood into the tray beside his head. "You are Rh-null."

Anubis blinked back his surprise. "And?"

"Your blood is more valuable than the gold in these hills."

"You thought you could sell my blood on the black market?" Anubis had never imagined that scenario.

"Selling human organs is extremely profitable. It has made me very rich. The homeless street people usually have acceptable organs. But, why not the rarest of all blood? I'll use you until your daughter is old enough." A lecherous sneer passed over Faas's face. "She is a pretty girl. I'll find her. She can't hide."

"You're dead. I killed you." Anubis took a quiet pleasure as the finality of his statement registered with Faas.

The man shook his head as if by doing so he could negate the truth. "Why are you here?" Faas coughed again and spit into the dish next to him. His little trough was filling up with blood-laced mucus.

"Closure."

Asp's voice came from behind him. Anubis turned slowly. He nodded once at his co-worker. "Closure." Anubis turned back toward Faas. "Justice was served, my family is safe. This conversation is my closure."

"What is your name?"

Anubis looked at the withered shell of a man on the hospital bed. "We have many names." He glanced at Asp. "We are the Shadow Guardians."

Faas closed his eyes. The monitor bleeped in an irregular rhythm, his heart no longer fueled by the small amount of adrenaline that Anubis had used to wake the man from his drug-induced haze.

"If he ever regains consciousness, he might not remember this." Asp opened the door, and they exited the room.

Anubis paused and looked back at the man he'd killed. For the second time in his life, he'd killed without direct orders, but with purpose and intent that morally defied the laws of man. Faas might not remember. "But I will."

He followed Asp down the stairs and out into the light of the day. Suriname was experiencing one of the few days of sunshine it had in October. The brilliant blue sky, unfettered by rain clouds, allowed the sun to shine down on the men as they walked away from the facility.

"Are you satisfied now?" Asp asked as they strolled down the street.

"I am."

"You didn't do anything stupid. Actually, that shocked me, you were pretty messed up."

Anubis nodded. "You spoke the truth. As angry as I was, I couldn't fault your logic. Crossing the line, taking unnecessary risks, did nothing to further my purpose." He glanced over at Asp. "Why are you still here?"

"If I left and something happened to you…" Asp didn't finish the statement, but Anubis got it. The man was all about doing the right thing. He motioned toward a small restaurant. They made their way into the establishment and sat down. Asp ordered the daily special and Anubis declined. "Have you checked in lately?" Asp asked around a mouthful of bread and butter.

Anubis shook his head. A sudden thought struck him. "Why? Kadey… Sky?"

"They're both fine. Bengal contacted me looking for you."

"What did he want?"

"The dossier on Faas was approved, and he's worried about your situation."

"Did he say that?"

"Fuck no. But I could tell." Those words came from around half a roll that Asp had slathered in butter and shoved into his mouth.

Anubis shrugged. It didn't matter that the hit was sanctioned. He'd done what he needed to do. He'd protected his family, and he'd gained the closure that he needed. Although the rationale for Faas going after him, and ultimately Kadey, was mind-boggling.

"So, your blood is that rare?" Asp asked as if he could read Anubis's mind.

"Less than one percent of the population has it, and we are a universal donor for all RH negative blood types. Scientists always want a supply of Rh-null blood to study, but…no, I had no idea selling my blood would be a profit-making venture. The bastard actually tracked me down for it, not for killing his uncle. I'm going to have to hope bringing Kadey into it was just his sick way to torment me from his deathbed." Unfortunately, he knew in his gut the bastard wasn't tormenting him. Sick fucker. Dead fucker.

Asp leaned back as the waiter placed a huge plate of chicken, rice and green beans in front of the big guy. Asp waited until the waiter left and spoke low. "Not so sure about that. While I was waiting for you to fuck up, I read his dossier. I think initially you were what he wanted, but he would have taken Kadey and used her, too. Guardian did well in getting the community to code the guy." Asp grabbed a chicken leg and tore into it, taking a huge bite that pulled almost all the meat off in one motion. He chewed twice and spoke around his food, "What are you going to do now?"

Anubis shrugged. Wasn't that the question of the day. He didn't have to 'do' anything. He had enough money to take care of Sky and Kadey, but he did need to present some front of normalcy. "I don't know. Maybe I'll sell insurance?"

Asp pulled in a sharp breath of air and started coughing before he went silent. He clutched his throat, and his face turned a dark red. Anubis was up in an instant. He placed his fist on Asp's diaphragm and pulled sharply three times before the chicken lodged in Asp's throat flew from his mouth. The giant of a man grabbed the edge of the table and took several shuddering breaths. Anubis fended off the waiter and the manager, assuring them that Asp was fine.

"Holy fuck, Ani."

"What? I take it you don't like the insurance idea?"

Asp wiped his chin with his napkin and leaned back in his chair. "You, behind a desk? Never going to happen."

Anubis shrugged and motioned toward Asp's plate. "Are you going to eat that?"

Asp's eyes popped as he switched his gaze from his plate to Anubis. "Don't tell me you suddenly want some?"

Anubis slowly moved his head from one side to the other. "No, what I suddenly want is to go to South Dakota. Thought you might like to join me. I'd like to introduce you to two ladies that are pretty special to me."

Asp blinked at him, the surprise on the man's face was as obvious as the fact that he'd been choking not two minutes ago. "You'd introduce me to your family?"

"I would," Anubis confirmed.

"Why? You do know what I do for a living, right?"

"I do. My family would have no better protector in the world, should I happen into misfortune." He could never one hundred percent guarantee that someone or something from his past wouldn't reach out and tap him on the shoulder one day. He'd take every precaution, but life in the Shadows wasn't escaped easily. He knew the righteousness of the man across from him. His honor and his sense of duty would forever link him to Sky and Kadey.

"If you get over yourself, you should be fine."

The jab was half-hearted, but a reminder of all that Anubis had been willing to put on the line and lose to face off with Faas. Anubis was damned glad he'd listened to Asp and waited. The closure was just as sweet and slipping into the hospital versus going into a heavily armed compound was the smart play. Anubis shook his head. Yeah, he'd been stupid. Emotion clouded the mind, and he was full of emotion. The foreign type of emotion that had him thinking of a future and of a family. It fucked with him in ways he couldn't explain. He needed to get back to Sky and Kadey because the world didn't make sense without them next to him. His family. *His life*.

"I'll have you around to knock some sense into me if I slip up." Anubis pointed at the plate of food cooling in front of Asp. "Are you eating that?"

Asp stood and reached for his wallet. "Nope, I think I can get some food at the airport."

CHAPTER NINETEEN

"SHE IS IN GREAT CONDITION. THE TEST RESULTS and scans show the repair to the ASD is solid. The valve that suffered from the Ebstein's Anomaly is also repaired and no longer an issue. She shows no signs of injury to the brachial plexus—"

"Wait, what is that?" Sky jumped in before the Air Force cardiologist could say more.

"It is a rare and minor concern, but we check for it. The brachial plexus is the main nerve that provides sensation and muscle function to the arms and hands. We knew before we discharged her that her arm and hand functions weren't impaired, but we did check today to make sure she had sensation in her fingers, specifically the third, fourth and fifth fingers. When we did the surgery, we moved the nerve to open her chest cavity, and that is always a risk. As I said, it is a minor concern and one that we don't need to worry about with Kadey. She's doing great."

"Oh… okay." Sky filed the information away, grateful she didn't know to worry about that item, too. She was exhausted from watching for all the other things they'd told her to watch for… infection at the incision, fever, trouble breathing. Even with Doctor Cassidy watching over her, Sky was a nervous wreck.

The doctor continued, "She'll probably always have a small heart murmur, and you should follow up with annual check-ups, but overall, Kadey is almost ready to go play with the rest of the kids her age. She'll become winded quicker because she's not had any strenuous exercise for such a long time. Don't stress that, she'll get stronger. She can have a bath now that the incisions are healed. I do need to remind you to make sure she doesn't try to pick up anything heavy for at least another month."

"I'm doing that. Nothing more than her Barbie dolls or her stuffed animals."

"Perfect. We need to let the sternum heal, and it will take time, just like a broken bone takes time to mend, but other than that, she's doing fine."

"So this is pretty much… over?" Sky looked up at the doctor.

He smiled as his kind eyes met hers. "Yes, mom. Your baby is going to be fine. I've been told I'm on call to fly to wherever you are should there be any concern, but in my professional opinion, you won't see me again."

"I hate to say this, but that really makes me happy." Sky leaned in and hugged the man before she stepped back, embarrassed by the impulsive action.

"It makes me happy, too. Now I believe there is another patient they want me to see before I have to go."

Sky took that as her dismissal, said thank you and goodbye again, and headed back to the ranch house where Keelee was keeping Kadey and Lizzy occupied so Sky could talk with the doctor. Keelee and her step-mother Amanda had been a source of continual support. If she'd been here for any other reason, Sky would have enjoyed the stay. She stopped about halfway to the house and drew a deep breath of the crisp autumn air. A cold front had rolled through, leaving the skies under a blanket of grey clouds. Sky swept the vista and hugged her arms around her. Kadey had cleared the final hurdle. Sky lifted her eyes towards the heavens and said a prayer of thanks.

What did she do now? Kaeden had once again fallen off the face of the earth. Zane hadn't been able to reach him. Everyone told her not to worry... and in reality, she *wasn't* worried. This was her life as far as Kaeden was concerned. He showed up, and he left. There was no permanence. She knew from the beginning he wasn't sticking around. The hard part was going to be explaining to Kadey that her dad was once again out of the picture. But Kadey didn't ask about him much anymore, her attention diverted with the multitude of new things to play with and explore with Lizzy.

The problem now was she had no money and no idea where to go even if she had the means. The house in California held a few possessions she'd have to return to retrieve. Putting the house on the market would provide a nest egg. The prices of property in Sacramento had skyrocketed since she'd bought. She'd take the lifeline Kaeden had offered her, just not in the form he set up. She needed to stand on her own two feet, and for the most part, she had until Kadey's health issues sat her on her ass. No, first she'd figure out a way to start again, and when the house sold, she'd have a foundation to build on. She'd reinvent herself and make a good life for herself and Kadey. One without Kaeden. She couldn't be at his beck and call any longer. The pain was too much. She loved Kaeden, but a one-sided love wasn't enough to carry a relationship. She had little doubt he'd call her again, but Sky couldn't... not again. Her heart wouldn't survive being left... again.

She ran the problem through several times before she made it to the house. She had one option. She'd ask Keelee and Doctor Cassidy to front her some money. Just enough to get her and Kadey to her father's house. Sky's mother and father separated when she was twelve. Her dad was... well, he wasn't a pleasant man, but Sky hoped he'd allow them to stay with him until she found employment. She couldn't work as an office manager any longer, not after what happened in Sacramento at the DA's office... but she could wait tables until she found something else.

~

"Say what, now?" Doctor Cassidy lowered his fork and looked across the dining room table at Sky. They were once again eating dinner at the Cassidys. Sky had waited until the girls had asked to be excused before she brought up the topic of a loan.

"We wouldn't need much. I swear I'll pay you back every cent, with interest." Sky lowered her own utensils and glanced from Keelee to Doctor Cassidy. "You don't know me very well, but I swear I'll pay you back and somehow I'll pay Guardian back for the medical bills."

"It's not the money. Hell, I'll give you whatever you need. Why are you leaving before Kaeden gets back?" Doctor Cassidy asked.

Keelee placed her hand on her husband's arm but looked over at Sky. Keelee understood. Sky could see it in her eyes and that gave her strength to speak the words. Sky straightened her shoulders and told them the truth. "Kaeden isn't going to come back. He has always been straightforward with me. He said he'd only stay until Kadey was through her surgery and recovering. He didn't ask for this, for us."

"Sky..." Keelee started and then stopped. She glanced at her husband and they communicated silently with just a look. He nodded. "We'll give you one of our vehicles, and I'll get you money tomorrow when the bank opens. How much do you think you'll need?"

Sky let out a breath and deflated. They weren't going to ask for specifics. Thank God. "I have a three-day drive, so enough for a hotel, gas, and food?"

Keelee nodded and placed her fork on her plate. "When do you want to leave?"

Sky gave her a sad smile. "Tomorrow. If I can follow you to the bank, we'll leave from there."

Doctor Cassidy leaned back in his chair. "I think you're making a mistake."

Sky bit her bottom lip and looked at the Doctor. "How many times have you told Keelee that you love her?"

He blinked at her question. "Too many times to count." He looked at his wife. The love between them was a tangible thing, something that Sky didn't have and never would have with Kaeden.

"I love Kaeden; I always have. I know he cares for me and for Kadey, but he's never said he loves us. Kaeden helped Kadey, and I'm eternally grateful, but I can't live a life where Kaeden is a question mark. I believe he cares for us, but he can't physically be here for us, and it isn't fair to either Kadey or me to pretend that he'll change. Kadey deserves a full-time father. I deserve a man who will be there when I need him. I'll forgo my needs, but not Kadey's. She deserves better."

Doctor Cassidy stared at her for a moment. "I know what I saw. I believe he cares for you."

"I think he does, in his way, but it isn't enough. I need to make arrangements to take care of myself and my daughter." Sky wiped her mouth with her napkin. "I'm sorry for dropping this on you, but you were the only ones I could ask."

"It isn't a problem. Have you told Kadey you're leaving?" Keelee pushed her own plate away from her.

"No, I'll explain it tomorrow morning."

Keelee nodded. "I'll explain it to Lizzy. Well, okay. I'll meet you here at eight tomorrow morning? We'll get you packed up and on your way. I'm sorry to see you go."

Sky smiled and reached across the table, squeezing Keelee's hand softly. "I never meant to be here permanently. I don't know what I would have done without you two. I appreciate your friendship and hospitality." She turned to Doctor Cassidy. "If you would let me know how much I owe Guardian? For the flight, the medical expenses? Your time?"

The doctor brushed away her concerns, "It was all donated. You don't owe us anything."

Sky blinked back tears and nodded. "Then thank you very much. I'll grab Kadey, and we'll go."

"Let her spend the night? I know Lizzy will be heartbroken when Kadey leaves." Keelee glanced into the living room where the two girls were brushing the manes of Lizzy's toy ponies. "But children are resilient and so are you. I'm glad I got to know you Sky."

"And I you." Sky hugged both the Cassidys, made sure Kadey was okay with staying, and then made her way back to the main house. She'd be able to pack faster with Kadey not 'helping.'

"WHY CAN'T LIZZY COME WITH US ON OUR adventure?" Kadey sat in the borrowed booster seat that Doctor Cassidy had strapped in. He added foam to the seatbelt across Kadey's chest to prevent any rubbing or chaffing of the incision site.

"Because her mom would miss her the same way I'd miss you." Sky watched the bank doors as Keelee exited the facility. The woman headed straight to the SUV that Sky was borrowing. She'd figure out how to return it once they got situated. Keelee assured her they rarely used the vehicle and they had other ranch trucks they could use if needed.

"Here you go. I added some in there to keep you going for a little while. That's my gift to you. Pay this forward. I'm blessed that I don't need the money or the vehicle and I don't want repayment. I signed the title over to you last night. It's in the glovebox. Register it in whatever state you end up in. It's yours."

Sky took the envelope with shaking hands and brushed away the tears that fell.

"Momma, is it dusty again?"

Sky nodded. "Yeah baby, it's really dusty today." She looked up at Keelee. "Thank you. For everything."

"You take care of yourself. I put my number on the back of that envelope. Call me and let me know you made it alright."

"I will. Thank you." Keelee smiled sadly and blinked back tears. "Take care of yourself, Kadey. Maybe come back and visit, okay?"

"Okay! Bye Miss Keelee."

Keelee tapped the side of the vehicle twice and turned away. Sky put the truck in gear and headed south. They had a long way to go.

"She's gone?" Zane glared across the desk at Adam Cassidy.

"Yes."

"Why did you let her go?"

"Right. I'm supposed to make her stay when she obviously believes this guy has been actively avoiding her. The man hasn't even told her that he loves her. What would your woman do if you fucked up and treated her like she was a convenient hole? I know what Keelee would do. She'd pick up, take off and make a life for herself. And I'd be lucky if she didn't castrate me first. Sky is protecting herself. This guy is someone you used to work with, you deal with it." Adam got up and stormed out of the small office that Zane was occupying.

He rubbed his hands over his face. *Damn it, Ani, you really fucked up.* He grabbed the secure line and dialed Asp's number. Since Anubis had gone silent, Zane had communicated through Asp, who wasn't supposed to be out of the country on a mission without going through his psych eval. The line rang and rang… and rang. *Fuck!*

Zane got up and walked to the next office where Jewell was working. Her hands flew over the keyboard as she looked up. She continued typing as she smiled at him. He had no idea how she did that. He'd end up typing in hieroglyphics if he tried.

"Babe, I need you to do something for me… off the books."

Jewell's hands stilled, and she cocked her head at him. "What?"

"I need you to find an asset that has gone silent."

"Kaeden?"

"Yeah."

"Well, it just so happens when he didn't answer your call when you told Sky you'd talk to him, I started working on that."

"Have I told you how much I love you?" Zane bent down and laid a long, needy kiss on his woman.

"Many times, but please, by all means, tell me again."

Zane moved around her desk and sat on the edge. He lowered and brushed his lips against hers.

"Oh, if going off the books gets me kisses, how about I break a few more protocols and then maybe we can make love in this office?" She waggled her eyebrows at him.

"Anytime, babe… well, after Jacob gets here, because I'd hate for him to walk in on that."

Jewell scrunched her nose. "Mood officially ruined. So, why do you all of a sudden need to know where your asset is?"

"Sky left this morning." Zane watched Jewell process the information.

"No."

"Yep."

"Fuck me." Jewell leaned back in her chair.

Zane chuckled. "Again, I will, but not here."

Jewell popped forward and punched him on the arm. "Be serious."

He rubbed the spot where she'd hit him. The woman had some strength in her. He'd make her kiss it better… later. "From what I got from Doc, she was pretty damn sure he wasn't coming back for her. He fucked up and didn't bother to tell the mother of his child that he loved her."

"Does he?" Jewell leaned back in her chair and looked up at him. "You told me that the men in your old profession were wounded, that some were too fucked up to walk in the light again. We all know Joseph's wickedly fucked up, but he's adapting." Jewell's brother was a Shadow that had portrayed his own death on a world stage. The assassin known as Fury was officially dead, yet very much alive. His wife and son were the tethers that kept that loose cannon from exploding. Everyone, including Joseph, understood that fact.

Zane grabbed Jewell's hand and held it while he examined her fingers. He'd like to believe Ani had the capacity to care for his family, but the truth was he wasn't sure. Ani had been in the dark for so long that maybe the woman and child were better off without him. He brought his eyes up to look at his fiancée. Thank God, he'd been able to make the transition back into the light. "I don't know."

"You can't save everyone, Zane. If Kaeden wants this life

with Sky and Kadey, then he's going to have to fight for it, like you did." Jewell stood up and scooted between his legs before she looped her arms around his neck. "Maybe your friend needs a wake-up call. Sounds to me like Sky is giving him his critical moment."

Zane smiled and moved in for a kiss. Jewell leaned away from him. "You need to let him figure this out for himself. You can't force him to become a family man."

"I know, but God, I hope Anubis finally catches a break."

CHAPTER TWENTY

Anubis sat in the passenger side seat and watched the pine trees go by. Their flight had been delayed by two days out of Suriname due to heavy rains. They'd missed their connecting flight and had been booked onto a flight that had been oversold resulting in them getting bumped. To say his patience was at an end would be a critical understatement. Asp had taken every setback in stride, but *he* was fucking over it.

"This place is way the fuck out in the middle of nowhere, isn't it?" Asp slowed as they approached the turnoff to the Marshall Ranch.

"It is." He couldn't wait to see his girls. He should have called when they got back to the States, but he didn't know Sky's new cell number. He could have called the complex and been patched through, but seriously, after almost a month, what was a couple more days? He'd see her in person soon, and they could sit down and figure out where to go from here. Anubis stared at the cattle that dotted the vast expanse of rolling hills. Walking away from the Shadow World would take determination, but Bengal had done it. Fury had managed it in a way that nobody expected. He was at least as intelligent as those two. He'd figure it out. Somehow.

"Wow. Would you look at that?" Asp pointed at the front windshield.

Anubis gave an internal snort of laughter at Asp's reaction and turned his head in the direction of the man's gesture. The mansion. Granted, it was a log cabin, but the place could have housed royalty. Word on the street was that the King's stepfather had built it by hand. They drove through a small valley and past the ranch buildings at the base of a large hill.

"Fuck me, standing." Asp slowed down and gaped at the vast expanse of the training complex behind the ranch.

The change that had happened since Anubis had left was awe-inspiring. There were at least twenty new structures since he'd last visited almost six years ago. The airstrip now had a small control tower. Fields of solar panels spread to the east and several large wind turbines dotted the field. Anubis picked out the hospital, and the comms facility was easy to spot with the array of antennas and security fencing around it.

"Park over there." He directed Asp to the closest parking lot. He'd start at the hospital. Doctor Cassidy would be able to tell him how Kadey was and where he could find his woman. Asp followed him up the stairs and into the hospital. There wasn't a waiting area, just a long hall that housed the doc's, PT's, and pharmacist's offices. Anubis walked down the hall until he reached the office door that proclaimed Doctor Cassidy's name. He knuckled the doorframe and waited.

"He's on rounds. Can I help you? I'm Doctor King." Anubis and Asp turned at her voice. The curvy red-head smiled at them.

"I'm looking for my daughter. Kadey…" Fuck, he didn't know if Sky had used the alias or not.

"Oh."

That single word brought Anubis to high alert. He snapped his head toward the doctor. "Is she alright?"

"Oh, she's fine, but she's not here anymore."

"Excuse the fuck out of me?" Anubis growled the response at the woman. Asp put his hand on Anubis's arm. He shrugged it off.

The woman straightened her back and lifted her hand. "Don't. Don't use that tone with me. I'm not the one responsible for Sky and Kadey leaving."

"Then who is?" Anubis would find the fucker and take him out.

"I believe that would be you." Zane's voice shattered the tense moment.

Anubis spun on his heel. "What the fuck are you talking about?"

"When was the last time you talked to Sky?" Zane crossed his arms over his chest and glared at Anubis.

"What the fuck does it matter to you?"

"Oh, it doesn't matter to me. It mattered to Sky. She assumed that you did what you always do, that you left her... again."

Asp sucked his teeth and shook his head. "Fuck, that's brutal, brother. He's been cleaning shit up so they could have a life."

Zane turned on Asp. "You are supposed to be on domestic R&R. I don't want to know how you know that."

Asp smiled at Zane—a wide smile filled with white teeth. "Then don't ask."

"Shut the fuck up!" Anubis cut the banter with his words. "Where is Sky?"

"Don't know. She borrowed a vehicle and cash, and she left. Three days ago."

Anubis snapped his mouth shut. She'd left and taken Kadey with her. He nodded his head. "It's for the best. They don't need me."

"Bullshit," That was the red-headed doctor. "Men. Are you all fucking idiots? Pull your head out of your ass before you lose that woman." She turned on her heel and headed down the hall, disappearing into an office. A loud slam of the office door put a period on her angry statement.

"She's right," Zane confirmed the woman's comments.

"Who the fuck is she because *daaamn*. All those curves. Oh, how I'd like to know them up close and personal." Asp looked down the hall after the woman.

"That is Fury's wife, so stand down, stupid," Zane growled.

"Wait? What? Fury's dead."

"You want to test that theory?" Zane arched his eyebrow in a challenge.

"Ahhh… that would be a no." Asp put his hands in his pockets like a kid caught with his hand in a cookie jar. Reprimanded but still wanting the treat.

Anubis had enough of the bullshit and took off down the hall. He needed to get away from people. He had to think. Asp's footsteps beside him brought him to a halt. "I need some time."

"Cool. I'll keep my mouth shut, but I'm not leaving you alone, or you'll do something stupid, and then I'll have to fucking clean it up."

Anubis glared at the man.

Asp shrugged his shoulders, his hands still in his pockets as he spoke, "Don't try to deny it."

"Fine. We passed a bar in the small town before we turned off to the ranch, I'm going there, and I'm getting drunk."

"Right, because you should be getting drunk instead of finding out where she went."

Anubis stopped and turned on Asp. "I have ways of making you shut up."

"Pshhh… you love me, but what's more important is you love that woman and your daughter. If it were me, I'd be calling in every favor I'd ever accrued. Hell, you don't even have to do that. All you have to do is ask Alpha to let you use Guardian's resources."

"Right, like he'd let me do that."

"I would."

Anubis closed his eyes and then opened them to glare at Asp. The shit-eating grin on the man's face proved the motherfucker knew Alpha was standing behind him the entire time.

"See how fucked up this has you? You didn't even hear him coming down a gravel path. You need to find her and settle this one way or the other. At least you'd know that she isn't running away from you before you can run away from her."

"What the fuck does that even mean?" Anubis swung to include Alpha in the conversation. Jacob King's expression was hard to read, and that was never good.

"I think he's trying to convince you she bailed on you before you could bail on her again." Alpha looked at Asp. "Food—that way." He pointed toward another building, and Asp spun on his heel, abandoning both of them without another word. Asp whistled as he walk-ran to the promise of food.

"Come with me."

Anubis watched as the man did an about-face with every expectation that Anubis would follow. He rolled his shoulders and groaned inwardly. He needed five minutes of peace and quiet to figure out what the fuck he should be doing, but it didn't look like that was going to happen anytime soon.

He followed his boss into the comms facility and processed in through security. He trailed Alpha into a large conference room and glared at Bengal. His woman was sitting beside him. He'd seen them together when he'd been given Boa's assignment. Fuck, that seemed like a lifetime ago.

"Sit your ass down." Alpha plopped into a chair and grabbed the nearby bag of chocolate. He poured a few of the mini-bars into his hand and tossed the bag back to his sister. Bengal reached down to the chair beside him and produced a tin of nuts and a bottle of water. "Dinner will be cooked by my mother, from food raised on this ranch. It will be safe for you to eat." Alpha unwrapped a piece of chocolate and popped it in his mouth. "Faas died. Yesterday."

Anubis nodded. The man hung on longer than he'd expected.

"Why use Polonium 210?" Zane spoke as his eyes focused on a tablet in front of him.

"If your woman was targeted for assassination and your child was to be used as bait to lure you out, what method of death would you have used?" Anubis asked.

"I would have peeled his skin off, one inch at a time." Bengal growled as he grasped Jewell's hand, "but I wouldn't have risked radiation exposure to others and myself."

"There was little to no risk. The limo had a rear ventilation system, and the driver was using it. I'm well versed in security precautions. It was the most miserable death I could imagine for the bastard."

"We are considering that kill as a mission, so standard protocols will be in place. You've had two dossiers now without going through a go/no-go evaluation. You'll stay here until you've met our requirements."

Anubis stared at his boss. He wanted to rage at the order, to tell the man to go screw himself. He crossed his arms and leaned back in his chair instead. His anger at having his hands tied hinged on the fact he wouldn't be able to go after Sky and Kadey. His brain told him that letting them go, forever, was exactly what he should do. Then why the fuck did he want to tear down the building they were sitting in with a sledgehammer? Anubis dipped his head once, acknowledging Alpha's command.

Zane cleared his throat and pushed a folder across the table. Anubis flicked a look at Alpha and pulled the folder to him. He'd just been told he wasn't going out on any other missions until he had his fucking psych eval done, so what the fuck was this?

He lifted the cover and glanced at the top page. He looked up, his eyes shifting between Alpha and Bengal before he pulled the folder in front of him and read the words again. Alpha was restructuring the Shadow World operation. There were three positions that worked directly under Alpha. Bengal's name filled one block. The line of authority under his name ran through several people with CCS under their names. Computer specialists no doubt. Bengal would also be in charge of all the administrative functions, although Anubis had no idea what that would entail for an organization that didn't actually exist.

The second line of authority led to twelve boxes. He recognized Asp's control number. His wasn't included in the diagram. The line of authority also trailed through several blank boxes that had Logistics placed in the duty position.

The third line of authority under Alpha was one block. It was marked as the Architect. All the other lines of authority had broken lines between the leads and the down channel personnel showing a cross-management function. The identity of the Architect was a closely guarded secret, for obvious reasons. Who the fuck wouldn't want to know every deep cover identity and alias for all of Guardian? Hell, it was rumored the Architect performed duties for other agencies, too. The man was a priceless asset.

Anubis closed the cover over the paperwork and leaned back in his chair, waiting for someone to tell him what the fuck was going on. Alpha popped another piece of chocolate into his mouth and pointed to the folder. "I want to know if you would be interested in heading up the personnel and logistics section of the Shadow World. I can't do it all anymore. Zane was brought on to CCS and has made a case for the need for better management of the assets we have assigned. You'd be here at the complex. He'd be in D.C. You'd travel as needed."

Anubis glanced at Bengal and then to his woman. She was busy scrolling through her tablet, ignoring the entire conversation. Bengal leveled his gaze and waited. Anubis leaned forward and placed his forearms on the table. "Why me?"

Alpha reached for another piece of candy. "You are one of the most experienced Shadow Operatives I have. I've never worked in the shadows. I'll be the first to admit I run a blind operation in several areas and that shit needs to stop now." He waved a finger between Bengal and Anubis. "Having you two available will streamline the red tape of building dossiers and assigning them to the correct skillset after they are coded. Gabriel, Archangel and I have been considering the benefits of teaming up our assets. For certain cases, joining the assets makes the most sense. You would be responsible for making that work."

"You'd be able to stay in the shadows, but walk in the light." Bengal tossed the final salvo over the bow.

Anubis shook his head. "I'd like to say yes, but I need to take care of something first." He shifted his eyes to his boss.

"Thank fuck, finally. Jewell?" Alpha looked at his sister.

"I can find her. She has Keelee Cassidy's truck. It could take a while and one hell of an algorithm, but in reality, a nation-wide system to link all the traffic cameras so law enforcement can track scum from municipality to interstate to municipality, is long overdue. The parameters and inclusionary data are overwhelming. Some systems are incompatible with our hosting platform so there will be gaps, but the concept is exciting, and the applications for law enforcement will enhance current capabilities exponentially. Fortunately, I won't need any of that because Keelee Cassidy put a tracking device in the SUV."

Anubis cut his eyes to Bengal. The big guy smiled indulgently at the woman who didn't even seem to register anyone else was in the room. Her fingers flew over the tablet, and she mumbled something before she grabbed one of the many pencils that stuck out of her messy up-do.

"Do you think she'll go back to California?" Bengal's question redirected his attention from the man's hot mess of a fiancée. Thank god he didn't have to understand what the woman said.

Anubis considered Bengal's question for a moment. "Maybe, but other than a house, there is nothing left for her there. If she hasn't been fired, she will be. She was trying to track me down and used the DA's assets without approval. I need to call in some favors to get any charges against her dropped."

"I'll call Jared and Nic. They can clear that up with one call." Alpha grabbed another piece of candy.

"Thank you. I know she'd probably want to make a fresh start, but I have no idea where she'd go."

"Family?" Bengal pulled out his tablet, and he and his woman tapped away at the faces of their electronics.

"Mother's dead. She's been estranged from her father. No other relatives." At least none that he knew about.

"Okay." Jewell glanced up at her brother. "Permission to cross a few boundaries in the name of the greater good?"

Jacob snorted. "Like you've ever asked before. Just don't get me fired."

"Again." Jewell and Zane both commented at the same time.

Jacob flipped them off, stood up and stretched. "Go check in and get a bunk. They'll figure out where your family is located."

"Hey, it could take a hot minute. This program is massive. Don't get me wrong, we're good, but dude, we are talking about an effort that could take months." Jewell looked up from her tablet when she spoke. "We can't trace the truck. I checked that already. It is too old, and doesn't have GPS tracking. Of course, I'll be running every other program I can think of to find her, we'll monitor financials, social media, cell phone contracts, law enforcement, hospital, and social security numbers... we won't just wait until we get this program done."

Anubis nodded and gave the woman a genuine smile. "I know you are very good at what you do. Thank you for the effort you're about to expend on my behalf."

Bengal's woman blushed and dipped her head. "You're welcome."

Alpha gathered the wrappers off the table. "Get on Doctor Wheeler's calendar; tell him I want your evaluation done ASAP."

"Roger that, sir." Anubis stood as he spoke.

Alpha reached out his hand. Anubis clasped it. "Welcome to the back office."

"Thank you, sir. For everything."

"Meh, I'll make sure to make you pay for it... eventually." Alpha cuffed him on the shoulder and headed out the door. "Oh, dinner is at six thirty, sharp. Main ranch house. Don't be late or my stepfather will have a cow. That is something you don't want to see. Bring Asp. I want to see the man explode when he tries to out eat Double D." The door closed behind the man as he laughed.

Anubis turned to Bengal. "Who or what in the hell is a Double D?"

"The guys that run the training side of this complex. Dixon and Drake. They're called the Wonder Twins or Double D. They fly anything that has wings or a rotary blade, are experts in demolitions, and are the brains behind the solar and turbine power that keep this entire facility off the grid."

"Damn. That's impressive." *Was he in over his head, or what?*

"They've been with Alpha since the beginning. You'll get to know the main players. Chief runs the complex from a management and logistical standpoint. Adam Cassidy runs the medical facilities, although he has a large staff of experts working with him. You'll have three facilities here, and we'll get into that tomorrow. For now, go get bunked, find Asp before he eats his way through South Dakota, and both of you get on the doctor's calendar. We have one hell of a lot of work to do and a dossier that we believe the combined council will drop within the next twenty-four hours. I'm going to need your help until we find your lady."

Anubis nodded, trying to take in the major league shift his world had taken in the last fifteen minutes. "I'm not sure I'm the person you need for this job."

"Why's that?"

"Those people in the field depend on Guardian to keep them safe. Their very existence is on the line every day they are hunting a dossier. The smallest thing could jeopardize their lives." *Things that would seem inconsequential to most people. The wrong intel on known associates, a lapse in the Shadow's background or even a change to the target's inner circle could start ripple effects that could be deadly to the Shadow working the dossier.*

"How many administrative types in this organization would know what those small things are?" Zane leaned back in his chair and put his arm around his woman's shoulders. She didn't even acknowledge he was there but just kept working on her tablet, apparently oblivious to the conversation around her.

Anubis pushed his chair in and leaned on the back of it as he regarded Bengal and his woman. Since Alpha had asked, and Bengal thought he could do the job, he'd go all in and fucking work his ass off to be what they needed. Although he still wasn't convinced he'd make the impact they seemed to expect.

"Alright."

A shit eating grin spread across Bengal's face as his fingers threaded through the hair that had fallen across his woman's shoulder. She glanced over at him and smiled before her electronics once again consumed her attention.

Anubis felt a rush of longing. He wanted what they had. He wanted to be able to have a relationship with Sky, to share a simple look, a touch, or even a smile. The question was would she want that with him? He extended his hand to Bengal. "I'm still not calling you Zane."

CHAPTER TWENTY-ONE

SKY HIT THE EMPLOYEE BREAKROOM AND IMMEDIATELY KICKED her heels off.

"They are fucking animals tonight." Sky jumped and looked up. She hadn't notice Beatrix in the far corner of the room. Her new friend had been a lifesaver, showing her the ropes and even helping her find childcare so she could work the later shifts.

"Two bachelor parties on the same night. It's insane out there." Sky padded across the floor and flopped onto an old fold-out chair next to Beatrix. The 'gentleman's club' was the best gig she could find when she moved out here. She'd attempted to contact her father, but the man wanted nothing to do with her, so Sky used the money Keelee had given her and rented a tiny one bedroom apartment. Beatrix's son was about the same age as Kadey so she knew of pre-school options that Sky could afford. Beatrix's mom was willing to watch Kadey at night while she worked since she was already watching Bea's son.

"Sean cut me loose. The crowd is dwindling." Sky rubbed the arch of her foot. She needed a better set of heels. Heck, she needed a better job. They'd been in Phoenix for just over a month, but she was still looking for an office job. A receptionist, secretary…anything would be better than what she was doing now, but she had rent to make, and while the tips here were great, the groping, propositions and outright lewd and disgusting behavior of some of the customers was reason to keep looking.

"Yep, he cut me too, but I'm so damn tired I've just been sitting here." Bea dropped her head back against the wall with a thud.

"Come on. We can walk out together. It's safer that way." Sky was only partially joking. She had a regular that was very persistent and had followed her to the employee parking lot twice. The guy gave her the creeps, but so far, he'd listened when she said no. The small spray container of mace in her purse was for the day he didn't. She prayed it would never happen, but she carried her keys in one hand and the mace in the other.

Sky got up and walked across the room to the small lockers to retrieve her purse and sweater. It got cold in the desert at night. "Come on, girl, time to go home."

Bea stood and stretched her hands over her head stretching. "Mason has T-ball in the morning." She glanced up at the old clock on the wall. "Check that, Mason has T-ball in seven hours. Uggg... does it make me a bad mom to wish he didn't like sports?" Bea pulled her purse and coat out of her locker.

"No. You're tired. Get some sleep, and you'll enjoy the game." Sky put on a pair of ballet slippers and swooped up her heels, shoving them into her purse. She slung it over her shoulder. The keys went into her right hand, the mace into her left.

"God, don't tell me Jordan is still following you out when you leave?" Bea looked over her shoulder as they exited the employee lounge. They turned right, heading to the back of the building toward the employee parking lot. They both swiped their employee IDs and exited the club.

"He's followed me twice. He creeps me out." Sky whispered the comment. The customer parking lot was between the club and the small graveled lot used by the employees. There were always men in the lot, which meant lewd comments and propositions as the servers walked to their vehicles. Management refused to take action unless there was unwanted physical contact. Bea assured her that she'd never heard of anyone being assaulted, but Sky hated being vulnerable. Working for the DA for five years, she knew what could happen. Maybe that was why she was so nervous.

"Hey, sweet cheeks! Want to come party with us?" A group of men gathered around a clump of cars near the entrance to the employee parking lot.

"Just keep walking," Sky whispered and put her arm through Bea's, and they ignored the catcalls.

"Hey pretty momma, don't be like that. We'll make it worth your while!" A loud chorus of laughter sent a shiver up Sky's back.

"I'm here." Bea pointed to her beat up Toyota.

"I'll walk you over." Sky stood beside the car while Bea opened the door and got in. The darn thing was notorious for not starting. She turned the key, and it jumped to life. Sky waived and headed across the parking lot. The headlights of Bea's car illuminated the rear of her vehicle. Sky stopped so suddenly she slipped in the gravel. A lone figure leaned against the rear of her SUV.

Bea pulled up and rolled down the window. "Do you want me to call Sean or the cops?"

Sky shook her head but didn't take her eyes off the man in front of her. "No, I'm fine. I know him."

"Are you sure?"

The wariness in Bea's voice pulled Sky out of her shock. She turned and nodded. "Yeah, I'm sure. Tell your mom I'll be there in just a couple minutes."

"Sky…" Bea obviously didn't want to leave her alone.

"He's Kadey's daddy. I'm fine. I'll be over to pick her up in just a few minutes." Sky tugged the strap of her purse further up on her shoulder and headed to her truck. Her back stiffened with resolve. She wasn't going to fall into the trap again. Not this time. He was bad for her, and she wasn't going to live waiting for him to decide to drop into her life again.

Bea's headlights arced around the parking lot, leaving the dull yellow light of a distant streetlight to illuminate her way. Sky stopped about four feet from him. He shifted off the back of the vehicle where he was leaning. "Why did you leave?"

Sky crossed her arm, still clutching her keys and mace. "Because I had to protect myself and Kadey."

His body went stiff. "From what?" He growled the question as if he didn't know.

"That would be you." Sky walked past him and unlocked the truck. She threw her purse up on the center console.

"You think I'd hurt you? Again?" The disbelief in his voice lit a fuse that took less than a second to ignite.

She turned and stared at him. The words she wanted to say were vicious and cutting, but he wasn't responsible for her weakness when it came to him. She was, and she was responsible for stopping her irresponsible longing for something she could never have.

"Kaeden, you were honest with me. Now it's my turn to be honest with you. You told me you were leaving, that you couldn't stay. I'm not living in denial here. I get that I'm nothing more than a hook up to you, but for some reason, even though I know that, I still come running when you want a convenient fuck. And still, every time I wake up, and you're gone, a small piece of my heart dies. Can't you see what you are doing to me? You can't keep doing this. It isn't fair." Sky's voice shook with emotion. "I will be forever grateful that you saved

Kadey for me. She's my world, but Kaeden, you're killing me. I can't do this anymore. You can't love me. Okay, I get that, but for God's sake leave me alone because as much as I've tried, I can't stop loving you!"

Kaeden lowered his head and looked at the ground. "You were never a convenient fuck."

Sky looked up at the sky and tried to stifle a sob. "Great, nice to know you had to go out of your way to fuck me. I've got to go." She reached for the door handle only to have his hand cover hers. "For God's sake, Kaeden. Let me go." She whispered the plea. She'd bared her soul to him, and all he had for her was that she *wasn't* convenient. How appropriate. She gave, and he took.

"I can't let you go, Sky. I'll never let you go."

The heat of his body behind her made her curl in on herself. "I don't care if you will let me go because I have already gone." The tears she'd been holding fell down her cheeks, and her shoulders shook with her suppressed sobs. His hands ran up her arms and pulled her back to him. Sky tried to pull away, but he wouldn't let go.

"I can't let you go because I need you. I've never been able to stay away because you are my soul and my humanity. The only happiness I had in my life were the memories of us together. I won't let the warmth of my life leave me. I can't." Sky spun in his arms. The stricken look on her face was sharper than a knife and cut him deeper than any blade. "But you can't stay. You've told me that countless times. Don't you see that I can't live like this anymore? It's killing me, Kaeden and what about Kadey? You can't ask me to do this anymore. If you care anything for me, for us… please, let me go."

Anubis lowered his forehead down to hers and wrapped her in his arms. "Sky, I'm not leaving. I mean, we're leaving, but I'm not leaving you."

"WH... WHAT?" HER BODY SHOOK WITH SOBS THAT she was trying to stop. He pulled her into him, holding to his chest. "I want you and Kadey to come live with me."

Sky pushed him back and bowed backward to look up at him. "What?" The suspicion in her eyes was enough to make him ill. He'd done that to her. She didn't believe that he was telling the truth.

"I'm not doing the job I used to do. I've taken a desk job. I'll be working from the complex in South Dakota. I may have to leave occasionally, but I'll be with you and Kadey every day. I want us to be a family." He held her face in his hands and wiped the tears from her cheeks with his thumbs. The utter sadness that emanated from her entire being confused him.

She shook her head and pushed him away. "I can't."

Fuck, his heart stopped in his chest, and he dropped his hands in shock. "Why?"

"Because you don't love us."

She started to turn, but Kaeden stopped her. "Haven't you been listening to me? What more do I have to do?" Fuck, he'd do whatever it took. He'd move the continents and rearranged the oceans if that would make her happy.

Sky turned and shook her head, defeated. "I'm a lot of things Kaeden, but I'm not stupid. Eventually, the sex wouldn't be enough for you." She lifted her hand and cupped his cheek. "I can't live with someone who doesn't love me."

His head snapped back as if he'd been slapped. "Sky, why do you think I've done all of this?"

She dropped her hand and lowered her head. "Because you feel guilty, but you don't have to, Kaeden. I love my little girl, and she doesn't need a daddy who is there just to make up for the difficulty I've been through."

Kaeden wrapped her up in his arms and looked to the heavens. He was a fucking stupid bastard. "Sky Meyers, I am completely, passionately, and permanently, in love with you. I'm all in, babe." He lowered his mouth to whisper the words into her ear. He heard her breath hitch. Her small body tightened in disbelief. He tucked his hand under her chin and elevated it so he could see her eyes, but more importantly so she could see his. Her searching gaze met his, and he smiled at the hope that he saw. "I love you."

"You do?" Her shaking hands sought his.

"Yes, I do." Kaeden lowered his lips to hers. Hers were wet with tears, and the taste of her misery was one he never wanted to experience again. "I will always love you." He breathed the words against her lips again.

Sky pushed up onto her toes and circled her arms around his neck, pulling him down to her. Her small, soft body melded into him, and at that moment, Anubis felt complete. There wasn't any portion of him that he kept hidden from her; nothing that he guarded so he couldn't get too close; nothing that he held in reserve in case she would meet someone else while he was gone. For once, he could be honest. He loved the woman he held in his arms. Describing the freedom that gave him would take a lifetime. She'd literally freed him from the darkness, shattering the shackles that kept him bound to the loneliness he professed to enjoy. But he had no idea of the power of true, uncensored love. It was a force that would take a lifetime to examine. He would gladly spend that time—with Sky and with Kadey.

He took her mouth, grabbed her thighs and picked her up as he straightened. She circled her legs around him. A loud cheer from behind them brought Kaeden to his senses. He slowly pulled away from the consuming kiss and just held her to him.

"Is this real?" Sky's head tucked into his neck, and her lips caressed his skin as she spoke.

A shiver of ecstasy ran down his spine. This was his reality, now. "It is as real as it gets." He lowered her to the ground and gave her another kiss before he pulled away. "Where's Kadey?"

"The sitter's." Sky leaned into him and wrapped her arms around him. "She's going to be so happy."

"Let's go get her." Kaeden walked her around to the passenger side seat and helped her into the SUV.

"You realize my apartment is a one bedroom, right?" Anubis detected both humor and resignation in her statement.

"You realize I have a two-room suite reserved at the Hilton, right?" He drew up her hand and kissed the back of it as he pulled out of the parking spot.

"You were pretty sure of yourself, weren't you?"

Sky's question was said in jest, but just in case she needed more reassurance, Anubis stopped the vehicle at the entrance to the parking lot. He turned to her and leaned close so he could see her expression in the dark. "I was never less sure of anything in my life. I only knew I didn't want a life without the two of you."

Sky smiled and pressed a kiss to his lips. As she pulled away, she whispered, "That was the right answer, Mr. Lang."

Anubis felt his chest swell. He wanted to have the right answer for her every time. Her happiness fueled his, and the emotion damn near clogged his throat. He gave her a wink and asked, "Which way?"

CHAPTER TWENTY-TWO

ANUBIS CARRIED HIS DAUGHTER INTO THE SECOND BEDROOM of the luxury suite that he'd reserved yesterday. Kadey hugged his neck as if she expected him to disappear into the air. He rubbed her back and laid her down on the bed.

"Are we really going back to the ranch?"

"Yep." Anubis took off her tennis shoes and pulled back the covers. He could sense Sky behind him watching.

He made a move to pull up her covers, but she stopped him. "And I can play with Lizzy every day?" Kadey put her hands on his cheeks, keeping him from turning his head.

He smiled down at her. She was an amazing little human being. He was truly in awe of the beautiful soul Sky had raised. "If your momma and Lizzy's momma say it's okay, then yes." Anubis bent down, kissed her cheek and then blew a raspberry on her neck sending her into a fit of giggles.

"I'm so happy, daddy! You're going to stay with us, too, right?"

The look of adoration in her eyes made him feel about forty-feet tall and bulletproof. "That's right, princess." He kissed her forehead again and stood. "The sooner you go to sleep, the sooner morning will come, and we'll get on the airplane to go back home."

"Yea!" Kadey flopped over and pulled her covers over her head with an excited squeal.

Sky moved beside him. A soft smile played across her face. She put her hand in his and gave his a squeeze. "I think it might take a minute or two to get her settled down and back to sleep. Go relax, and I'll be out as soon as she's asleep."

Anubis bent and kissed Sky, sending Kadey into another fit of giggles. Anubis felt himself laughing against Sky's lips.

"I see where she gets the giggles from." Sky laughed out the reprimand.

Anubis tried to feign shock, but couldn't manage it. He was too damn happy.

He left Sky to get Kadey settled and went through to the main bedroom. He smiled at the box that sat beside the bed. Anubis carried it out to the living area and quietly emptied the contents, arranging them on the small table. He nested the bottle of champagne in a bucket of ice. Miss Amanda, Alpha's mother, had packed him a picnic of finger foods from food grown and raised on the ranch. Since she learned of his food phobia, she'd worked tirelessly to gain his trust, and she had. He emptied the box, making sure all the covers had the marks perfectly aligned before he took off the tops. He did leave the food alone in its insulated box, so the inspection was mandatory. He was getting better, but he doubted he'd ever trust without verification.

Anubis washed the champagne flutes—three times, and dried them before he popped the top off the bottle. The soft pfft noise muffled by his hand wouldn't be enough to bother Kadey as she struggled to go to sleep. The smile on her face when she'd seen him tonight was a priceless memory he prayed he never forgot. He glanced around the small table and nodded. It was the best he could do. Hopefully, it would be enough.

Anubis sat down on the couch and immediately popped back up. He paced the room and sat down again. His knee bounced as he waited, and he ran his hand through his hair for the twentieth time. He stood back up and re-checked the table, then checked the ice in the bucket and paced the room again. He knew it was insane to be so nervous, but there was so much on the line. The stakes were higher tonight than they'd ever been. Anubis dropped into the large armchair and scrubbed his face. Fuck, he hated not being prepared. He should be able to detail the events of the night, know the exact way things would unfold. This feeling of unease was foreign and decidedly unacceptable. He launched from the chair and went to the table to check everything again. The door to Kadey's room opened, and Sky slid out before shutting it softly behind her. Anubis moved before she could turn around.

When she spun, she stilled and raised her hand to her mouth. On one knee Anubis held a black velvet box up to her. "Sky, I've been a complete and total failure. I've made you doubt my love for you and for Kadey. Sky…" Anubis stopped as she dropped to her knees in front of him. She put her small hand on his cheek, tears crested in her eyes but they didn't fall. Anubis swallowed hard and lifted the ring from the box. "Will you marry me?"

Sky bit her bottom lip and shook her head. "You don't have to do this."

"I need to. I don't think I could live without knowing you were mine. Forever." Anubis sat the box down, still holding the ring in the other. "Sky, please. I know I don't deserve your trust, but I love you and Kadey. I will protect you both with the last breath in my body. My heart and my life are yours. Please, baby, let me cherish and protect you both. Let me take away the worries of your life and give you a place to find peace. You and Kadey are the only light I have in my life. Marry me?"

"Say yes, Momma!" Anubis turned and reached out his arm to his daughter. She flew across the room into his arms. She reached out to Sky. "Please, Momma! Say yes!"

Sky laughed and nodded. "Yes."

Kadey squealed and lunged toward Sky, throwing her arms around her mom's neck. Anubis wrapped his arms around both of them. There, on the floor of a hotel room in Pheonix, in the middle of the night, he found the most brilliant light in the world and embraced it.

Sky lay on the king-sized bed and watched the sunlight start to peek through the curtains. Instead of trying to make Kadey go back to sleep, Kaeden insisted she be allowed to stay up and celebrate, too. He had a marvelous array of finger foods and a bottle of champagne. They opened an apple juice from the small hotel refrigerator for Kadey. After Kaeden meticulously cleaned a glass they all toasted getting married. Sky's cheeks hurt from smiling and laughing. Kadey had lasted far longer than she'd expected, the excitement of having her daddy back and going back to South Dakota seemed to energize her like that fuzzy pink bunny on television, She kept going and going and going until she hit the wall. One minute she was telling Kaeden all about the Barbie dolls that Lizzy had and the next she was yawning and leaning against him. He winked at Sky and scooped up his daughter into his arms. Sky cleaned up the small living area and made her way into the larger bedroom.

Kaeden asked her to marry him. That she loved him was a foregone conclusion. The fear surrounding her love was what she needed to talk to him about, without Kadey present.

She heard Kaeden open and shut Kadey's door and then heard the front door to the unit open and shut. The lock turned, and she heard his footsteps coming towards their room. "Is she finally asleep?"

Kaeden chuckled and dropped to the foot of the bed and crawled up over her. "Sound asleep." He dropped to his elbows. His eyes traveled over her as if he'd been gone for months instead of minutes. "I will make up for not being here for you and her."

"I don't need you to make up for anything, Kaeden. I just need to know that you'll be here."

He dropped to his side and pulled her into him, tucking her against his chest and under his chin. She relaxed into his body. This felt so right... so good. "I told you I took a new position within the organization. I may have to travel for meetings in D.C. or maybe a trip out to meet with one of our...employees, but I'll be there for you. I promise."

"Are you sure you'll be happy?" Sky clenched her eyes shut. Please God, let him say yes.

"I'll be happy if you and Kadey are there with me." Sky let out the breath she'd sucked into her lungs and said a small prayer of thanks. However, there was still that lingering question. "Are you ever going to tell me what you do for a living?"

"Baby, if I could, I would, but if I told you anything, it could endanger the lives of other people... of my friends. I swear to you that what we do is for the greater good and I swear that's all I can tell you."

Sky let his words soak in, but more importantly, she let the emotion behind the words fill her. Kaeden was a good man. She knew it, and she was willing to forego a detailed explanation because of the love she knew he held in his heart.

With a spark of mischief, she teased, "So... *now* can you tell me what your real name is?"

"Kaeden Lang." It wasn't of course, but it was the name of the man that Sky Meyers loved, and that made it good enough for him. She eyed him suspiciously. "Some of your co-workers didn't recognize you by that name." "Baby, all they ever knew me by was my number. It was safer that way." "Oh." Her face brightened. "Hey, we're getting married." Sky changed the subject and lifted her left hand as she gazed at the huge diamond. The beautiful setting framed the round cut gem, and it glistened in the small amount of sunlight filtering into the room.

"Do you want a church wedding?" Kaeden's chest rumbled under her ear.

"No, I don't need a fancy ceremony. I just want to get married."

"Vegas isn't far."

Sky pushed away and looked up at him. "Yeah?"

"I've been told I have the plane and crew at my disposal until I have my private life straightened out. I won't add the adjectives my boss used when he told me to get off my ass and go get my family."

Sky examined the top button of his shirt, running her fingertip around the smooth edges. She didn't want a big church wedding, but Vegas? Elvis impersonators and drive through chapels? She didn't want that either.

"Could we maybe get married by a justice of the peace back in South Dakota?" She peeked at Kaeden to gauge his reaction.

"Baby, if you wanted to get married at the North Pole on Christmas Day by Santa Claus it wouldn't matter to me. I don't care where we get married as long as we do." Kaeden dropped a kiss on her lips. "You're wearing far too many clothes."

He rolled her onto her back and straddled her. His fingers trailed the edge of her white t-shirt and lifted it up slowly. She moved to allow him to pull it up over her head. He traced the edge of her bra with one hand before he lowered and tugged the elastic waistband of the short black skirt over her hips. He caught the top of her panties and pulled them down with the skirt. She sat up and unhooked the back of her bra, slipping it off her arms.

"Now *you're* wearing too many clothes." She unbuttoned the front of his shirt and pushed the cloth down over his shoulders. He'd gained weight since she last saw him. The firmness of his muscles was still there, but he looked... healthier. She leaned forward and kissed his chest. Her hands fell to his hips, and she looked up at him. "Take off your jeans, Kaeden." She watched as he moved away from her and stood beside the bed.

He unfastened his jeans and dropped the zipper, but that's as far as he got.

"Are you teasing me?" She lay back on the bed and slid her fingertips over her breast and down her abdomen to her sex.

With the exception of his eyes, Kaeden remained frozen, watching their journey.

"Kaeden?"

His eyes flew to hers.

"Take off your jeans."

He blinked and then shoved his jeans and briefs down his legs. His hard, long cock slapped against his abs. He grabbed his cock and stroked it twice before he lowered and crawled back over her.

"No. On your back."

Kaeden quirked an eyebrow but dropped to his side and rolled.

Sky moved down to his knees and wiggled in between them. Kaeden was up on his elbows watching her in an instant. She smiled at him and kissed the inside of his thigh. It quivered at her touch and a drop of clear liquid formed at the top of his cock. His dick held a deep red hue and pulsed when she dropped her lips to the juncture of his legs.

She licked the seam, and Kaeden groaned, "Fuck, baby."

Sky loved that she could make him shake with desire. They were explosive in bed, and this part of the relationship wasn't going to be a problem. She licked a stripe from his balls to the tip of his cock and swirled her tongue around the head of his shaft, taking in the glistening drop of pre-cum. He sucked air in on a hiss, which made her all the more daring. She swirled the head again and dropped down, taking him into her mouth. Holding the bottom of his cock she worked to take as much of him as she could before she started jacking the bottom of his cock to meet her lips. His hands found her hair, and he held her, careful and gentle. Sky loved the taste and smell of Kaeden, but she wanted more. She lifted off him and crawled up his body straddling him. She held his shaft as she lowered onto him and sank over his hardness. She moaned… or maybe he did, Sky couldn't tell. The sensation of him splitting her, filling her, was so damn good.

When she'd taken him all, she moved her hips in a figure eight, grinding her clit against his pubic bone before she rose, sank down, and shifted her hips again. The sensations of his hands on her body as she rose and fell, coupled with the way the nerves of her body sang from the sex was too much. She leaned forward and placed her hands on his shoulders. "Fuck me," she panted, as her body trembled with need.

"No. Never again. But I'll make love to you forever." Kaeden rolled, while still inside her. He held on tight and slowly stroked into her. His kisses promised everything they couldn't before.

Sky ran her hands over his body, claiming the man that loved her. Since he'd left Fresno, she'd never given herself permission to dream of the possibility of a life with him. Her body strained toward its finish. The kiss broke so they could breathe. Their lips barely separated, their breath co-mingled. She arched into him and clawed at his back trying to get closer.

Kaeden thrust into her, deeper and harder.

"Yes, more… like that." She begged him for the release her body demanded.

He held her tighter, his hips pounded into her, and she bit his shoulder to keep from screaming his name. She rode the waves of sensation as they pulsed through her. Kaeden found his release, his muscles tightened in a glorious display above her.

Sky panted under his collapsed weight until he rolled to the side and pulled her with him. She kissed his chest and tried to catch her breath.

"I love you. I always have, even when I thought I could never have you." He whispered in her ear.

She gasped and pulled away, gazing up at him. "Why didn't you tell me?"

"It wouldn't have been fair to you. What if you met someone else?" Kaeden smoothed her hair with his hand.

God, she'd tried and failed miserably. "I realize now that was never an option for me. I looked, but it was impossible to find what I was looking for. Nobody compared to you."

"And nobody could eclipse the light you've brought into my life. I love you."

Sky nestled into his chest and murmured her own words of love. She had everything she could ever ask for in life. A healthy child and the man she loved. All the hardships, the loneliness and the heartache dulled in comparison to the emotions that filled her life now. She sighed and let herself drift. If this was a dream, she never wanted to wake.

Chapter Twenty-Three

Kaeden glanced at the paper again. "Are we ready?" Zane's voice cut through his thoughts. He glanced up at the eighty-inch screen in front of him. It split into four sectors. Zane's mug was in one, Alpha, Archangel, and Gabriel filled the other three. Having Gabriel, the founder of Guardian Security, in on-call drove home the importance of the reorganization of Guardian's Shadow World.

"Ready here." He pulled his paperwork closer to him and looked up at the screen. "Alpha, all parties are on the line. The video call is secure." Zane facilitated the call.

"Great. Alright, Kaeden and Zane, this is your baby, so let's get started."

Zane pointed at the screen, and Kaeden took his cue. "Sir, I've sent the brief to you, but I'd like to run through it so I can answer any questions. First, we have the initial layout of the organization. We suggest the lines of authority be altered to accommodate the organization's organic flow. Both Zane and I need access to all lines of support at any given time. Having one section report to him and the other half of the section report to me may cause delays. We suggest a co-command if you will."

"Will accountability or masking our Shadows be affected?" That comment came from Gabriel.

"No, sir. The system we have in effect to mask the Shadows is solid. Of course, we will continue to ensure our entire operation remains off the grid. We will utilize only standalone systems with cryptology that will fry the internal hardware if not accessed correctly. The operator system works very well, and reporting in will continue through those secure communications lines. The majority of the changeup will be the way we assign dossiers and the potential for teaming two or three assets together depending on the mission."

"How are the facilities coming along?" Archangel's gravelly voice chimed in.

"Since it is twenty degrees below zero, there isn't a lot happening. Chief has the plans drawn up, and we've made some changes based on the unique needs of our assets, but when we have them up and running, we will have a safe place for our assets to rehab without exposing them to the general populace of the complex."

"How are you going to do that?"

"Underground tunnels, sir." Anubis smiled when all three of his bosses shot their eyes up to the camera.

"Double D came up with the idea. They want to upgrade the water and sewer capabilities by adding a water treatment plant in the spring. Using that construction as our cover, we will build tunnels from the flight line to the Shadow facilities and from the facilities to other structures as needed. There will be four points of security before anyone gets into the facility so the assets who are more… recognizable, shall we say, won't be identified as our assets."

Anubis glanced at the folders on his desk. He now knew the identity of every asset Guardian employed in the Shadow World. Three of the assets… fuck, he had no idea how Gabriel managed to obtain them. The implications of what the man was building were extraordinary—

and frightening if in the wrong hands.

"Alright. Well, unless anyone has any objections, I vote we give them the go-ahead to construct the facilities and realign the lines of authority." Alpha spoke to the others.

"Approved." Archangel concurred.

"I'm no longer a voting member, just an interested bystander." Gabriel smiled when both Alpha and Archangel snorted. "Alright, I'll concede to a pushy bystander."

"That's the truth," Alpha mumbled.

"What was that?" Gabriel asked.

"Nothing, sir." Alpha's smirk belied his answer.

Jason snorted. "Right, be careful, or you'll get fired."

"Again." Everyone echoed the word at the same time. Laughter at his boss's expense followed the comments.

"Zane, give us a rundown on the build-up of personnel," Alpha barked over the dying chuckles.

"Roger that, sir. We have four more computer programmers in the vetting process. Two won't have any problems qualifying for the security clearance we need. I'm waiting on information about the other two. One has some background issues that could be exploited. I'll probably farm him out to one of the outlying detachments. The other I'm having Jewell put through the paces. No formal education, but he's off the charts smart when it comes to coding, programming, and cyber warfare. I'm talking spooky smart."

Jason leaned forward and tapped his pen on his desk. "I want a brief on this guy. Tell Jewell I want to know the smallest detail. Anyone *that* smart could either be a priceless asset or a formidable enemy."

"Roger that, sir."

"Kaeden, the council is meeting tomorrow. There are three

dossiers on the table. Be ready for the cases to drop." Alpha glanced up from whatever he was reading after he spoke.

"Roger that, sir."

"Alright, it looks like we are set. Unless there are any other questions, I'm giving the new Shadow World Operations Center a thumbs up." Archangel glanced up at his screen. "Good. Kaeden, Zane, make this work. Take care of my people, and they will take care of you." Archangel reached over, and the screen went black on his and Gabriel's camera.

"Where's Asp?"

Zane's question surprised him, but Anubis rolled his eyes and answered, "Probably eating the boss's mom out of house and home. He passed his eval after his last mission but doesn't show any signs of leaving. I think the guy likes it up here."

"Don't let him out of the area." Alpha leaned forward. "One of those dossiers is on a rogue agent. One who stole some of this country's top weapons' intelligence and is rumored to be in the process of setting up an auction. Asp has personal knowledge of the man."

Anubis leaned back. "His old handler?"

Alpha nodded confirming his guess. "I don't think it's wise to give him the case."

Both Bengal and Anubis leaned forward, but Anubis beat his friend to the punch. "That's bullshit, sir. He has a personal interest in this case, granted, but that man used Asp. If the council drops this dossier, Asp has earned the right to go after him."

Bengal broke in before Alpha could speak, "I concur, sir. If I were in Asp's position and I found out the man who used me to kill one of his political obstacles was given to another asset, I'd walk away from the organization. You've basically stated you don't trust him, and that means he can't trust you. You don't want Asp out there on his own. Hell, none of us want Asp as a potential enemy."

"Agreed," Anubis chimed in.

Alpha blew out a long exhale and nodded. "Agreed." He leaned forward. "You're sanctioned and endorsed. Call if you need me." The screen went to black and Anubis turned his gaze to Bengal.

"We have a shit storm coming down the pike." No sense sugarcoating the truth.

"Asp can handle it." Bengal acknowledged the essence of the problem.

"I hope you're right." Anubis glanced at his friend. Asp wouldn't survive the consequences if he wasn't.

The End

About the Author

USA Today and Amazon Bestselling Author, Kris Michaels is the alter ego of a happily married wife and mother. She writes romance, usually with characters from military and law enforcement backgrounds.

Kris was born and raised in South Dakota. She graduated many years ago from a high school class consisting of 13 students (yes that is thirteen, eleven girls and two boys… lucky boys). She joined the military, met her husband, and traveled the world. Today she lives on the Gulf Coast and writes full time.

Kris is an avid people watcher and dreamer. The stories she writes are crafted around the hopes and dreams of a true romantic. She believes love is essential, people are beautiful, and everyone deserves a happy ending.

When she isn't writing Kris enjoys a full life revolving around family, friends, laughing, whiskey, and cold red wine. (Yes cold… don't judge.)

Email: krismichaelsauthor@gmail.com
Website: www.krismichaelsauthor.com

Printed in Great Britain
by Amazon